TROPHY

TROPHY

A Novel

Michael Griffith

TRIQUARTERLY BOOKS / NORTHWESTERN UNIVERSITY PRESS

TriQuarterly Books
Northwestern University Press
www.nupress.northwestern.edu

Copyright © 2011 by Michael Griffith. Published 2011 by TriQuarterly Books/
Northwestern University Press. All rights reserved.

Printed in the United States of America

10 9 8 7 6 5 4 3 2 1

Library of Congress Cataloging-in-Publication Data

Griffith, Michael, 1965–
    Trophy : a novel / Michael Griffith.
        p. cm.
    ISBN 978-0-8101-5218-2 (cloth : alk. paper)
    I. Title.
PS3557.R48928T76 2011
813'.54—dc22

2010050767

∞ The paper used in this publication meets the minimum requirements of the
American National Standard for Information Sciences—Permanence of Paper for
Printed Library Materials, ANSI Z39.48-1992.

For Nicola and Bix

By indirections, find directions out.

—SHAKESPEARE

Contents

Epilogue: When the Going Gets Tough, the
Freaks Perish Weirdly   3

1   The Cusp of Corpsedom   5

2   Certain Harsh Judgments of Recent Vintage   7

3   He Thought as Much   9

4   Forward Progress for Positive Yardage   11

5   Midwife to Giants   13

6   A Note to the Timekeeper   18

7   Second Seat, Back Fiddle   20

8   Near-Zero Turning Radius   23

9   Nevertheless   25

10   Book Learning Is the Pink Fiberglass of the People   27

11   The Juicing Muse   32

12   The Next Ludicrous Failure Waiting in the Wings   34

13   Femme Fatality   36

14   Vomitus Mundi   38

15   The Several Faces of Celeste   45

A Perfectly Respectable O'Clock for Your Turkey
Ink-Pen Tracheotomy
The Firebrand's Candlepower

16 Stuck a Feather in His Cap and Called It Cannelloni   54

17 WoE Is mE   56

18 The Silky Smooth Drawers of Ghoulie the Cricketer   58

19 Hussies of Cellblock DD   63

20 The Casserole Parents   64

21 More Sowbellies, Less Style   67

22 Forebear, Afterbear, Present Bear   70

23 God and Man at Denny's   71

24 The Milk of Magnesia of Human Kindness   74

25 Smurf 'n' Turf   76

26 Flying the Coop de Grace   80

27 A Metaphor from the Theater, Vada's Main Experience of
    Which Is Playing Skate Punk #3 in One of Those High School
    Productions in Which the Bard Is Made Relevant by Having
    Mercutio Wear Painter's Pants   81

28 The Last Half-Inch of Life   82

29 Biography-Scotch   83

30 Attestations of the Party of the First Part   85

31 The Last Leak   86

32 The Streep of Death by Canned Beer   87

33 Lumpkin's Choice   89

34 Above Covenants   93

35 That Damned Lissomeness   95

36 Where It Says the Heavy Head of Pablo the Possum, Read . . .   97

37 Sorry for the Interruption, Which Only Serves to Prove That
    Philosophy Is the Last Refuge of the Sphincter-Loosened and That
    Vada Can't Bear to Yield the Spotlight, Even to His Beloved   116

38 Armageddon on with It   118

39 You Are Here   123

40 Isn't It Ironic? Don't You Think?   126

41 Charity Begins at the Top of the Cup, Little Dude   127

42 Your 20, His 30   128

43 Death and All Its Serifs and Portals and Butterscotches   130

44 Unglesby and the Caramel Corn   133

45 The Hexagon of Friend-Having   135

46 Sackcloth and Ashcans   137

47 Tintinnabulation   138

48 How Droll!   140

49 The Pocket-Pool Talisman   143

50 Ollie the Punt Returner   144

51 Death the Disambiguator   146

52 Taking a Vada from Vertex to Vortex   148

53 The Difference Between a *Fascis* and a Fucking Mess   150

54 Immortality via Duotone Resin   153

55 The Central Axe   155

56 Lacuna Beach   157

57 One Practical Lady   159

58 Tapping the Bladder   164

59 To Action!   165

60 OK, So It's Pretty Sorry Action   166

61 Late Mom   167

62 Lingua Vada   168

63 In Defense of the Pun   170

64 A Buttload of Bottlecaps, a Big Basement   171

65 Two Films, Summarized   173
    We'll Always Have Plaster of Paris
    Lodestone

66 Strange Attractors   177

67 United in Love and the Rheumatiz   178

68 The Underwater Undead   180

69 A Shining Subdivision upon a Hill   182

70 Piscinity: A Strained Metaphor (Gotta Charge
    Extra for Artistry)   186

71 A Truth Universally Acknowledged   188

72 The Thunder of Disclosure   190

73 No Man's Napkin   192

74 Mr. Jefferson's Colossal Cowpie   194

75 Spreading Thin the Raspberry Corps   196

76 Smart Capitalism   198

77 Führer Bee   199

78 Under the Microscope   201

79 Revenge Is a Double-Edged Sword Best Served Cold   204

80 Nanook of the Penumbra   206

81 Yahweh's Subtrahend, Mommy's Monster   208

82 Toshiro from Encino, Malfeasant Flumist, Toting WMD,
    KO'd by WY, VIP   215

83 Vada, Come On, It's Time   218

84 The Hero Accountants of the Apocalypse Crunch Their
    Aftermaths (Biff, Pow, Nnnfff)   220

85 Under's Easier (A Tale from the Age of Shivery)   221

86 The Meat Journalist's Chauffeur   224

87 Baker's Man   227

88 Dorito Ergo Sum   230

89 That Little Tricorn Glow   233

90 Aubergine Trebuchet   234

91 Busman's Holiday   237

92 Five Snapshots   238

    Love Makes a Hash of Our Metaphors
    A Man Called Intrepid
    Learn the Litterbox
    Telltale!
    Sitting on Something Too Deep for You

93 A Dental Irony   244

94 What True Love Looks Like   247

95 Pièce de Vichy   248

96 Black Panther, Brown Bear, White Devil   250

97 Gravity's Slack   253

98 The Antonym of Shipwreck   255

99 Wedding Cake   256

100 Giddy   258

101 No Juiciness   260

102 Vada Was an Angel   261

103 The Five Sacraments of the Apocalypse   262

    Gobblers in Throws
    Scrabble
    Gather Round the Tube
    Story Hour
    Cookies for Christ

104 Subtract One   274

Acknowledgments   277

TROPHY

Epilogue:
When the Going Gets Tough,
the Freaks Perish Weirdly

To the Editors of the *Lexington Gazette,* Lexington, S.C.
Re "Freak Mishap Claims Lake Man, 29"

July 23, 2007

Dear Editors:

Yesterday's article about the death of my friend Vada Prickett makes it sound like he was just some loser who spent the last ten years with his thumb up his ass, waiting for Freak Mishap to sort out the paperwork and get around to making its Claim.

I object.

For starters: If *you* got crushed to death, would "Mishap" seem the right word to cover it? Also, what's "Lake Man"? I picture a sci-fi creature, fishlike head and gill slits big as a/c vents, a rubber tail that drags when he runs. Snarky robot critics stand in front of the screen in silhouette, making fun.

Finally, is "freak" an adjective modifying "mishap," or is a "Freak Mishap," as you imply, a Mishap that happens to a Freak? Your reporter seems to think that anyone who died the way Vada did must be a joke, must *always* have been a joke—how else can the dead man explain perishing weirdly? (He can't, Eds. You're right about that. Yours are the last words on this. Freak. Mishap. When the going gets tough, the freaks perish weirdly.)

For the record, I want to state that Vada Prickett was a kind, gentle, intelligent . . . oh, what do you care? You've assigned him punchline-for-eternity status, and there's no taking it back now: Lake Freak Snuffed by Stuffed Bear. Ha damn ha.

What I mean to say here is mainly good-bye, Vada. I thought somebody besides Freak Mishap ought to Claim you. Well, then . . . mine!

Love (note to the Eds: I'm not talking to you assholes anymore; you can get your love elsewhere),

Tisha Alston
Charlotte, N.C.

P.S. Re: "mine!" above: Sorry to be your nearest thing to a loved one. I would have left the claiming to the Happy Couple—but I didn't think you could count on Darla and Wyatt. They have a wedding to get through. As I told you, two's company. And what's three?

Not your problem anymore, I guess.

1

The Cusp of Corpsedom

Vada Prickett is a corpse.

Oh, but that's showy . . . it's more accurate to say that Vada is on the cusp of corpsedom. He is enjoying—or, rather, not enjoying: what kind of man would take pleasure in an end so early and grim and flat-out *painful* as this one, especially if it's his own early, grim, and flat-out painful end?—his last instant of life. Dear God but that's a mess. Think straight, Vada. Uncomplicate, unravel.

What Vada is doing is dying.

Actually, at this precise sub-instant what he's doing is wondering: Does "cusp" mean what he thinks it does? Seems like it might have to do with the cauliflowery tops of teeth. Or it's a poisonous snake from Bible times. Does a cusp have something to do with Amontillado, whatever Amontillado is? Or it's one of those snapped-together words, one that applies to the wretch who *lisps* when he *cusses*. Vada can empathize: The world gigs you again and again, waits till dark and shines a bright light in your eyes and runs you through with a sharp stick, and then even your rightful rage becomes fodder for chuckles. You wriggle; they haw. It's not fair. Up your ath, world. Kith thith.

Vada has no dictionary on hand as he lies here broken, ebbing away, his sternum crushed, the foul beast's breath mingling with his. He finds himself in a place where Webster dares not tread, so "cusp" it is. Who'd begrudge him, in the last flicker of life, a solipsism? Is that the right word?

5

Vada, one's dying quiver is no time for horsing around. Do this right, with the seriousness the situation requires, with *gravitas fortissimus*. He doesn't know Latin either, obviously, except to understand that it's more ceremonious than English, and moments in extremis call for the grandeur of a foreign tongue. This is *it*, after all. No reason now to hold anything in reserve. Don't act like the cheapskate at Halloween who hoards the last few Goo-Goo Clusters for himself, who tries to mollify straggling lumberjacks and Orphan Annies with elderly caramels and the heat-warped chocolate doubloons the lube shop gave him with last summer's radiator flush. One shouldn't hold out on kids who've been lugging rubber axes for two hours or are wearing hair made out of a mop-head dyed orange—what kind of jerk would do that?

It boils down to this: Your next thought may be your last, Vada, so for once, please, make it good. There are pleasures to bid adieu, memories to sift. There are loved ones to apostrophize (screw it if that's not the right word—*you* try waxing eloquent when your lungs are hemorrhaging and there's a sliver of rib invading your heart and you're held fast in a fatal drawer-sachet made half of musky fur and half of the onion-and-salad-oil sandwich you ate for lunch).

So back up. Start again, and zap the foreign shit this time. All the memorable last words have one thing in common, whether they're cries of anguish ("Et tu, Brute"), pronunciamentos (Darwin's "I am not the least afraid to die"), grumblings (Marx's "Last words are for fools who haven't said enough"), or ordinary utterances given weight by nearness to death (Goethe's "More light," Robert E. Lee's "Strike the tent," Vada's mom's "Hey, look out . . ."). There's Casanova, in whose last words one hears a gotcha to God, the smugness of a man who believes he's made and won Pascal's wager: "I have lived as a philosopher and die as a Christian." There's John Henry's defiance: "You cain't drive steel like me, Lawd, Lawd, / you cain't drive steel like me." There's Tallulah Bankhead and her tidy list of needs: "Codeine, bourbon."

What do these share? Last words must be pithy . . . and not in Vada's lithping way, cut it out, not pissy but *pithy*. For lo, the good Lord offers the corpse-to-be a final dignity, the chance to edit oneself down to a few brave syllables by which to be remembered. Vada, make like stout John Henry or like Tallulah, who at least knew what she wanted. End this now. Start it over and get it right.

2

Certain Harsh Judgments of Recent Vintage

Vada couldn't tell you how many times, in his thirty years topside, he's heard that saw about your whole life flashing before your eyes when you die. It's a movie cliché, like amnesia, multiple personalities, Neanderthal lardos with slumming starlet wives, villains shot and shot and shot until they're human colanders, but who always rise amid swelling music to pose one last threat before being impaled on something weird, a weathervane or hood ornament.

To learn now, almost the last thing Vada will ever discover, that God doesn't work in the vaunted mysterious ways but rather like a Hollywood paycheck-whore . . . it's a disappointment, especially for someone who has spent his life—oops, chuck that—someone who *spent* his life waiting for the thing to get a proper start.

Villains are like lovers, in a way. Their urge to do you in is a sort of affection radically misapplied. You probably don't want to be dead, but in weak and lonely moments (and what else is there?) you might welcome the rare attentiveness a true nemesis can offer. To the Antagonist, yours is the only heart worth perforating, yours the only skull that makes his cudgel twitch. Every throat cut ear to ear begins—this is physiology—with a hickey, even if (granted) the love-bite is erased or superseded after a hundredth of a second by a ragged wound and geysering blood. Eventually the special-effects boys and girls take over, and after that, who cares?

Vada has until now believed at least in a malign God; an indifferent one is too much to bear. One wants the reassurance of knowing one's death serves *someone's* ends, that it's not just the outcome of stupid, graceless, all-canceling chance.

It would be bad enough if, as promised, your whole life flashed across the backs of your eyelids like a high school hygiene film: "Next puberty, with its joys and challenges, lay in wait for young Vada. Would he prove a goofus or a gallant?" But the cliché is wrong on three counts, if not more.

1. That last instant of perfect lucidity isn't perfectly lucid. In truth, Vada's no less confused than he has been all along.

2. Your life passes not before the eyes but well behind them—an inch, two? Vada, gracious to the end (or merely accustomed to getting screwed, see above), is willing to call that a good-faith mistake, an error in translation.

3. God turns out to be not only uncaring but also a bit of a weasel. He's shortchanged Vada, who's unable to cast his eyes (see, here's where mistakes start: he's unable to cast whatever you call that mind-seeing spot that lies an inch or two behind his eyes, what he'll dub the Prickettus Memorious, and who's to stop him?) over all his days. What unreels in the Prickettus Memorious is nothing like his "whole life." No, Vada's reverie begins not at the beginning, when he popped like a squalling pink cork into the klieg lights and chirping monitors of the world (Lexington, S.C., 7/26/77), but just twenty minutes back (Vada's front lawn, Lake Murray, S.C., 7/21/07).

Twenty minutes! Held out on again. And when life gives you lemons . . . when life gives you lemons, avuncular Uncle Vada always unclishly offers, make preparations to pelt any motherfucker who strays into range and looks like he might be improved by lemon-pelting.

Vada is, alas, citrus-deprived just now, and in any case his arms are pinned, which would nix any chance of pelting more than feebly, a pelting that would hardly deserve the name. And Vada, for one, pays strict attention to names, to the promises contained in words: He's not of the ilk that would hornswoggle or boondoggle or plain goddamn *cheat* a dying man. (May he *please* start over, Lord? Please? He's willing to take back certain harsh judgments of recent vintage.)

3

He Thought as Much

He thought as much.

Even left-handed pelting is out of the question. In his lamentable situation, corpsecuspdom (either see chapters 1 and 2 or start paying attention), Vada can neither feel nor see his left arm. The right hand knows not what the left is doing, though it seems a fair bet that it's lying idle over yonder, prematurely dead.

He has warm regard for it anyway, the hand that would fain have worn Darla's ring; the hand that, at the carwash, worked out slack in the high-powered hose while his right got the glory; the one that ticked the turn signal, pinned countless chicken breasts to countless plates, tilted yogurt cups so he could scrape out their lasts, steadied penny-nails or matchbooks.

What distinguishes lore from hokum? Is it that they're both bullshit people knowingly try to pass for truth, counterfeit that's spendable if the folks you pay it to are willing to call it an artful, amusing fake? Vada doesn't know; those of you with more than a half-second to live figure it out. In any event, during his brief stint at vet school he heard a bit of hore or lokum, take your pick, about bears having one forepaw that was tenderer and more aromatic than the other because it had been sweetened by being soaked again and again in honeycombs and then sucked ecstatically dry. (That last phrase doesn't sound like Vada, which probably means the story came from gross anatomy class with that reprobate Dr. Veen, the softness of whose hands derived from a different sort of steeping, from other acts of ecstatic suction.)

Even now, under all this weight, as Vada simmers (despite the expensive climate control Wyatt has in his trophy room) in a potpourri of wild bear and sweet onion, he thinks he detects a whiff of sugar and wood pulp and industry. But—and think about this, please—the hard work doesn't belong to the bear. The *honey* may be his now, possession being some obscene number of tenths of the law, but the *industry* belongs to the workers fated to die for their queen, having spent their stings on the unfeeling skin of blissed-out Yogi, who's snarfed the work of all their lives in five seconds and now is going nappy-nap.

Then the whiff fades, and with it the thought, and with the thought the hand. How he used to love that mound of muscle he could raise in the back of his left hand's lower right quadrant by pressing his thumb hard against the base of the index finger; it was what he had instead of a bicep, this bump—the product of thumbal opposability, the only triumph he could point to.

So . . . gone now forever, his coddled left, the soft and honeyed hand. Farewell, south paw. Farewell.

4

Forward Progress for Positive Yardage

Enough preliminaries. Vada's weary of them, too . . . but please don't hurry him. On what grounds does he ask this? It's not because he thinks you should consider him well enough hurried as it is, thank you—and by powers greater than yourselves. That Vada's got plenty trouble already should be evident, but why should that stop *you*? After the mob in Naples shot and piñataed and hanged Mussolini, did the Duce's shade wail and bitch when they gouged out his eyes or plucked out his tongue by its root? Did he complain that hanging his gooey remains upside down was a humiliation too far, as right side up would have been plenty bad? The corpse doesn't get to decide.

Nor will you hear Vada invoke "respect for the dead" as a reason. For one thing, he's not (quite) gone yet. For another, the respect due isn't for the dead but for death. It's ridiculous to believe that somebody who stunk it up in life is to be accorded reverence for having gotten himself under the wheels of a streetcar, or for at last having made his alcoholism pay off in a spent liver, or, yes, for being crushed under an animal weight and having one's left ventricle invaded by the fifth anterior rib—wherever he is, Dr. Veen may now congratulate himself on this specificity (you were useful after all, you old muskhound).

"Death before dishonor"? Don't fool yourself. Death *is* dishonor, no matter what the stonemasons say. You count your luck by whether (as will be the case for Wyatt, fifty years from now) death is your *first* dishonor, and not the end of a clown's parade of them. Vada's life has been a fire drill with midget cars, a vast richment of embarrasses, and here he lies, twenty-nine years old, dying beneath three hundred pounds of grizzly pelt and weighted urethane on the trophy-room floor of his lifelong friend and rival, Wyatt, on the eve of Wyatt's marriage to the woman Vada loves, Darla. If you can find silver in there, by all means pry it out like a filling, rush on down to the pawnshop, get yourself something nice. It doesn't have to be black; life is for the living.

What Vada asks is indulgence of the digressions of the corpse-to-be—he'd like a slightly protracted version of the thirty seconds you give more or less willingly when a funeral procession passes. You know: those purple pennants snapping imperiously above windows, ordering you to sit tight or you're a heel.

Vada understands you want to get on with it. Your own lives are more important to you than his is. You're overdue for a cut and color. Your cat needs a cranberry pill before it pisses the sofa again, and there's no fresh side of the cushion left to turn up. Your kids, in soccer togs, are squawking in the back, not yet propagandized into the idea that the dead need deference. (Bravo, children, and good luck.)

It's time, as the gridironists say, to make forward progress for positive yardage. Time to get on with dying, and Vada's first step—patience, please!—is to squeeze what he can from the fraction of memory he's been allotted.

It started, as he's already complained, just twenty minutes ago.

5

Midwife to Giants

Twenty minutes ago. Another steamy Saturday in endless July, with the push-mower flipped on its side and fuel leaking from the cap's shoddy seal. Vada braces his belly against the left front wheel, reaches up the chute, and probes. The blades of this cheapie are fouled almost constantly.

He'd like to think he might look, to a passerby, like a vet yanking a recalcitrant calf. As a boy, Vada dreamt of hauling a black bag—a well-worn accordion bulging with utensils (goat forceps, emasculator, speculum the size of fire tongs), with phials, syringes, knuckle-sized horse pills, souvenir calendars (a cockatiel riding the nose of a tabby cat, perhaps a moose wooing a jungle gym in lonesome Maine)—down rural roads before dawn. He'd give his satchel a fond pat as he shaved a corner at speed, on his way to minister to large animals: carnival elephants, emus, yaks, orcas, triceratopses, whatever sort of colossus fate laid out for him.

It was an appealing fantasy: urgent errands, a trusty sack of tools, a road all his own. Dr. V, Midwife to Giants, would be hale and cheerful. In manger, mid-crisis, he'd be prone to step back and wink at the farmer in whose hands a portable spotlight quavered. Then Dr. V would nudge his glasses up his nose, grasp those frail forelegs again: *Come on in, my shy friend. Oho, the water's fine.*

Like every promise of childhood, that turned out to be a joke. Vada's hardly the one to usher reluctant creatures into this world. Turns out that womb-clinging is the last wisdom a creature is permitted before being hauled up into a lifetime of harsh light and agony. Instead of dipping buckets of spermaceti like Queequeg, as he once imagined (and a honking fuck-you in passing to the publishers of *The Boy's Golden Illustrated "Moby-Dick"* for promoting professions long passed from the world and, one discovered, no longer smiled upon by teachers or peers as subjects for schoolboy rhapsody) . . . instead of milking whales, Vada whiskbrooms the condoms blocking the drain in wash bay #3 at Caw-Caw Car Cleaners. He's fallen far, spermically speaking: from the majestic *Physeter macrocephalus* all the way to what his friend Tisha calls the "urban whitefish," examples of which have been either vacuumed from backseats or tossed aside by the teenagers who tryst by night in the privacy of the bays.

Oho, the water's . . . What a jackass he was.

Far from fine, the water is soapy brown, and it sluices to foaming grates clogged with—besides those city-fish—cigarette butts, desiccated fries, promo postcards, smudges of moth. In his sweeping, Vada is cheered on only by the massive rotary mops that buff windshields and hoods and quarter panels. The closest he's come to veterinary heroism is ministering with a spray nozzle and a rag to Mustangs and Rabbits.

Vada Prickett, DVM, has devolved into Vada Prickett, HA. The capitalized laugh is thanks to Wayne Albergotti, owner of Caw-Caw, who's crazy for titles adapted from the geniuses of WalMart or Starbucks or Fascist Italy. After two years on the job, Vada has yet to advance beyond Hose Associate. He's afraid to ask for promotion; it's dangerous to tempt the nomenclaturist. His friend Lem's campaign for a raise got him no extra money but, as a sop, the new title he wears on his special extra-wide nametag: Maestro of Squeegee, which he accepted in preference to Squeegeeista.

Wayne, meanwhile, insists on answering to DUCE: Director of Undercarriage, Carriage, Etcetera. It's thanks to the DUCE's cinderblock-sized employee manual, which includes a long and spectacularly irrelevant biography of Mussolini, that Vada is able to provide a catalogue of Benito's wounds. How can you wax a car if you don't know that the Leader's body was kicked to a pulp, after which his shirt was set on fire and fed to him? If you're going to dust the dash without disturbing the trip odometer, surely you have to know that Mussolini was shot with a borrowed pistol that sported a tricolor Italia ribbon on its trigger guard, and that some modest bystander cord-tied the skirt of the Duce's mistress to her legs so as to deny the mob any looky-looky. The lesson here is discretion, men, *discretion*. This is the watchword of today's Auto Detailing Technician. Whatever secrets you learn from your expert reading of a car—its seat stains, the suspiciously clean and lemony ashtray, the wrack and ruin of the way-back, the scratch marks on the trunk's interior—are protected by client–Auto Detailing Technician privilege.

Still Vada's traitorous synapses keep firing, bringing back his Dolittle fantasy. It's better to face facts. Fact: the only animals in Vada's life just now [Corpse's Note: that is, gentle reader, twenty minutes ago; keep up, please] are the cartoon tortoise and hare on the mower's throttle, a foot to the left of Vada's cheek as his hand roams up the debris chute and reaches, at last, the clotted blade. This lever is the manufacturer's little joke: The only difference between the two settings is how high the engine revs. The mower roars more ferociously on bunny than on turtle, but it cuts no differently.

Vada has always been able to count on his timing, and sure enough, thirty seconds ago, as he pulled on a canvas lawn glove nubbled with polka dots, hitched up his shorts, wrestled the mower onto its side, and hove to, he saw Wyatt—lifelong neighbor, boyhood companion, and betrothed of the incomparable Darla Dietz—flying down his driveway in a customized golf cart, on his way to fetch the mail. Wyatt's initials are painted on the cart's side in a curlicue script, and they spell out a retort to the scoffing noise any sane person makes when confronted with the vehicle's orange paint, its fringe-top surrey roof: "No way!" Yes, WAY.

WAY, HA. The world insists on insults in uppercase. Vada gets it. How could he not get it by now?

Wyatt (what was he doing here? he was supposed to be away for another six hours) tooted the horn, a custom-made that alternates between the opening bars of "The Battle Hymn of the Republic" and "Witchcraft." This noon it was the chairman of the board rather than the Lord a-trampling out his vintage.

That Vada knows this history—he was consulted on the question of "Witchcraft" versus "Suspicious Minds," "Papa's Got a Brand-New Bag" having been eliminated in the prelims on the grounds of James Brown's poor driving record—serves as a painful reminder that he's always been stuck here, in this lakeside neighborhood of doctors and lawyers and pilots, a place where every soul's cry against injustice or ostentation ("No fucking *way*, man") is hurled back pronto in cursive capitals.

And where next Saturday, a week from today, Wyatt is scheduled to marry Darla, the most adorable woman in the world. Speaking of which, where was she, who *was* supposed to be here now?

The neighborhood association plans to hang a congratulatory banner across the entry to the subdivision. They asked Vada to kick in twenty bucks, but he refused, wouldn't budge . . . or wouldn't answer the phone at least, just stood trembling over it, rocking on his heels, as Juanita Proehl prattled to his machine: "Vada, you know we just hate to fundraise, but the price of banners these days is a scandal. They didn't used to be so dear. There's like a lamination shortage, the guy in town said. We're just plowing through the world's resources, it's a shame, but this is *important*. Now as you know, the association doesn't have money for extras like this, and if we don't get donations we'll have to cancel the fall pig-picking, and nobody wants that. By the way, will you help us dig the pit? Wyatt would do it as usual, but he'll be in Antigua with his bride. You could borrow his backhoe, maybe?" Vada, summoning every reserve of courage, refused to call her back. Which didn't stop Juanita, of course. Even now the guy in town (almost certainly Il DUCE's adjutant over at Jax' Plax-Max) is brushing on his precious laminate. Soon this mockery, too, will find its four-foot letters. OK, OK—back to the matter in hand. Thanks to Wyatt, the idlers at the local breakfast joint, Skink's, would soon be calling Vada "Lawn Proctologist" again. The analogy wasn't, sad to say, inapt. He was wearing the glove because what clogged the blade might not be grass alone. There was Kendall Proehl's Great Dane to contend with, its crap Matterhorns. Surely Vada couldn't have zoned out and plowed into a turd alp again. Surely he could have.

These twit musings were to blame. They're the fate of the solitary man—just as the errant moose has no choice but to size up a swing set as the best available mate ("She looks fine to me too, my brother. Oh, those mazy antlers . . .").

Here came Wyatt, back from the box with his bouquet of mail, which no doubt didn't consist of overdue bills, tire-recap circulars, and canning-supply catalogs sent, it seems, to remind him to keep mourning his parents, nine years gone. The horn sang out again. Vada knows where the motherfucking grapes of motherfucking wrath are stored, thank you. But—what else to do?—he waved halfheartedly with the fistful of glop and then flung it toward the back of the cart, one hundred yards away, after it sang past.

Wyatt's pavement was perfect, unlike Vada's buckled and crumbling driveway. If Wyatt Yancey needs fifty thousand pounds of gravel and asphalt, he can call in a favor. Easement, fire permit, cushy job for a druggie cousin: the favors are there to be plucked. A living parent, ten days of rain, an untroubled soul—let me make a call or two. Where there's a will, there's a . . . oh, screw it . . . WAY.

Vada wrestled the mower onto its wheels and yanked the cord, and the din drowned out all thought.

6

A Note to the Timekeeper

You dry-souled pedant. Yes, it's true—if you're going to be a stickler—
that Vada has ventured farther back already than the time allotted. He
didn't attend either vet school or carwash orientation in the last twenty
minutes, didn't celebrate last Halloween at noon this July 21. He hasn't
had his birth-slimy rump slapped by Dr. Sowell in nearly three decades.
It's even true that Wyatt's ride *to* the mailbox lies beyond the pale,
though his trip back is in bounds.

But memory, dear timekeeper, is a pouchy, convoluted thing, like
those valises you see salarymen toting on trains. Or it's a fruitcake,
dense and indestructible, studded with green cherry hemispheres and
shreds of nutmeat and dried-coconut confetti. Or it's an infinite intestine that absorbs what it will and then doubles back on itself to close its
loop—though the loop isn't closed in the sense that you can't still always
add more, there's a tube leading in, which is what makes it infinite, it's
just closed in the sense that nothing is lost or voided, only absorbed or
passed around the circuit again and again—an ever-lengthening turd-
train of memories one can't leach any good out of.

Oh, forget it. Metaphors aren't Vada's gift, clearly. It isn't an intestine.
It is a mystery, for God's sake, a mystery, and surely you know that the
right thing to do with a mystery is to stand before it in awe. Yes: awe-
struck, awe-inspired, awe-smote or smitten, awe-full. If you aren't on

your knees before a mystery, you should at least be on your heels. In any case, Vada only got to those anachronistic things—the goat-forceps fantasy, the tenderized paw—by way of where he was precisely twenty minutes ago. Time's not as simple as you make it out to be. It's hard to stay on the reservation.

Timekeeper, a plea: It's not like you don't have plenty to spare. From each according to his endless stores, to each according to his meager needs. Take a cue from the Italian communists, please, for once. Wait until Vada's dead before you piss on his face and set his shirt on fire and make him eat it.

One other thing: please grant Darla a long life and no guilt. If Vada's death needed hastening, Darla would be his hastener of choice. She isn't responsible. She was merely fate's instrument. Let her know that, OK? Surely holding a stopwatch isn't a full-time job, and you can spare a consoling whisper? Vada will keep things moving along here while you're gone. Trust him. Go, go.

7

Second Seat, Back Fiddle

Wyatt's life has rolled out before him like a movie star's gloating tongue of red carpet. Thanks to Reid Yancey's connections, Wyatt's birth was heralded by a proclamation of the legislature: edged in gold, sealed with scarlet wax, encased in glass, and mounted on the wall of his bedroom. When he was six months old, an adman spotted him, all but snatched him from his stroller, and hired him on the spot to be "spokesbaby" for a local company introducing a new molded-rubber infant chair. The chair looked like a Day-Glo pillory in which your baby might, in Puritan New England, have been punished on the town square for tippling or calumny, but it made *any* kid into a phenom who could sit upright at eight weeks. Parents will pay anything for precocity, and the chair became a national hit. Throughout his childhood, Wyatt would receive every quarter a residuals check. Even in his young-adulthood, people would stop him and turn their heads sideways and swear they knew him from *somewhere*. Once, at the caramel-corn stand in the mall, Vada had stood by a woman with a scoliotic daughter who'd "fought through it" thanks to the injection-molded prison Wyatt had advertised. While this misty-eyed mom pumped Wyatt's sixteen-year-old hand and pinched his sixteen-year-old cheek, she said, "Your posture meant so much to so many people. Bless you."

Wyatt was one of those blond kids whose arms are a fine-downed brown, the kind whose heads get tousled even by strangers. Vada still recalls the way Ms. Gillum, their sixth-grade math teacher, ushered them back into the room after he and Wyatt winged erasers at Curtis Behre, who'd been at the blackboard flaunting his skills at digit-carrying. Wyatt had collected the missiles, double-dipped them in dust from the little-used rear board's trough, handed one to Vada, and given the signal. Wyatt's clocked Curtis in the ear, and Vada's drifted three feet right and thunked uselessly into a map, leaving an imperialist smudge on Africa. Wyatt, glibly apologetic, was spared, but sullen Vada was sentenced to cleaning his schmutz off the Third World after school. After their hallway talking-to, on the way back to class, he couldn't help noticing the tender way Ms. Gillum cupped Wyatt's skull with her right hand. Her left was planted, blunt palm foremost, between Vada's shoulder blades, like a gangster's gat.

Adults adored Wyatt. He could pull off the supercharged politeness they were mad for, and without seeming a suck-up. His "sirs" and "ma'ams" had an undertone, noticeable for some reason only to the young, of insolence, or maybe not insolence but merely confidence that this was *his* world, and soon he'd come into his inheritance. The attitude gave him the air of a revolutionary. He was the schoolyard's Che Guevara, but a Che who could have buttled. "Yes, Ms. Gillum. Thank you, ma'am. The fault is mine. I accept full responsibility."

Vada, on the other hand, felt *guilty*, an emotion inconceivable to Wyatt, but his shame took the form of a hot-faced, shifty scowl. He knew better than to voice his defense: Nobody's aim was that squirrelly. Hadn't he missed Curtis basically *on purpose*? Couldn't Ms. Gillum see there'd been no malice in his heart, toward either blond boy or Dark Continent?

Vada was cowed by grownups, but when he watched Wyatt parley with Ms. Gillum or the fire chief or the principal, it became possible to see their vulnerabilities. Wyatt had the power of laying them bare via manners. It was like an X-ray, and it thrilled and horrified Vada to gaze at the bright bones thus revealed. Chief Gressette's golf pants were relics from a svelter time, too-tight Sansabelts with odd horizontal pockets that bore finger stains, and maybe there was something less than awe-inspiring about his candy-red Caprice with the gold-lettered doors and a siren he'd let the kids set off. Two of Principal Shuler's fingernails were clubbed and yellow, and it seemed sad to see her tuck the bad ones behind their betters as she chortled at Wyatt's jokes . . . could the old bat, with her lopsided shoulder pads and Pilgrim shoes, be *flirting* with an eleven-year-old?

When one stood next to Wyatt, it was possible to see in adults what *he* must: paunchy frauds playing out the string, people who'd given up on their own ambitions and were now hunkered in the last ditch of vicariousness, praying their zitty, gawkward children would do better. This illusion was hard to hang on to—hence Vada's father's consternation. Only Wyatt the paragon kept hope alive: Maybe, just maybe, their children would wake up and buckle down and, one of these days, look alive. Maybe the next generation's lives wouldn't be so paltry and cheap, so second-seat and back-fiddle, so *small-time*. This next generation might bestride the town like . . . like Wyatt Yancey.

Wyatt trounced Vada in every game they played, and he was endlessly gracious, which sucked even more. Didn't he have the decency to be a bad winner? But victory was no less than Wyatt's birthright. When Vada was ten, he pleaded with his father to buy him a space-age orange kicking tee, then spent a month in secret practice at the high school—but when the Punt, Pass, and Kick competition came around, Vada hit three skitterers that rattled among cars parked by the band shell, and Wyatt boomed one that bounded over the fence and ended up between the tank and the World War II bomber that were the centerpieces of Yancey Park. While Wyatt accepted his prize, camphor-smelling Mrs. Seibelson was making Vada help adjust her passenger-side mirror, which one of his kicks had knocked screwy. Then she made him erase his traces with a wet-wipe.

8

Near-Zero Turning Radius

It cranks the first time, and back inside his cocoon of racket, Vada gladly returns to the thoughts of a lawn-mowing man: *Is that a root or a rock? Should I reverse and go counterclockwise a bit, for variety? When I encounter a lost-dog flyer or a cheeseburger wrapper, do I let go of the handle and endure the automatic shutoff?* The answer is almost always no. To do so would result in the cessation of holy noise, a silence that seems a defeat. In the sudden quiet he feels exposed, like a teenager who's been crooning falsetto in his car on a summer afternoon, pouring on the emotion, clenched fist and shut eyes and all, and then the radio blinks off at a stoplight and he's caught out by everyone in neighboring cars. Vada doesn't scream underneath the mower's covering noise, but he adopts the mower's scream as his own. He keeps both hands firmly on the handle, which shudders like something he's choking the life out of, and he leans into his task like a cartoon of weariness and downtroddenness and lets the mower roar for him. He has only the tiniest measure of control over the timbre and fury of the sound, but he uses it from time to time, like an inside joke—*terp, terp, terp, terp; BUNNY, motherfuckahhh.*

So he blasts bits of napkin into confetti, fertilizes his beds with Big Mac clamshells. When he encounters teens' discarded forties or one of Wyatt's stray golf balls, he grumblingly halts his progress, turns the mower aside, and contorts himself so he can kick bottle or ball out of the way without cutting the engine. He looks forward to the big powdery mushrooms he can explode into chocolaty spores, and he deftly edges around the poop that lurks.

He's not bored out here; it's too loud for boredom. And, too, there are other questions to entertain. He always starts on the perimeter and works inward. But once one's narrowing circles have cut off some smaller section of yard—the result of irregular geometry, a flowerbed, a staked Bradford pear that needs skirting—does one proceed according to plan, or, a prisoner to compulsion, does one find oneself spun on heel as if by the will of the lawn itself, forced to make the series of short and ever-shorter turns that by the end look jerky and angry and frantic, as if the ragged grass is an affront and must be expunged, expunged, *expunged*?

One is always spun, of course, and then abruptly finds himself at the center of his obsession, amidst a massacre of shorn blades, wondering what's happened to the plan and feeling like the trip across already-cut spaces to the rest of the task is shameful, a perp walk with sneaker tips stained green.

There are other questions for the lawn-mowing existentialist, thinks Vada as he cants his right hip and shields his face from the sasanqua hedge along the road. *Do my swaths overlap too little (which will leave a fringe) or too much (which makes me overcareful and a waster of time and energy)? And what does it mean that I even have such a task to do? What does it mean that, in a way, I enjoy it?*

Because who wants to be the kind of guy who not only has a lawn (bad, as it makes him a suburbanite drudge) but has to mow it himself (he's cheap, he's poor, he doesn't want to give a hand up to the boys who rove the neighborhood with their creaking rattletraps, pleading for business and poaching one another's yards), and with a power mower (bad Earth citizen) that's not a ride-'em (in which case he could at least look masterful, a man *astride* something—Hannibal bunching an elephant's silky ears in his fists, a Blackfoot brave in stirrups, Peter Fonda on a chopper). Riding a mini-tractor—it's the posture of the smug: knees spread, feet flat on a metal deck. Oh, to be a man with a near-zero turning radius.

9

Nevertheless

Let it be clear: Vada is not a bard of lawn care, and he takes no special pleasure in or notice of mowing, unless and until it's the last pleasure he's allowed to cling to in this life. Before now it's been just another task that gets him an hour down the line. As he staggered through the noontime glare, he would never have guessed that philosophical thoughts were occupying his attention. His mind felt pleasantly empty . . . but in retrospect it turns out that he was, by God, pondering the verities—second-string verities, perhaps, inexpertly pondered, but still.

Vada's not suggesting that he's profound; he's been hardcore antifound for as long as he can remember. Mainly he was pondering the sweat dripping itchily down his neck, spinning out his fantasy of devising a turfgrass hybrid that recognizes squatting Great Danes and delivers a massive anal shock, wondering what time the Canadian lumberjack championships are on this afternoon (he loves the sound of spiked shoes biting into wood in the climbing events), speculating whether he's out of the good mustard, the one with the specks in it—and is the bread green again? Most of all, asking *Where is she, where is she, where is she? And what's HE doing home?* Philosophical hoo-ha is not his bag, is what he's saying. The big ideas are like background radiation. They provide an imperceptible baseline of warmth, the remnant of a long-ago big bang that keeps the temperature of Vada's universe of contemplation a couple degrees above absolute zero.

Depth: last refuge of the desperate, a place no one would go by choice. If there were another option, would the Loch Ness monster and giant squids and underwater zombies and so on live in cold and total darkness, their skins squeezed by pressures of a bajillion pounds per square inch? Vada can relate, guys—he and the squids and the swimming undead form a brotherhood of the compressed.

"Nevertheless." A lovely word, the contrarian's friend. "That's stupid, Vada. It's pointless. Why on earth would you want to do that?" "Nevertheless."

"Only a retard would believe that." "Nevertheless."

"Sinner, why should ye be admitted at the gates of heaven?" "Sir—nevertheless."

Confess it. As the area still to be mown shrinks to the size of a baseball diamond, then a sedan (such as might be circumnavigated at Caw-Caw, hose blasting), then the girth of a bulging black vet-bag, what dominates Vada's attention and drowns out every other thought, from sweat and mustard on up to Kierkegaard, is two people. As usual, two people. Two people, not one couple—they are to be held apart resolutely, in his mind's eye and in life.

Darla and Wyatt.

Darla, and Wyatt.

Darla. Wyatt.

Darla.   Wyatt.

Vada, the Vada of twenty minutes ago, has a plan. Today is Implementation Day. And if Darla rejects him . . . what will he do? Why does he do any of the idiotic things he does? Why conceive and execute a plan you know must fail, and one whose failure will drive you away from the one place you know, the spot where your parents set you down and where grief and habit have kept you for the years since they died? Why do something to guarantee that you'll be banished from the Eden where, over years to come, you might at least watch Darla and privately pine . . . where you might be allowed to be her friend and see her, talk to her?

You know why as well as Vada does. *Nevertheless.*

10

Book Learning Is the Pink Fiberglass of the People

Ten days ago, late afternoon, Wyatt's yard. The gazebo is a cross between bandstand and dovecote, twelve feet in diameter, that Wyatt's mom put in years ago and promptly forgot, perhaps because it commands the same lake view that every other spot on their lawn does, only two feet higher. Penny's Folly, Wyatt's dad called it, and its only uses were as cache for the skin magazines Wyatt was always finding in the woods (he had a nose) and as setting for boyhood play (everything from Castle Siege to Fotomat, a game that, though boring, turned out to be prophetic [see Vada's résumé, 2000]).

When she moved in with Wyatt, Darla reclaimed the space. She draped diaphanous pale-green muslin around the perimeter, scattered cushions and wicker furniture over an outdoor rug, laid in earthen smudgepots full of incense. The effect is vaguely haremlike, and surely, Vada thinks as Darla rolls off her throw pillow and starts doing side leg-lifts, that's one step more inviting than she meant. You know what word you don't see often enough, hear often enough? "Tautening." As Darla levers her leg up and down, that's how he'd describe what it's doing: tautening. Vada is needled by a memory of the rain-damaged French-maid pictorial that once resided on the underside of a bench just about where her feet are now. He can't remember the pictures, but he liked the title, which was . . . what? He doesn't want to know. Did you hear him, memory? He doesn't want to know. This is his friend's fiancée. Stop it.

He sits forward, straightens his spine, raises himself to his chastest, most formal height. Beneath him the papasan chair crackles and groans.

A flash of thigh and feather duster, and there it is: *Bone Soir.*

Next week this gazebo will serve as the platform on which preacher and betrothed will stand for the ceremony, and for the last few minutes Darla has been talking through details of décor. Wyatt asked for bunting, but Darla says bunting is appropriate only if you're awarding medals or selling cars. She wants a bare stage, just a waist-high wrought-iron table, tasteful, with a vase of wildflowers. Meanwhile Wyatt's envisioned a thick shag of petals sprinkled from baskets by cherubim; an orchestra; a phaeton driven by some rat-faced drunk in silk stockings and a plumed cap; sky-writing; a blimp. But Wyatt doesn't actually *care.* His job is to suggest romantic grandiosities and have her veto them. The decisions are hers. Besides, he's not here to hash it out.

"Hopeless," Darla says. "Barely two weeks till D-day, a zillion things to take care of, yet this afternoon he drove an hour to shoot skeet. Excuse me, 'sporting clays.' What's sporting about shooting molded dirt?"

Vada glances at the dirt daubers blundering overhead, searching for adobe nests they won't find any trace of unless they check the knob of the whisk broom leaning against the column across the way. Darla's been taking down some clays of her own.

"What's the deal with men and hunting?" she asks. "You're the only guy I know around here who doesn't. You don't, right? Not ever?"

"No." It pleases Vada to give a right answer, but he can't risk a lull. There's no good in having her consider whether that leaves him out of the category *men.* She licks a droplet of perspiration from her upper lip, and he slumps back in the chair, looks away. "And you?" tries Vada. "Have you ever?"

Darla lies on her left elbow, left hip, and scissors her right leg up and down, a metronome keeping perfect time. A broad smile tells him he's asked the right thing. *Thereby hangs a tale.* "Only once," she says. "Indoors."

The story doesn't interrupt her exercise. Like a backbeat, her parachute shorts billow and fall, billow and fall. "My uncle was an exterminator out in Ellicott City, and when I was fifteen and looking for summer cash, he hired me for an after-hours job. There was this home-improvement warehouse infested with a couple dozen pigeons. They were freaking out customers: flapping around, dropping bombs on the merchandise, roosting in the eaves. The *cooing* was the worst. You get enough of them in an aluminum building, and an echo starts up, and then people go all Tippi Hedren on you. Which is bad for business, so they called my uncle.

"Annoying noises might have done the trick, except that the racket would just chase the birds into walls, and if you scare them away they go out in a hail of guano. No easy way to poison, either. The usual methods would have meant feet-up birds in the aisles or sick-kid lawsuits. So one night after closing, my uncle and I put on every light in the place. It was like an alien autopsy room in there, unbelievably bright. He gave me a sack and gloves, and then he went up in some sort of cherrypicker thing they used for restocking, and he knocked off the pigeons one by one with a shotgun. The gun was loaded with what he called 'popcorn,' hard enough to pierce bird skin but not the roof, and not toxic like lead. It was like grit, and the stray ammo came right up with a shop-vac afterward. The weird thing was that he'd take one down, and the one a foot away seemed not to notice. The birds didn't *budge*. 'Fish in a barrel,' he kept saying. My uncle took pity on me: I was garbage detail only. If he didn't kill one cleanly, he'd whir himself down in the bucket and twist the neck himself. One started flapping down the paint aisle, and he had to stomp it with his boot. At the end he ran the cherrypicker all the way to the roof and pulled down three nests with eggs in them. It all went into my sack."

"You did this *why*?"

"For the life-lesson, mainly."

Vada raises his eyebrows and waits.

"OK, sure. A hundred bucks for two hours' work. I had my eye on a boss stereo. If only I'd known . . ."

"Wait, I've heard this one. You got the stereo, but the tweeters always had this distortion that sounded like cooing, and when you took it back the salesman claimed not to hear anything wrong, and then you noticed the weird way he moved his neck and tucked his head under one arm. And you decided, for your karmic good, to sell and give the proceeds . . ."

"I'm serious. It was traumatic, and I've hated hunting ever since." She pauses, smiles. "Though I have to admit the stereo was *awesome*. Sometimes life-lessons don't work out as neatly as in sermons. But it's a principle now. No hunting."

"Even hunting that nets you fifty bucks an hour?"

"It's an *expensive* principle."

Vada has begun to hope that Wyatt—expected any minute—will be delayed, just for a decade or three. Here at last is the life he's been wishing for, waiting for. A beautiful woman, tautening. Breeze-stirred muslin. Yarn-spinning. He just spoke about fifty words in a row, without stammering. They weren't *smart* words, or *funny* words, but maybe he's working up to that.

"Your turn, V."

"Hunting story? Uncle story?"

"Take your pick." Darla switches to right elbow, right hip, and left leg, resumes her exercise.

Vada tries to find a comfortable posture, but his chair has stayed stubbornly wicker. He knows just the story. "My father's brother," he begins, "built a woodshop in his yard, and he insulated the walls with two hundred copies of *Das Kapital* that he got at the flea market. He used to say [here Vada adopted a voice that was much more Foghorn Leghorn than Uncle Gene], 'I figured it was about time that windbag did somebody some *good*. Practical good. You know what they say, boy: "Book learning is the pink fiberglass of the people." You take that down. You listen to your uncle, you'll go places.'"

Darla, bless her, laughs. "You made that up!" she accuses.

"I swear," says Vada. "Back in the '60s, the Anti-Red League over in Florence bought a whole crate of the books for their Know-Thine-Enemy campaign, but they didn't mean to know their enemy *in German*. Any enemy that wants knowing is gonna have to talk English. My uncle got the whole lot for five bucks."

"Did he put them in shredded, or whole?"

"Whole, I think, but I didn't ask. Book shredding's easier said than done, unless you're a carnival strongman."

"Was the shed warm?"

Vada can't resist. "Do you mean what's the Q rating of communism?"

Darla laughingly corrects him. "Insulation has an R value, not a Q rating. Q measures the popularity of celebrities."

"Q, R," says Vada. "I've never understood ratings. AAA bonds versus A-1, PG and PG-13. Crash tests, meats. It's all German to me."

Darla, having completed a hundred lifts with each leg, stands, sets hands on hips, and starts rotating her torso at the waist. She looks like she's shadowboxing with the paper lantern she's hung from the eaves. "F ratings are for fire retardant stuff," she says. "Windows have U ratings. Tires take H." Every time she leans back, her T-shirt rides up and exposes her belly.

R, NC-17 . . . Vada dares not let it go higher. Those striae of muscle, that winking horizontal innie. His F-rating is being tested—and here it comes, right on time, the fire brigade of shame providing its usual dousing.

"See," he says. "Ratings all up and down the alphabet. And every one another way to be found wanting."

Darla stops swaying. There's a coin-sized spot of sweat on her T-shirt, just below her throat. "See?" she says. "*That's* what we need to overcome. If we're going to find your dream-girl, you need some self-confidence."

I've found her, Vada says, only to discover that he hasn't said it aloud. But of course he knew that. He feels restored, in a way. Here's the topic he knows most about. His failure—home ground, home truth. "I'm not rated for self-confidence," he says. "Foundation's too weak. You pack that on, it could cause a catastrophic structural failure."

"I'm no psychiatrist," says Darla, "but I'm pretty sure that if your deflecting joke contains the phrase 'catastrophic structural failure,' it's not enough of a joke. You know what? Once the wedding's over, I'll make you my next project."

"You should know," says Vada, "that muslin gives me a rash. I can't be trusted around open flames. And doc? I think I might be prone to transference." This is the boldest thing he's ever said to her.

"Ha ha," says Darla, in a tone he can't read. Just then, a quarter-mile down the driveway, there's a series of honks, and Vada swivels to see Wyatt's yellow Hummer.

"Home is the hunter," announces Darla, "home from the hill." Is that weariness in her voice? "Project"—he likes the sound of that. He'll be her Galatea. He jumps up, grabs the broom, and starts sweeping.

11

The Juicing Muse

So in summary . . . in the first ten minutes of the last twenty minutes of his life, Vada flipped the knob to off and stilled his synapses. Because he shut it down for those minutes, there's little for Mnemosyne to fasten on—but she, thorough girl, insists on trying to squeeze blood from the turnip that is Vada at Contemplation. Vada would like to stop her, for your sake if not his own, but he's in a weakened state, and anyway fears to cross anyone with hands tensile enough to draw blood from root vegetables. So, Mnemosyne: You go, girl.

What might she find, the Juicing Muse?

a) Glimpses, as Vada skirted the driveway, of the prodigiously blossoming peanut tree, soon to be bowed by the weight of hundreds of seedpods. If no one plucks the pods, the shallow-rooted tree may be tipped by autumn wind. Now there will be no one who knows this or cares. The real-estate agents will be busy burning beeswax candles, buffing floors, clearing clutter; Darla and Wyatt will have all their time taken up by wedded bliss. Who pays attention to a plant once its blooms are off? No one heeds the dormant.

b) As he negotiated the house's southwest corner, a view next door of Zorba the dalmatian in his pen, doing his low-slung version of a prisoner's pacing, his usual whines and howls drowned out by the mower yet somehow audible anyway.

c) Yet another dirt dauber nest in the eaves, to be poked down later—or not, it turns out—with a noodlish twenty-foot length of wood lath from his father's workshop: a task that always seems embarrassing because Vada has to brace the thing against his pelvis. He feels like the flag-bearer in a high school band, or perhaps a porn star in troubled late career.

With that Mnemosyne gives up, washes her hands of Vada's unpromising corpuscles. Let's give her thanks for trying, though. This stuff's boring even to Vada, not worth revisiting even when one has only a lousy third of an hour available for revisiting before shuffling off this mortal coil. Farewell, hard-to-pronounce muse. Farewell, butter-yellow cassia, badly named dog, bendy codpiece. Farewell, mortal coil.

12

The Next Ludicrous Failure Waiting in the Wings

If Vada yawns, he's dead. Those are the rules. Those must be the rules. God sits vigil at his bedside, an angel of unmercy, eager for any excuse to yank the plug, twist the neck, flick the hatchet. Maybe he's already flicked the hatchet, and this is just Vada making a last headless circuit of the yard, and he doesn't have sense enough to realize that his path is guided not by conscious thought but by an imploding nervous system that's jerking him in ever-smaller circles. Human consciousness, he remembers hearing somewhere, may continue after death by momentum. But Vada *had* no momentum.

Or God is behind a TV-game-show desk, holding a drumstick, and behind him is a gong. He's watching Vada juggle chainsaws while singing falsetto, and as soon as God gins up a cutting witticism he'll swing the stick and bang the gong and he and the rest of the celebrity panel will move on to the next ludicrous failure waiting in the wings.

And Vada? Poof.

God appears to be indifferent, either paring his nails or, Zeuslike, nailing his pairs. But just in case: Vada's kidding, Your Lordship. Really, he is, all that about game shows and chicken necks and that crack about lusty Jove and his bolts. Vada's not quite ready to go yet. Stay the gonging hand. Give him one more sprint around the henhouse, with feeling.

Yes, skeptics, it's easier to whip up ideas when the penalty for not whipping up ideas is death, *prontomente*. But Vada's tired of this question, whether he's inventing depths just to make the draining of the swamp of self last an instant longer, and the question will answer itself. Soon Vada will be gone, and you can congratulate yourselves on his having proved himself wrong and you having proved yourselves right, temporarily (you'll be gone too, someday, and your ideas with you, and those who survive you will congratulate themselves likewise on your having deluded yourselves into thinking you had substance when, as your corpse attests, substance is merely a lumplike remainder of what you used to have, or what used to have you).

13

Femme Fatality

A non-Platonic barely dialogue from a chilly January day at Caw-Caw, six months ago.

Tisha: "Same old story. A pretty woman shows up, and you rush to get underfoot. I can *see* it, Vada. I went out with a guy once who told me—we were watching *Double Indemnity*—that Fred MacMurray was doomed from the moment Barbara Stanwyck's ankle bracelet entered the film. Say what? Doomed to have a hard-on, maybe. But doomed to off her husband? Come on. If he was doomed then, he was doomed *before* then. He was an anklet waiting to happen. You are, too."

From underneath the SUV, Vada can see Tisha's feet. She's wearing canvas tennis shoes, and her ankles are wrapped in three layers of rolled coverall. She's not the jewelry type. "What brought this speech on?"

Tisha: "Oh, I can't *imagine*. Beautiful woman shows up for a wash, and you immediately prostrate yourself before her."

Vada: "How else am I supposed to give her an undercarriage spray?"

Tisha: "She didn't *ask* for one. You volunteered to throw one in for free."

Vada: "Road salt is awfully corrosive."

Tisha: "And isn't used within five hundred miles of here."

Vada scooches out from under the car by wriggling his hips. Beneath his goggles, his face is soaked and grimy. A chill is setting in. Vada thinks it's physical, but can't absolutely rule out existential. He tries to rally with a joke: "She looks like a worldly woman. The kind who would have an anklet. Think she has a husband?"

Tisha: "The dual car seats say yes."

Vada: "Then I may not live to star in *My Three Sons*."

Tisha: "I'm serious. What I'm giving here is advice. Some of you just can't be helped. Every woman is a femme fatale. And what you want isn't the femme. It's the fatality."

Vada peers through the window and beckons Ms. Stanwyck, who's sipping coffee from the mug he poured her.

14

Vomitus Mundi

Outside a zoo, Vada has seen only one bear before. He was ten.

A mid-spring Saturday. His father, in his role as wildlife conservation officer, had been called to investigate a farm-pond fishkill, and Vada was along for the ride, a rare foray with Vic into the world of men. He wanted to feel flattered, but the reason was that his mom was in Columbia on errands gynecological. There'd been a row, easily overheard from his room, that ended when Celeste barked, "You think seeing dead fish is going to damage him more than seeing his mother in stirrups? He goes with you."

Vada knew his job today was to be mature, the measure of which was manful silence. The farmer who led them down the narrow berm between fields set a solemn example. He must have been millennia old, to judge by the depth of his quiet. He rarely answered a question except by turning his watery eyes toward Vada's father and letting his chin rise or swing or sag almost imperceptibly. No wasted motion. He was a man made of earth, and to move was a task of seismology. He seemed to be stirred only by tremors born miles deep, and his swallowed rumbles or groans might have been the grindings of tectonic plates. The wad in his cheek was not tobacco but humus. He was a man who had mastered the art of even *spitting* thoughtfully.

Vada recalls being both excited and repulsed, as they topped the dam, by the sight of hundreds of fish floating belly-up around a spillway cap protected by wire mesh—a bobbing sheet of white, gill to gill, tail to tail, as if the fish were flashcards unsteadily held just under the murky water's surface. (*Perhaps,* the thought flitted through, *by zombies?*) These cards might be flipped at any moment to reveal . . . what? The usual "Go Tigers" in orange, maybe; or "Osteichthyes," the taxonomic class of bony fishes, part of a lesson arranged by his father and the programmers at South Carolina ETV. Or perhaps as the three men (*three men!*) approached, the fish would leap in unison, splash down and disappear, like frogs quitting the reeds when a boy crashed along a pond-bank.

But then the first tendril of stench had risen to Vada's nostrils, and with it the realization that "fishkill" meant what it said (an unfortunate property of words, he was finding). The thought of that malodor, held under the water for days on end, months, years, made his stomach clench. What were zombies, after all—once you divested them of their cool—but corpses, and what was a lakebed but a boneyard, the final rest of things sunken and reeking? What was the mud made up of that one let ooze between toes or hurled at a friend as he dove for cover?

The only flashcard lesson to be learned from the gas-filled bags before him, the ex-bellies of ex-fish, was *We Are Meat,* and that thought had cramped him and knocked him to his knees and lunged forth—though he tried to keep it quiet, quiet—in the form of his breakfast.

When he was done, he felt his father's hand cup the back of his head. "It's all right, son," Vic whispered. "Go on to the car. I'll be there directly." Vada sensed both tenderness and embarrassment, and he turned as his father stood up from his squat and sighed. The farmer gazed discreetly into the distance, a thousand-year stare. His shoulder blades projected from the back of his tight shirt like twin dorsal fins, and Vada noticed he was assless, the seat of his jeans caved in like a mouth barren of teeth. His right rear pocket bore a perfect circle of white, a snuff tin's halo.

Vada spat once more and wiped his mouth with a hand-shaped leaf his father ripped from a nearby bush. Meanwhile Vic and the farmer scanned the water. Nobody spoke. Nobody budged. A tableau: the hot puddle on the grass of the dam; the skeletal farmer, an exile on his own land, peering hard at the horizon. The father, the son, the holy bloated ghosts of fish. Vada wanted to gargle, but gargling would break the silence. He used the leaf's last clean point to brush a string of spittle that wouldn't let go. He floated the leaf on the puddle.

Not long before, Vada had prepared a Just So Stories report for Mrs. Ashley on the Congolese god Mbumba, who after ages feeling sad and queasy was said to have solved both problems at once by chucking up the universe. Here was a creation myth Vada could get behind, one that made sense: a world born of lonesome heart and sour stomach. He presented the case with relish, and was even ready, provisionally, to believe what he was saying, but his classmates and teacher had howled at it.

"That's enough, Vada," chid Mrs. Ashley. "Let's have no more mention of bodily fluids. You know my policy on suchlike talk."

"Them Africans is backwards," hooted Sam Chisum, whose mother, once a mermaid at Weeki Wachee Springs, later shed her rubber tail and her bubbler and got right with God. Now she was often quoted in the paper about how fluoridation was a satanist plot to leach the Jesus out of your teeth. Sam went on: "No wonder they don't have rocket ships, or guitar amps, or pants."

"I think you mean 'Those Africans are backwards,' Sam," Mrs. Ashley corrected. "They may not be as advanced as we are, but many Africans nowadays are Christians just like you and me. They have cities and shoes and everything. And they understand that we're God's children, not God's throw-up. You remember that."

"I bet the whole country stinks," added Graham Gossett. "It's like a bus station, only without the buses and stuff."

"Africa is more than one country, Graham," said Mrs. Ashley. She smiled: another misconception dispatched, another teaching moment seized. Then she noticed Vada still at the board. "Thank you, Mr. Prickett, for that provocative report. You may retake your seat."

Vada trudged up the aisle. Baines and Vesta, the black kids in his row, kept their eyes on their desktops. He wanted to let them know that he thought Mbumba a true god, as good as any other, a vomiting god who deserved his share of the limelight. He was certainly as plausible as pale-faced Zeus, that wife-fearer who slunk around costumed as a swan or a lightning bolt. Vada tried to beam this thought, but transmission was hopeless—Baines was the son of an A.M.E. minister, after all, and Vesta had quit paying attention years before, a policy being amply rewarded now.

Vada found it hard to relinquish his admiration for Mbumba. He liked the idea of a god who created the universe in an act only partially under his control. The Big Barf Theory: what made it less believable than Yahweh throwing together all creation in a frenzied week, out of what . . . boredom? How could an all-seeing, all-powerful God produce a world where the stegosauri got killed off and Graham and Sam were left alive?

And then, alongside the fishkill pond, Vada had to pay for his heresy. He'd brought up not a cosmos but only the recognizable remains of fried egg, red-pepper-flecked patty sausage, and toast—a dialogue bubble in which a single word could be read: "Weak." He stood and went. The world resumed its noise, and Vada cringed to hear behind him the rasp of his father's boot as he kicked dirt over the sick like a cat in a box.

For the first few miles of the trip home, Vada nursed his sour mouth and sulked. What could be less adult than the act his mother called "waldoing"? What ruder betrayal of silence was there? What must his father think? It was clear that Vic felt no anger, but neither, thank God, did he stoop to giving comfort. Vic was no soother. He wouldn't ply Vada with pop-and-sonny-boy inanities. He knew well, a block off the old chip, that comfort can't be given; it either is one's birthright or isn't.

Vada brought his knees to his chin, pressed himself against the door, twitched when his father flipped the new auto-lock and the car's innards seemed to convulse in belated sympathy with his. As they approached a small depot town, Vada glanced sidewise and saw Vic's eyes locked on the road ahead, keeping the wheels between the lines . . . conveying them from this moment to the next, which might turn out to be more congenial. A competent man, one who could hold his tongue, his liquor, his food—the kind of father who when his son yaks at pondside quickly identifies a tree with absorbent leaves, plucks one, and hands it over.

In the years since, Vada has sometimes wished for a father capable of making a joke to save the day. But what could he have said? No, the only line that seemed right was the one he'd actually whispered, providing the balms one could count on from Vic: taxonomy, expertise. "This is a swamp mallow leaf, *Hibiscus moscheutos;* it's not poisonous. Go ahead, blow your nose into it. It's safe." A father whose idea of consolation was Linnaean Latin and the promise that there would be no schnozz-rash to compound your misery.

"Look a-here!" said Vic now. Vada felt the brakes drag. "How about that? Think we should stop?" They were on the outskirts of the junction town, and Vada wondered why his father would get so excited about just another cinderblock cash-and-carry—Jeffy's Jiffy—that leaned toward the street as if it might tumble. Two forlorn gas pumps; a vat of boiled peanuts, big as a cannibal's pot, under a tin umbrella. And chained to a telephone pole at the street, a portable trailer sign, two bald tires and a yoke balanced on cinderblocks. Rimmed on two sides by an arrow of orange lights, it pointed you not into the lot but away, on down the road, and featured either a Bible verse or an ad for cardiology (BLESSED ARE THE P ACEMAKERS). The place was spilling over with itinerant workers, Hispanic men who sat atop the ice machine to cool their thighs or perched on their feet, squat vultures, on the curbs; only their eyes moved. They were eating Nekots or Slim Jims and drinking malt liquor while they waited for the slat-sided trucks to be emptied and brought back for another round of peach picking.

Vada couldn't help noticing, as the car slowed, that the pickers carried all their fat in swollen cheeks and gourd-hard bellies; everything else was sinew. They didn't have the glossy all-over chubbiness of the country club set. They carried those pockets of lard around their waists like bullion belts, insurance against leaner times. To think what these men might have done with the good food Vada left on that dam. Was it gross to think this, or stupid, or kind? Vada couldn't say.

But the car veered left rather than right, and when Vada turned, he saw his father pointing to a banner strung across the main street: RAYLRODE DAZE, it read. Vic pulled into one of the plentiful diagonal parking spots along the street. It was late morning, and but for the waiting pickers there seemed no one around.

Vic opened his door, beckoned Vada out. Several white men, uniformly elderly, were spilling out of an old hangar or switching barn that was, Vada could see through the door, filled with model trains. Most wore engineer's caps of blue-and-white twill; a red bandana clutched one guy's neck, as if to choke him into self-awareness—but this seemed a corner of the world that irony hadn't reached yet. A midway had been erected across from the square, but the rides wouldn't run until evening. There were a few people over there, sitting in lawn chairs and reading magazines while waiting for customers to come and buy their henna tattoos, their painted crabs, their biscuit tins and glass insulators.

Miss Scuppernong, identified by a hand-lettered sash, staffed a bake-sale booth, hawking the cobblers and wines of her dominion. She gave a corkscrewing pageant wave that Vada shyly answered.

Vic led his son past the Confederate War Memorial statue, which faced north, as always, to keep an eye on those sneaky Yanks. Beyond the statue was a truck dispensing name-brand chipped beef. Past it, ugly wood-burned signs (THE SMITH'S) to hang on your mailbox so punks could ride by and take baseball bats to them; a booth specializing in patriotic windsocks; an exhibit of choppers and sidecars. Vada saw rhinestone-studded T-shirts (Ride My Hog), old German helmets made of chrome, biker wallets on chains. CASH IS GOSPEL read one sign. There was a signup table for the John Birch Society, which seemed to be a club for stringy oldsters in hound's-tooth fedoras, clashing plaid shirts, and black-framed glasses. Under a canopy sat a zoot-suited minister huffing an asthma inhaler. His table was bedecked with a purple felt cloth on which was written, in fat yellow letters, FIRST CHURCH OF THE FACTORY SECOND: TO GOD YOU'RE NOT IRREGULAR. Just up the way—partially hidden by the snowball stand—sat a beefy psychic behind a card table. She wore a purple caftan and a jeweled hat, and gave a rumbling belly laugh when she saw Vada read her banner: MEDIUM LARGE. "Hey, kid. Read your palm? See your fyoocha."

Abruptly Vic grabbed Vada's collar and yanked him back from the curb, which kept Vada from being bowled over by a small brown bear on a bicycle. Dragged by a long leash, the bear made a wobbly turn. Its hair was matted and thin, skin slack. "One dollar for you boy pet him," said the man holding the bridle in one hand and rattling a red satin hatbox in the other. A gold tooth shone beneath his upper lip. "For twain-ty I vrestle mighty Meska."

"We're going," said Vic, and he put his arm around Vada, propelling him across the street and down a side aisle. Vada glanced back to see the bear circling a fire hydrant painted to look like Uncle Sam, remnant of the Bicentennial ten years before. Meska did a slow spin around the hydrant's red-and-white trousers, its robotic-looking bolts and knobs. The man, grinning, held his leash arm high like a dancer's and watched Vic and Vada go. Thirty feet away, his gold tooth still shone.

Even now Vada recalls the dingy rawhide tassels hanging from the handlebars, the animal's worn and dirty muzzle, like that of a teddy gnawed and drooled on for years by some mama's boy. He can still feel the tug of his father's hand. "I *said* come on!"

"Sorry about that stop," said Vic when they reached the car. "It made *me* want to throw up."

Twenty minutes into the drive home, Vada could hold it in no longer. "Pop," he announced, "when I grow up I'm going to be a large-animal veterinarian." It sounded ridiculous aloud, this title he'd heard on the radio one day. Were there small-animal vets? Amoeba vets? *Medium Large*?

But Vic didn't make fun. "Good for you," he said. He didn't ruin it by looking up from the road, much less by the chin-chuck of condescension. Men don't spare each other glances, not at the important moments. Which, oddly, this turned out to be. A smile twitched at the corners of Vic's mouth. The rogue emotion met resistance there (as was proper among men), but for once emotion won.

"Good for you, son," Vic repeated.

15

The Several Faces of Celeste

A Perfectly Respectable O'Clock for Your Turkey

Yes, Celeste tended to wear three-dimensional seasonal sweatshirts, for instance the one featuring Rudolph's nose, a red honkable cottonball uptilted from her bosom. Yes, she drove a car with wood veneer and the word "Estate" in its name. Yes, she tended to gabble, keeping Vada floating through the world on a tide of bright badinage. "I love these holiday plates. Look at all those symbols; nothing like a good symbol. That beaver with the big teeth is Punxsutawney Phil. He's for Groundhog Day. The flag is for Independence Day—no, wait, it's for Flag Day, and the scroll beside the tricorn hat is for Independence Day. My turkey is right at the top; Daddy's is, too. Is your turkey at the top? No, your shamrock is at the top. You should turn your plate. I know that puts the yams closest to you, but maybe that's where they should be. Yams are yummy, really they are. Yums are yammy. Don't cry. Quit your crying. OK, maybe you're right, sweetie, maybe you're right. Leave the turkey at seven o'clock. Seven is a perfectly respectable o'clock for your turkey. And maybe having the shamrock at the top will bring you good luck . . . not that the luck of the Irish isn't to eat potatoes every day and to like it, or at least try to like it. The poor children in the famine didn't dare turn up their noses at good starch, and they didn't have marshmallows and their potatoes weren't a festive orange like yours, either—no, of course I don't mean literally turn up your nose, get your fingers out of your nostrils *now*. [Pause.] But honey, Daddy and I have our turkeys at the top. Don't you want to match? It's Thanksgiving, after all. No, no, there's no holiday where you eat black people, silly, be careful what you say. That's the Reverend Martin Luther King Jr.; he symbolizes himself. The turkey symbolizes Thanksgiving, and the jumping electrified cat is Halloween, and Santa's for Christmas, but there's no symbol for Martin Luther King Jr. except Martin Luther King Jr., because racial justice doesn't have a mascot. It wouldn't be right. You know perfectly well who he is, Vada, he was a great man who had a dream about the contents of his character and got shot at a motel by a bad man. Stop asking questions and eat your yams. Just because you've got them hidden away at one o'clock doesn't mean you don't have to finish them. [Pause.] Vada, honey, don't you want your turkey where Daddy's turkey is? Most boys want their turkey where Daddy's turkey is. There you go, spin that plate. It's Thanksgiving, after all."

All these things are true, were true. But don't get her wrong. Yes, Celeste cared deeply about her Velcro advent calendars and her cypress knees baked in thimbles, dabbed with gray frosting, and deployed in a rough circle around Vada's swamp-tree birthday cake. But hers was the zeal of the convert who has time to make up, years of tchotchkeless, chatter-free unbaking to be shriven of. Celeste was like the undercover cop who gets in so deep that she forgets who she is, or who comes to rely so heavily on the role that the rest of her identity shrivels away. You know, like that former straight-arrow in the movies who finally gets so mobbed up in his mind that when his wife asks him to deadhead some daisies he reaches into his waistband.

Except that Celeste would be like the opposite, the ex-mobster (OK, psychologist) who when ordered to ice a snitch heads out to the guy's house with a bag full of compresses, throw pillows, and lollipops.

Ink-Pen Tracheotomy

But even though all that's true, it's also false. There was the other side of her, too, the side that made Vic call her, in tones of admiration, a "baby-faced chicken killer."

Take the time when she was ready to puncture her own throat with an ink pen. She'd inadvertently eaten something with peanut in it. Allergic reaction clenched her throat, and Celeste dropped her hand to the floorboard, fished up a ballpoint ("Dixie Hy-Test Meats, Highway 378, Batesburg, Meat Inspector On Site"), and poised it at her neck in case she needed to perform an autotracheotomy.

Vada still has the pen. A relic of the world's ass-kickingest saint, it's been niched for two decades now in a cedar-lined keepsake box, the kind of well-hinged ossuary in which one stores things kept for the sake of sake-keeping, to keep sakes alive, her sake or your sake or God's sake . . . they run together, which is good reason to lock them away in a box you never look into.

But of course it wasn't *his* idea to save the thing. Vada, at ten, wasn't savvy enough to see anything of note in a parent willing to perforate her windpipe with a linty pen fished from the floorboard as she sped toward town. Yes, he recalls being concerned—Celeste's inability to talk, her bugged eyes and splotchy face, made clear that this was not a drill. But certain factors mitigated his worry. For one, the attack happened on the way to the library, where Vada was to score another ten books on the borrower's card he'd begged for and recently been granted. The Case of the Mother Robbed of Breath? Pah. The mysteries captivating him at the moment were the three-minute kind that, if you got stumped, you could turn the book upside down and have solved for you ("The bank robber referred to a badly thrown tear-gas grenade as a fifty-eight-footer, so the thug is probably a baseball catcher. Look out for men with unusually developed squatting muscles . . . also possibly wearing wire masks").

Vada, preoccupied, at first thought Celeste's gasp was a show of appreciation for Dr. Haledjian, who despite the handicaps of eggheadedness and a weird foreign name with two dotted letters next to each other (*jiminy!*) had been able to call on a knowledge of our national pastime to snare the sturdy-gluted villain and his accomplice, a former fireballer fallen on hard times. How did this alien know the things he knew?

"HHHHhhhh!" applauded Celeste.

Vada turned the book upright and proceeded to the next case. He glanced up not when, in his peripheral vision, he saw his mom lurch forward, nor when she plucked up something from the mat and raised it to her neck. But there's something attention-getting about the clicking open of a pen.

They were halfway to Lexington, three miles out of town. "Hang on," Celeste rasped. "Allergy. Throat shutting." She reached across the bench seat and patted Vada's hand with the one that held the pen. "Be OK," she said, in a way that might be either a reassurance or a mother's dying instruction to the son she doesn't dare hope for too much from. Then she floored it.

Wyatt was in the backseat. He had tagged along not out of nascent book-love but out of a boredom so intense that even the library might alleviate it. Or maybe he came to convince himself that there were boredoms yet more unendurable than his, and that at least he'd never be one of the wraiths of late middle age who, instead of being abroad in the world, plumbing or comptrolling or assassinating or ordering others to do these things, sat at tables all day and read newspapers clipped to long brown wooden dowels. Even worse than regular newspapers, which were dull enough: *other cities'* newspapers. These were the last men in America to wear hats with feathers on the sides, and often their noses and cheeks bore the stigmata of newsprint over webs of broken capillary. They were literally ink-stained wretches . . . stained with ink that described the exploits of the people, elsewhere, who actually *did things*. Qaddafi, Reagan, von Bülow. Doug Flutie. Oliver North. You wouldn't find Ollie North cracking his bean on the *Sun-Sentinel* Mystery Quote. He had other people's beans to crack.

Vada knew the drill. When they got to the library, Wyatt would fling Vada's returns one by one into the metal maw of the depository out front, though you could simply fork them over to the librarian ten feet away. He'd snatch his hand back as if it might get snapped off by the chute and say "the man-eating jaws of knowledge" an irritating number of times. Afterward he'd curl up under a beanbag chair in the children's room and startle back to illiteracy the next kid who sat atop him with a book. Eventually he'd meet Vada and Celeste at the circulation desk and make a big show of misery. "What are you going to *do* with all those? Did you bring *matches*?" Vada hated it when Wyatt came.

When they screeched to a stop at Celeste's allergist's office (further proof, if such were needed, of her poise—death before emergency-room fees), she dropped the pen on the seat and sprinted up the steps, leaving an eddy of crape-myrtle blossoms behind her. Vada can recall that she was wearing schoolgirl saddle Oxfords—those pink soles always seemed too private, like looking at a person's insides.

If you live with a force of nature, you don't *act;* you are acted upon. You wait. Wyatt didn't abide by such rules, though, and when Vada heard his belt disengage, he knew he too should move. But gravity seemed to have increased tenfold, and by the time Vada leaned into the immovable boulder of his door, Wyatt was already kneeling on the vacated driver's seat. His eyes were wide with . . . was it fright?

It occurred to Vada that his mother had left that door open when she fled. The keys were still in the ignition, were only now ceasing to shake and jangle. The interior light blazed overhead, draining the battery. On the dash, the plus-minus icon blinked ominously. Now that he thought of it, he hadn't heard the pen click shut—somewhere amid the snarl of seatbelts and tissue beside him, its ink was even now beginning to dry up. How had he missed so many clues? She might be *dying.*

"Let's go!" said Wyatt. "Hurry!" He reared back and slammed the door.

With that the spell was over, the danger past. Celeste would be fine. Called to crisis by the pen-click; restored to normalcy by the door clunking shut, by the wind it sent Vada's way, the change of pressure one always feels in a closed car, alone. And, he was relieved to find, alone in the usual small-stakes way—lower-case *alone,* not the capital kind. He'd been right all along. Inertia had paid off. Sit tight and leave survival to the survivors.

Sure enough, just as Wyatt broke into a run toward the office door, a nurse emerged and said, as well as Vada could make out, "Your mom'll be fine. Got here just in time. We have to keep her a while, so come on in." She sounded muffled, mistranslated, like the ocean in a conch. She glanced at the car. "Your friend, too."

"Thank you, ma'am," said undersea Wyatt.

"You're a lucky boy," said undersea nurse. They'd met at the bottom of the steps. She cupped Wyatt's cheek.

Vada still didn't move. Was Wyatt, on top of everything else, *deeper* than he was? Vada had never felt fearful. It wasn't like Celeste could really *die.* The purpled face, the risky driving, even the pen's point digging into her windpipe? All *interesting,* no more. It had been movielike, a chase scene set to the castanet soundtrack of the hazard lights. She was as invincible as Haledjian. This was a three-minute adventure; when time was up, Vada assumed he'd flip the book and discover the brilliant way she'd saved herself.

Some rule of logic covered this. She was Vada's precondition: Without A, no B; therefore, without cease-to-B, no cease-to-A. QED. But what did it mean to have replaced mother-love with syllogism? How ashamed should he be that even now, he was holding his place in the book with a finger?

The driver's door opened, and Wyatt stuck his head in again. "I'm glad she's OK," he said. He knelt and reached across to chuck Vada's arm. Vada flinched. Wyatt turned off the ignition, pocketed the key. "Think she'd really have done it?"

Vada didn't need to answer. They both knew she would have. Now Wyatt rummaged under the lap belt, dug out the pen, held it aloft. He read the inscription with reverence, aloud. Here was *his* kind of literature. "Think I could keep this?" he asked. "That's like the awesomest thing I ever saw." He clicked the nib back into its hole, backed out, and shut Celeste's door.

Now Vada found that he could move, and he did. He scurried around the hood, which was still ticking like the one in a mini-mystery that proved the criminal hadn't been sitting home all day as he claimed. "She's *my* mom," he said. "That's mine."

And for once, sighing, Wyatt conceded. He reached the pen behind him like a relay baton, Vada took it, and they walked in side by side.

The Firebrand's Candlepower

Celeste was a gifted student. Vada has a hatbox full of brittle ribbons to prove it, plus a sheaf of certificates done up in calligraphy, a few of them pre-yellowed or factory-mottled to simulate age, and the pretense now long overtaken by the real thing. His favorite is a blue ribbon with flaking gold paint that reads "1963 All-Girls Spelling Champoin" . . . and there, snaked among the letters of the last syllable in black ink, is his mother's fierce squiggle of correction: sine wave, deep tilde, indication that she felt one's triumphs in this life, lowly and rare though they be, deserve not to become jokes that rhyme with "loin." (Which is not to say that Vada's mother's triumphs were either lowly or rare: Miss Peach of Greater Gilbert, Second Runner-Up, 1965; Dean's List, 1964, 1965, 1966, 1967; Magna Cum Laude in Psychology; seventeen letters published in *Newsweek*, 1971–1993; thirty-one in *The State* newspaper, 1966–1998; eight-time titleholder in the Lexington County Fair bake-off, most often in the lemon square division. No, her wins were frequent and impressive, with the exception—and there's no transposing squiggle in the world that could fix *this*—of what might have been her triumph of triumphs, who turned out rare and lowly indeed. Sorry, Mom.)

In school she was a firebrand, if militating for pants on campus and shaking hands with black people counted—and in 1960s South Carolina, in her circles, they did. Not long after her death, Vada found in the bottom of the hatbox a strip of card stock, framed with tape, with "White" neatly printed on it. It was tiny, the gauge of ticker tape, like a fortune-cookie slip shrunk by two-thirds, and its purpose baffled him for weeks, until one night the answer suddenly came to him.

In a fit of excitement Vada entered his parents' bedroom, a room he'd seldom ventured into when they were alive and that for the first month or two after their deaths he stole into on tiptoe, until he real-ized how silly this was and resolved to stomp in on seven-league boots from then on, as they were *his* parents and it was *his* house and therefore now *his* room . . . but the footfalls sounded ridiculous and false, differ-ent from the tiptoeing only in being a childish photo-negative of it, and it wasn't long before he went back to tiptoeing, which might have been craven and pointless but at least had the advantage—or had once had the advantage—of being ingenuous rather than plotted. He pulled out the hatbox and sat on his parents' nubbiny counterpane and pressed the slip to the spelling ribbon like a key to a tumbler. The fit was perfect; it had been cut to custom. Then he pulled his hand away, watched the label curl and warp, and cried.

The tears are complicated. It was only a month after his parents' death, so there was still the animal grief that had to be let off its leash now and again, lest it yank him around in public, bark his shins on car bumpers, make him close his eyes and slide his plate of eggs out of the way and cool his forehead (just for a minute) on the Formica of the din-er's counter. That's of no interest to anyone but Vada. There was also secret intimacy, this a way of communing with the girl his mother was years ago, when—he sees her tongue at the corner of her mouth, a button of concentration, a girlish trait she never shed—she trimmed each edge of the card with scissors, spinning it clockwise with her left hand and snipping with the right. Round and round, from the outside in . . . pretty close to the way Vada just mowed the lawn, if you think about it. But why should you think about it?

What else? What is there that you can relate to, that's a half-step closer to the universal? Oh, um, ho, hum—how about the sadness that always comes when one sees tape that's lost its stickum, that's gone gray and crazed and linty? Do other people feel that way?

There might also have been a hint of smugness on his part—that this was the far extent, in 1960s Dixie, of his mother's protest against racism. It's always a mistake to condescend to one's forebears, to imply you have some loftier perch. No perch could be less lofty than Vada's present one—pressed to his friend's slate floor by a killing weight, like a butterfly pinned to a board. But he may, as he sat crying on that bedspread almost a decade back, have had some illusion about the altitude of his perch, and pity may have entered the scene in an unforgivable way.

Now that the danger of loftiness is gone, Vada can see his mother, newly political at sixteen, spiral-cutting this index card, taping it to a ribbon that of course she didn't *wear*, didn't even display on her bureau mirror. She did this only for herself, so that when she sat—as he was now sitting, or as he was sitting almost nine years ago and is now sitting again in memory, and God strike him dead if He must—before her hatbox of victories, she didn't get, as she often said, "too big for her britches." And when she next stood upon the gymnasium stage with the principal, in a cozy envelope of applause produced by like-minded like-dressed like-complected schoolmates and their parents, she would be reminded that she was champoin of a diminished realm. She would be no vain Ozymandais, and no one, mighty or not, should look upon her misprinted laurels and despair.

So "firebrand" may be pushing it a little. The tape lost its adhesive, Vada assumes, because his mother didn't dare let her parents see her secret Second Correction. It was by her and for her, and of course it did little for the cause of southern blacks—if you judge such gestures this way, as Vada supposes you must, though he hopes you'll not begrudge his choosing another, more forgiving standard. African Americans might not have been comforted, when women were raped and men lynched and dogs were set on them and firehoses turned and bombs planted in churches, that the best girl speller at Nathan Bedford Forrest High (Go Night Riders!) was willing to acknowledge, on the quiet, that there might be a black girl out there who could do as well with "equestrienne" and "obbligato" as she did. In college, Celeste told her son, she left sit-ins as soon as she heard sirens; her father had said he'd cut her off if she were ever arrested, and the dutiful daughter complied. She allowed herself only miniature protests, fashioned with craft scissors and minced tape. But be careful about judging the firebrand by her candlepower.

16

Stuck a Feather in His Cap and Called It Cannelloni

In Vada's first few years, the wig boxes on his mother's closet shelf held not only the hair but also the heads Celeste chose to wear in public. He'd catch her unawares before her dressing-room mirror some mornings, wig agley, mouth open, puzzled expression, an eyelash perched on her fingertip like a tiny pet. Alongside her, a shapely white Styrofoam head on a slender neck.

Celeste looked pupal, stopped in mid-metamorphosis, but as soon as she caught sight of him the machinery clanked back to life, the eyelash was steered onto her head, the lips painted on, the role resumed: "Hey, sweetie. Mom will be with you in a minute." Mom will be with you in a minute. Then who was *this*, his pre-Mom, his non-Mom?

She was still working then. She was an advisor to the state mental hospital during his elementary school years, and when Vada overheard phone conversations with fellow board members or discussions with his father on the deck after dinner, Celeste was as soberly well-spoken as Banquo's ghost, an eloquence that registered to him mainly as a tone, the susurrus of mastery.

Only gradually did she leave that life behind and grow into the role that myth and social expectation assigned. We find roles, or they find us, and we fill them, gratefully or crankily, until at last the role is full enough all on its own, thank you, and then we can retreat inside ourselves and be our small and secret selves and no one will know or care because it's not our selves they notice, but our roles. And no matter what you do, you're always what you got labeled years before, justly or not. Everything you say or do is read in that context, passed through that filter: bemused idiot-son; gruff but tender dad; neighborhood hero-child, the patron saint of invidious comparisons.

"And you, ma'am? Who are you?" "I am a mom. A mom is what I am."

Vada remembers a line from a book he read once: "Eventually even Yankee Doodle learned to stick a feather in his cap and call it macaroni." What good does it do you, finally, to deny people what they demand? Did Vada's boyhood football coach *like* limping around atop that stacked heel and answering to "Shot," or would he rather have stayed plain Clarence, the buck-dancing hellcat he'd been in school? People want the injured and ruined to be good sports, to accept their fates or at least pretend to—so Shot it was, and godspeed to Clarence.

It may be beneath the dignity of one who's spawned a nation and ridden a pony and lent his name to the mighty New York baseballers—and who knows what hasty pudding is—but, well, the feather in your cap is still a noodle, Mr. Doodle, and nothing you can do for it. You're a prisoner of rhyme, and the best you might hope for is a change now and again, for variety, to "cannelloni." Shut up and deal.

17

WoE Is mE

Every time Vada went out with friends during high school, Celeste gave the same sendoff: "You know what we expect." Vada took this to mean that his parents required conformity to the rules, and he lacked the gumption or the imagination to do otherwise, except for a few bottles of pink Champale that he guiltily made himself vomit up (a *motif*, dear reader!) and a few tokes, once, of a fatty (false advertising—the thing was slender as a lollipop stick) that Sam Chisum shamed him into trying. But thinking back, can he hear sadness in his mother's voice as she delivered those rote phrases? The wording didn't seem ambiguous then, but it does now. Did they expect the best or the worst? Did she mean "We expect you to be no more than what you always have been" or "Though we know you'll always take the path of least resistance, please go out there and prove us wrong"?

"Vada, son," she told him when he came home and announced that his class had conducted elections and that, fifth grade being like Tammany New York and President Wyatt having offered patronage jobs to everyone for their support, Vada had earned the title Warden of Erasers . . . "Vada, son," she said, as he made a show of clapping his ceremonial erasers together like cymbals, a man delighting in the perks of High Office, "you need to cut a wider swath than that."

(Brief interruptive note: The present time is twelve minutes ago, give or take, and Vada—as he presses on in this attempt to create an eternal present, or one that may seem eternal to you, though he's under no illusions—is still mowing, hence "cut a wider swath." Do you get it? Sooner or later, dear reader, we *all* get it.)

(Brief additional interruptive note: That last note was a trick, Vada trying to justify with a pun the retelling of a memory he's not entitled to. Full disclosure: About thirteen minutes ago, Vada *did* recall that day in fifth grade. While edging the azaleas, he mowed over an old hacksaw blade. The screech made him wince and jump, turning his head and hip in the air, and it occurred to him—he'd let go of the handle, cutting the engine, and the silence was a *j'accuse* of cowardice—that this was his same response when, less than a week into the Prickett Administration, Tristan Soares had seized the ceremonial mini-bricks from Vada's backpack and declared a coup at the Wardenry of Erasers. Tristan clapped them near Vada's ear, in a vertical gator-chomp way, and Vada responded by simultaneously jumping and cringing sideways as if the erasers were made of brass instead of felt, which proved to any and all that he didn't have the right stuff to run a major wardenry like erasers. And thirteen minutes ago, as Vada sailed the mangled saw-blade into the woods and yanked the cord to restart, it further occurred to him [though maybe this time it was precognition—had he, in quailing before that two-dollar blade, been not so much an instinctive chicken as a man shrinking from death? Had he espied in that blade the shadow of Azrael's scythe?]—anyway, as Vada pitched death's hacksaw blade into the bushes and pulled the crank that would plunge him back into din and out of thought, it occurred to him that the DUCE would have anagrammatized Vada back then, at his peak of worldly power, to WoE. He'd gone in twenty years from WoE to HA, and was steaming now—though of course he didn't know it, or only half-knew it—toward RIP . . . End of brief interruption, with apologies that it turned out not to be so brief as the first and therefore might not have merited the adjective "brief," relatively speaking, but how is one to know in advance how long a path will take to retrace?)

18

The Silky Smooth Drawers of Ghoulie the Cricketer

Scene: The morgue. Hours after Vada's parents died. The attendant clicked his mother's drawer handle, which resembled the silver latch on Grandmère's old-time refrigerator, and Vada, caught off guard, was tricked into feeling the usual thrill—such an elegant mechanism, with its clean, rhythmic chii-chik—that flawless engineering always evoked in him. It took an instant, no longer than the instant that has filled and is still filling these pages, to realize that the sound this time was a traitorous, misleading chii-chik, unthrilling, anti-thrilling, the farthest thing there could ever be from thrilling. And so he was feeling shame as Celeste's trundle bed whispered toward him. It wasn't like on TV shows, he noted, where they always stashed dead bodies head-out so that the drawers needed only to be cracked a few inches to let loved ones see all they needed to see. Celeste, a breech death, emerged feet first.

Vada looked for the legendary toe tag, which turned out either not to exist or not to be applied until after a son made the official identification. He realized a split second late how idiotic this was, realized he'd had the fugitive thought that he might identify her by the label affixed to her toe and thus be spared seeing more. *Yes, yes, Celeste Prickett is her name. That's Mom, all right. No doubt about it.*

But the fruitless search focused his attention on the oddly proportioned big toe around which a silver wire was *not* looped, and Vada realized, with a suddenness like a sob, that he'd . . . never seen it before? Was this possible? Could one live in proximity and in love with a person for so long and through a combination of modesty (hers) and oblivious-ness (his) never see her feet? This made him doubt that he'd loved her, at least that he'd loved her the right way and at the right range of intimacy. There was no surge of hope, much as he would have liked one. He didn't imagine for a moment that these unfamiliar feet belonged to a stranger. No, they looked exactly like his, long, slender, and bony, like a map of South America if someone cast it in pink taffy and stretched from both ends.

How strange to learn only here and now that his mother had had surgery to correct an ingrown nail on the big toe of her right foot. The arc of unpolished pink was interrupted two-thirds of the way across, like the graph of a lifeline cut abruptly short, sob sob. Or not—Vada didn't cry, in fact suspected he was summoning up such metaphors to try to *make* himself cry, either for catharsis or to satisfy the cheer-ful, minty-smelling, cowlicked coroner's assistant ("Name's Trent, but everybody calls me Ghoulie") who was his Charon in this nether realm. Ghoulie was carrying not a tiller pole but the cricket bat he'd been holding when Vada knocked on the steel door. Vada presumed, from the rubber ball on the counter—it was, he couldn't help noticing, the pink of organs—that Ghoulie whiled away his shift playing a kind of ball in this cramped inner sanctum, but as he jerked his head back and led Vada to the side-by-side drawers in which his parents were resid-ing, the bat made him look like a man guarding against unauthorized reanimation.

Ghoulie let the drawer creep inch by inch into the room, at a pace that took ten seconds at least. Vada couldn't criticize this bit of theater: If he'd had access to casters silent as those, he'd show them off, too. There were flecks of blood on the sheet covering Celeste from ankles to forehead, and Ghoulie, showing a tact that belied his nickname but with his eyes flashing in a way that unbelied it right back again, drew down the sheet's edge to reveal her closed eyes and undamaged nose, but no more. "That should do her," he said, with his free hand holding the sheet tight to the deep groove above her upper lip, the body part Vada had never heard anyone but Celeste call the "philtrum." The word would fall out of the world with her, loss upon loss.

Celeste looked like a Hindu woman in purdah, looked like *she* was grieving for *him*. Vada tried not to look, tried to concentrate on the inappropriateness of Ghoulie's phrasing: "That ... should ... do ... her"? But he had no anger in him, didn't have much of anything in him.

He thought of the time when he and his dad had gone to Golden Kernel to buy a ten-pound croker sack of peanuts for boiling. They did this only when the deathly allergic Celeste was away, and their pleasure was more profound for the tinge of danger. Boiled peanuts were the Prickett version of blowfish sushi. Vic and Vada weren't just making brine and drowning legumes in it, weren't just eating something down-home and tasty. There was more at stake. A peanut could be either delicious or fatal, depending on the luck of the draw. Father and son had won that draw, and could celebrate—after several hours of rising steam and mounting anticipation—by tugging the purple baby-toes free with their teeth and tasting the earth in them, then flicking the shells at each other or into the flowerbed. But the peanuts never entered the house; Vic and Vada did their boiling in a propane-heated pot in the yard, and afterward swept and disinfected the deck, scrubbed their hands with a hard-bristled brush until they ached. The best pleasures, as Ghoulie had reason to know, are the ones backed by death.

Anyway, at Golden Kernel old Ray Chesnutt had uncinched the bag, opened its neck a couple of inches, and said, "There you go," and Vic said, "No offense, but I'm not buying a pig in a poke. Let me root in there a minute." At which point he stuck his whole head into the mouth, like a lion-tamer. Now Vada came to and saw Ghoulie's gloved hand still resting above his mama's mouth and wondered if he'd said it aloud: *No offense, but I'm not buying a pig in a poke, Ghoulie. Let me root in there a minute.* Seconds passed. "That her?"

"Kind of" seemed not the right answer. The veil; the long, thin, outturned feet; the sheet of paltry thread-count, like nothing Celeste would have bought; the whole, like, dead-and-gone aspect: all these were unfamiliar. Obedient Vada nodded, though, nodded and dropped his eyes. In some ways, not being able to see her whole restored his faith in death's majesty and mystery. It seemed right that passing over would entail a religious conversion, and that the morgue would be a foreign country in which custom didn't allow him to gaze upon the Lord's bride.

He heard the whisper of the casters again, a little deeper this time like thunder rolling away, then a secure and final double click, then the slightly higher-pitched whisper of the second drawer unfurling. Vada made a businesslike turn to identify his father, whose shroud Ghoulie smoothly and casually rolled down past the chin line. He seemed more comfortable, convinced that Vada wasn't going to go either weepy or apeshit, and so he'd allowed some of his stiffness to lapse. He was twirling the cricket bat expertly in his right hand, on his face a complaisant look edging almost toward a smile, and Vada wondered how loud the crack would be if he dropped the paddle. Now *that* would be a violation, Vada thought, and half-rooted for a mishandle. It seemed that something would be served by it. Vada would have an articulable complaint; he'd have the chance to lodge the only sort of protest available. *Hey, man, that's inappropriate.* O Death, be not inappropriate.

Ghoulie, noticing the visitor's trance, stopped in mid-twirl and pressed the bat against his hamstring like a con concealing a shank from a nosy screw.

Dad had died from the blunt force of steering wheel against sternum, and he looked the same as always, except maybe a hint jowlier. Vada vowed to exercise his neck muscles in the coming years, then retracted the vow as unclean, under the circumstances. After four or five seconds he heard the light, impatient whap of bat against pant leg—Ghoulie had a ballgame to play, life goes on—so Vada nodded again, then closed his eyes and let himself revel this time (we all have our weaknesses) in the smooth operation of the file drawers' hinges. They made a surflike sound, lovely: our tax dollars at work. If his parents had to exit forever, best to go out on a glide like that, on ball bearings rounded to the minutest tolerance. Bravo, state legislature. Kudos, procurement office. *Domo arigato, Koyo.*

Vada clamped his lips shut and tried not to think about his mother's corpse, tried not to consider what level of gruesomeness would call for compassion from a night attendant named Ghoulie. He didn't envision the battered lower face that must be under Celeste's veil. The words "agape" and "agog" did not flit through his mind. He did not think of cemetery flies, nor did he entertain the irony that she'd kept her feet encased all this time out of a fear of *lockjaw*, not its . . . opposite. He paid as little attention as he could: not to the wounds nor to the cowlicked kid's partially revealed concert T-shirt (Shallow Purple?) nor to the morgue itself (much better lit than on TV, and with a Nature Conservancy calendar on the wall: June, the photo of a rain-forest canopy so intensely green that it looked abstract, like choking smoke from a tire fire, only billowing emerald instead of black).

Back home, he fell asleep with his shoes on.

19

Hussies of Cellblock DD

Vada gives thanks for the prison slang above, shanks and screws and so forth, to the makers of *Hussies of Cellblock DD*, shown last weekend at Wyatt's bachelor party in the Austerlitz meeting room of a chain hotel in downtown Columbia. The venue was cramped, mainly because they switched at the last second from Waterloo—Darla having demanded it when Wyatt told her where to reach him in an emergency. The hotel had had only Austerlitz and First Manassas still available, an easy choice. (Memo to marketing: in the South, you might want to translate the Civil War battle names out of Yankee. Vada's guess is that the occupancy rate for First Manassas in Columbia is about the same as the occupancy rate for the Chevy No-Va in Tegucigalpa.)

It was a surprisingly OK film, with some lifelike scratch-fights and a rather tender interracial lesbian subplot . . . though there were others not so happy as Vada when it turned out to be secretion-free, just a tame, jiggly R from the early 1970s. After twenty minutes, when it became apparent that the inmates' unexplainable hotpants and bikini briefs would stay on even in shower scenes, a stockbroker named C. Bo Beckley shouted, "This ain't no stag, men! It's a goddamn chick flick with titties, besides which it's liberal. If I have to see race-mixing, I want to see race-*mixing*. There's better than this on basic cable, man. On *basic*. Where is the pussy at?"

20

The Casserole Parents

On the second night after his parents' death, Vada stacked all the grief casseroles. He was drunk, and had in mind some photography. His plan—if you could call it a plan: Vada went to fetch another beer and was confronted by foil-clad dishes that looked like small-scale coroner's drawers and suddenly was off his nut and off the rails and off to the races—was to haul the neighbors' pans out of the refrigerator (and out of his father's freezer in the basement) and to take pictures in various rooms. Vada's usual: a grandiose gesture devoted to no knowable purpose.

For five minutes, though, he was bursting with ideas. A family dinner shot from above, the holiday china, the candelabrum, cloth napkins in the white ceramic cinch-rings his mother had decorated by painting on holly sprigs and the family's first names in calligraphy (the fourth, fifth, and sixth in the set she had labeled for their most frequent guests: Reid, Penny, Wyatt). But in his father's chair, not his father but a teetering stack of comfort food topped by chicken tetrazzini with water chestnuts, and his mother's role played by her understudy, a tower featuring a nine-layer lasagna oozing ricotta.

Which would leave Vada's chair to fill. For that job he'd need something arty and heartbreaking, but in a way inexplicable enough (the essence of art being inexplicability) not to seem schmaltzy. A half-inflated tetherball cut loose from its rope? An oozing Virginia ham? Were tetherballs and hams arty? Vada didn't keep up with the downtown crowd, but he did know who would clean the ham gel out of the chair-bottoms once the art was over.

Three lousy minutes in, and already the will was wobbling, the appeal fading. For one thing, he had an odd number of food-solaces: which parent would be represented by nine and which by eight? How do you choose which parent to cheat by a casserole and thus imply to be lesser? It was like that parable they were always telling in church during his youth, about the trainman forced to choose between mangling his kid, who in a moment of paternal inattention had toddled out of the switching house to play on the tracks, or letting a load of innocents chug over a cliff . . . and you were supposed to be impressed that this guy quick-wittedly boiled the thing down to math, as Jesus required, and therefore didn't hesitate to snap his kid's femurs and then decapitate him with a thousand tons of locomotive and thus save The Greater Number, hurray. This seemed to Vada, if nothing else, questionable arithmetic—didn't the guy even stop to figure in additional variables? How high was the cliff, and did the train have seatbelts, and who could say whether these passengers were wife-beaters or maybe dictator-adoring carwash magnates who deserved a little escarpment plunge for their sins, or people who ate bag upon bag of pork rinds or smoked unfiltereds and wore asbestos undershirts or drank and drove and might kick off early anyway—and, more to the point, how many strangers would *you* kill not to rehear, for every second of the rest of your life, the brief wet thump of train meeting infant, Iron Horse v. Fruit of Loin?

But that's beside the point—sorry. How would Vada make *his* choice, nine casseroles on one side of the scale and eight on the other, given that the dishes were Pyrex and thus put anything Solomonic out of the question? Babies are much easier to split than tempered glass. Solomon never had to deal with space-age polymers.

In the light of practical considerations, in other words, inspiration failed. Vada remembered that he'd never liked setting the table, had done a shitty job of it all his life. He was always sloppy, the napkins wadded or crimped rather than folded into triangles, the forks often half-on the paper and half-off—and tossed down passive-aggressively with their tines to the cloth, inverted, like the postage stamps of that

kind of fearless radical whose fearless radicalism expresses itself in turning stamps upside-down. Take that, powers that be. Mom! Your napkin
is screwy, and your fork's on its side like a jackknifed trailer. What do
you have to say about *that*?

Why make the effort now? A well-laid *hôte* wasn't going to bring
Mom back to scold him for not being able, not even tonight, to make the
napkins look like scallop shells bursting from the tops of their rings. He
probably couldn't locate Dad's old Brownie, and if he did, could he spin
the gizmos and work the shutter-stop and keep his fingers from in front
of the lens for once? Besides, what would he *do* with the photos? Keep
them in a shoebox and draw them out, of a wintry night, to weep over
. . . thus to assure himself that he'd turned out after all to be the Good
Boy they wanted, nobler than those callous neighbors who tried to imply
that parents could be compensated for—replaced!—by foodstuffs?

That was the lure, more of the same bullshit: Vada as dutiful despairer,
boohooing while the winds howled down the lanes of pine outside. The
son alone, bravely carrying on in the face of hardship (his, not theirs),
even transforming his bereavement into art—bad art, sure, dippy out-
of-focus art involving borrowed serving-ware and tetherballs and meat
from cans, but still and all . . . art is in the eye of the beholder, and did
he ask *you* to behold it? He did not. Leave the man alone. Leave the man
alone with his grief. Can't you see the man is torn up?

21

More Sowbellies, Less Style

Sorry about that. Let us rejoin Vada in the kitchen on that second night after his parents' death. He had several casseroles out, and the open fridge was beginning to steam and strain. But the distance between plans aborning and plans aborting is never far. The idea founders, as he's suggested, on a silly detail: the difficulties of cleaning ham sludge from wicker.

Or on a digression. One gets sucked into musing about what would make a grown man, a father, save a *tetherball*, something fit for only one purpose, and that purpose so weak and transient that it hardly counts: Has anyone anywhere ever played tetherball for more than two minutes at a time? This morning when Vada brought the overflow grief casseroles down to his father's freezer, his foot dislodged from a junkpile of hose nozzles, duck waders, flowerpots, sagging rafts still half-filled after twenty years with his father's mentholated air . . . a surgically altered tetherball. Be practical, Vada sternly instructs: Think about this. *How* would you amputate the rope-holding eyelet, the loop that makes a tetherball tether? With what tool? And *why*?

Vada watched the ball wobble away in lurching semicircles, a drunkard's walk, and instantly remembered the winter night fifteen years ago when his father, who scorned parlor games, had played along just once with Celeste and Vada (and Reid, Penny, and Wyatt, who were over for dinner) and seemed to enjoy himself.

The game was called Bushwa. Its object was to make up fake definitions for real words and fool others into believing them. When Vic defined "cantle" as "a gait peculiar to three-legged horses," the only person who fell for it was Vada. Wyatt snorted when this was revealed. He of course had immediately recognized that a cantle was a saddle pommel, or a candle that will no longer light, or a kind of lever used in bridge-building, or whatever a cantle was and is in the humdrum. Vada has forgotten now and didn't care then. All the others had gone for dull, plausible answers ("a hard-crusted custard"; "a mesh used to wrap summer sausage") rather than whimsy, and Vada's answer, the perhaps overelaborate "a canticle with its middle edited out so that a church service doesn't go all the way until kickoff," had attracted no takers.

"How did you fall for that?" asked Wyatt, knowing full well.

Wyatt could try to suck the joy out of it all he wanted, but it wouldn't work, not this time. Who would ever have imagined? His father, playful! "It's what the word *should* mean," said Vada. "So it got my vote."

"Son, s'gonna be a hard life for you," said Vic, but he winked as he spoke, a wink that said he understood. What was the point of living in a world where everything turned out, in the end, to be the same old crap: saddlehorns, crusted puddings, wurst sleeves?

As the tetherball rocked to a halt, Vada flipped open the freezer and laid the neighbors' latest offerings atop the leavings from last year's bumper crop of butterbeans. He closed the lid, trying not to think of what lay at the bottom, Reagan-era venison that was now his responsibility. Back in 1987, ten-year-old Vada hadn't understood why his father consented to accept Reid's gift of Wyatt's first kill unless—certainly the freezer's location in his father's basement workshop played a role in this fantasy—Vic was going to thaw the animal, stitch it together, reunite it with its hide, and jolt it back to life with a tractor battery. But Vic never got around to this miracle, and now revivification was out of the question. Sorry, Bambistein.

Vada had a flash in his mind's eye of his father using the tetherball to test a new table-vise or acetylene torch. Yes, he sees it: Vada inching open the basement door to call Vic for dinner or maybe just visit. He finds his father's back turned, his welding mask down; he hears the alchemical whoosh of the canister (definition: "a sinister-looking can"), sees the blue flame, and retreats, knowing interruption would not be welcome. "Don't take it hard," Celeste says when he mopes back upstairs. "Daddy has important work down there."

Important work: disfiguring a tetherball. Which was useless, but kept anyway—a trophy. But of what? Vic never confided. So now Vada is left to speculate what was meant by the single word imprinted on that almost-orb, a word that Dr. Rosengruber, his mother's grad-school mentor, spoke to him a few years ago on the phone—well, spoke to the answering machine: "You must stay bissy, Vaaadaa. There must be some-tink to fill the Voit. Heff you any hubbies?"

Vada's hubby for the moment: the tetherball that hovers over the Voit.

Enough. You're quite right, reader. Vada can hear you chanting for substance, as Confederate soldiers were said to when yet another meal-time on the march brought only wormy hardtack and chicory coffee and, from the officers, talk and pomp and more talk and more pomp.

Sang the soldiers: "More sowbellies, less style!"

22

Forebear, Afterbear, Present Bear

One last metaphor—then it's sowbellies for sure, sowbellies until you ache and plead for more style. Really.

To tell the truth, Vada abandoned the idea even before he started removing casseroles from the fridge, was just letting his momentum, yet another wickless novelty cantle, sputter. He's always disliked indignation. What good does it do? What good does *will* do, for that matter? It's something in which the powerful can safely indulge, since they have the resources to bring about the desired end. Vada has always enjoyed, instead, the moment of letting seriousness go, of being returned to the comforts of his own triviality. He's had no choice but to enjoy it, if he wants to find enjoyment.

And so, like all its forebears and afterbears, like everything but his present bear, the photo-exposé idea curled up and croaked. Another crotchet that seized him body and soul for a second, that made him feel alive and willful and capable of heroic anger . . . and then turned out to be tame and teddyish, something he could knock the stuffing out of. *Good* bear. Not like—bad bear—the ursa major occupying his pectoralis minor.

The reader may safely skip this chapter.

23

God and Man at Denny's

It's official. God is out to lunch.

Vada imagines him down at Denny's on the bypass, savoring toast points dredged through yolk, the remnants of his Moons over My Hammy, which Yhwh orders not because he especially loves salt pork and hen bullets—he can take or leave food—but because He's partial to puns. (Vada has deduced this trait from heaven-sent Darla, the closest to God it's ever been his privilege to get. Like Father, like daughter.)

God likes to flirt with the waitress: "I'll have *Moons* over My *Hammy, Ham* under my *Moonies.* Dry toast, wheat. And a cuppa, *s'il vous* pretty *plaît.* Hon, this menu says 'bottomless.' Do you really mean it? I might test that. I'm what they call a stern test. If you put infinity on the menu for a buck forty-nine, you're *asking* for a test, right?"

On the way out, God always wastes two bits on the novelty construction crane while He sucks at his Starlight mint. He likes trying to maneuver the pincers to snare a small stuffed bear. Yes, a small one, attached to a keychain—he knows the game is rigged, and it's impossible to get the really *good* stuff: the hundred-dollar bill in a plastic pouch, the Yosemite Sam wristwatch. God has no use for timekeeping, it's true, but he loves that Yosemite Sam, whose likeness he'll never, never, never catch between the toy crane's jaws.

But for now He's still in his booth, holding that pleasure in antici-pation (the pleasure of disappointment, a rare and precious one for the omnipotent). The waitress proposes a final refill of joe; God disposes himself kindly to such a thing. When she's gone, though, He doesn't drink it. Instead He takes a last deep sniff, waves a wisp of aroma toward Himself, and pushes the cup across the worn Formica. The Lord moves in mysterious ways. He watches the tendrils of stream rise and merge into slanted morning sunbeams—poof. God never tires of the magic of physics. Oh, he was sharp back then, with his trim schemes and airtight systems—but micromanaging is for the young. He sighs, peruses the curling scroll of His bill. He loosens the belt of Orion, picks His teeth with the Sword of Damocles. What's 20 percent of $6.76? Oh, how the mighty have lapsed.

Sword of Damocles? Is that right, or has He confused His myths? The world has sputtered on for millennia now since the Greeks, a falling action too long protracted. God never meant humanity to drag on so, but in that heady week of creation he overdid both will to live and desire to procreate. They've gone forth and multiplied, all right, like rabbits or minks; actually, having no predator to cage them and skin them and sew them into capes, they make rabbits and minks look chaste by com-parison. Hard to screw like a mink when you're draped over a matron's bosom, jaw clamped round your tail.

So far *Homo sapiens* has held on fifteen hundred years longer than the Lord intended, and oh, the surfeit of human history; God's mind teems with trivia. Ancient Greece is so far back now, and these last few years have kicked up so many pop artifacts, so much dust and schnutter. It's a mishmash. Who was Archimedes? Something about baths. Maybe he was the guy who first mounted a hot tub on a limo and put it in a rap video? Orestes Destrade's tragic flaw? Easy—he couldn't hit the curve. Unless God's confusing him with Othello, hero of a tragedy set upon the moors and written by one of the Brontës, whom he could never tell apart. From schoolyard jokes God recalls the names of the great Italian trouser dramatists: Euripides, Eumenides. And the Platos: he's pretty sure Dana was the one on TV, sister to that funny black midget until she started robbing laundromats or something; *plain* Plato's the gabby one in the robe. He has a retreat, maybe?

Our Lord is like the indestructible centenarian who, rooting one morning in the medicine cabinet of her assisted living, plucks up the nitroglycerin instead of the vitamin C and pops two dozen pills more or less accidentally, as far as the coroner is concerned. Tired begets bored begets reckless, and honestly, whether you're God or man, what's the point of being slave to a heart—overengineered machine, fool of momentum, addict to beating—that has outlasted one's peers and plans and purpose?

Getting everything right is also a kind of prison-house. God gets sick of it. So it's possible that He accidentally on purpose flipflopped his myths, mistook Damocles for Diogenes for kicks, and now, in search of an honest man, the Almighty wanders the Denny's parking lot with a sword, scaring the shit out of the breakfast crowd, while what's left to hover frighteningly above Vada in his dying moment is Diogenes' lantern, reborn as the ultra-white recessed halogen lamps in Wyatt's trophy room—lighting that makes Vada's vision swim, or rather drown.

And you with him, poor soul. Glub, glub.

24

The Milk of Magnesia of Human Kindness

Vada would like to note that the preposition in "Sword of Damocles" is an act of cruelty. Tortures should take their names from those who devise them, not from the innocents to whom they're applied. We never speak, for instance, of "The Close-Range Fist-Sized-Hole-Producing Bullet of Abraham Lincoln" or "The Fire Hoses of Martin Luther King Jr." or even "The High Chopper of Billy Buckner." Such phrases are misleading, the lot of them: Sword of Damocles, Fall of Man, Death of Vada: as if *it* belonged to *him*. If the goddamned beast on his chest is *of* anyone it's of Wyatt, a technicality worth insisting upon.

God asks Vada to add that He too has a beef with humans and their possessives. Avogadro's number, Hubble's constant, Newton's Law: how dare they? It wasn't Langerhans who founded those islets, or Sharon who designed those convoluted roses . . . magnesia doesn't exactly milk itself, does it? And *Heisenberg*'s uncertainty principle? The hell it is. God beat old Werner to that by eons, has been unsure practically forever.

All these belong to Him, and once God held His secrets closely, resented their discovery and appropriation by mankind. But what's the point, anymore? Now He too has given in to the foggy ad hoc of age. He putters and crotchets and does the best He can. Memory is shot, will ebbing, and nothing seems anymore to be His and His alone. And you know what, they can *have* the secrets of the universe; they're welcome to them. As His servant Celeste Prickett used to say, you spend the first half of life accumulating things, the second half letting them go. She was a wise woman, that Celeste. You know (God asks Vada to ruminate in His behalf), maybe the experiment of humanity hasn't been a total loss. Celeste came of it, and Darla Dietz. Tisha, too.

And the Lord beheld His creation, and it was good.

25

Smurf 'n' Turf

Vada knows you're sick of listening to him, which is one reason he turned over the reins to God—to give you a breather. But maybe you'd rather hang out in the back of the Austerlitz Room, where the keg's in a tin tub of ice in front of hideous golden flocked-suede wallpaper, and listen to C. Bo Beckley. He's recommending his favorite off-the-menu special at the Short Stop Truck Haven off I-95, near Santee. The Smurf 'n' Turf, he says, features a country-fried steak and home fries smothered in white gravy, plus fellatio from a midget prostitute named Tina—and for dessert your choice from Granny Sal's pie safe. Thanks to an inquisitive lawyer friend of Wyatt's who was also bored with *Hussies of Cellblock DD,* Vada can answer what may be your next question: These pleasures may be partaken of either one by one or, for a small surcharge, simultaneously.

At this point last weekend, Vada—who'd also lost interest in the movie, probably during the third scene set atop the warden's desk: How many lamps and blotters and glass ashtrays could that satyr sweep blithely onto the floor before the guys in purchasing caught on? What a waste of tax money!—asked a follow-up, and though his query wasn't as warmly received as the lawyer's, C. Bo did finally grant him a reply. A sneering one, but a reply.

For dessert at the Short Stop, as Vada suspected, cobbler was also on offer. Granny Sal's turned out to be also a cobbler safe. Upon further questioning, C. Bo was forced to concede that there might be cake in there as well. Red velvet seemed a fair bet to Vada, who's no slouch when it comes to knowledge of roadside comfort food. He'd put even money or better that they had red velvet with cream-cheese icing.

"Dude, who gives a crap? I was busy feeding the *other* face," said C. Bo, to appreciative laughter. Up front the film was still going (why would a warden who looked like H. L. Mencken have Barry White on his office hi-fi?), but in the room's back half the overheads were blazing, to light fools the dusty way to drink. Only half a dozen guys were still watching, and they'd long since given up on shushing the others. It had turned into a singularly unclever episode of *Mystery Stag-Film Theater 3000*. Beyond C. Bo's left shoulder, Wyatt stood barely ten feet away, priming the keg. Vada tried to catch his eye, tried to tell whether his grimace was from exertion, embarrassment, or both, but Wyatt stayed unreadable, a man in a world all his own, pumping furiously, or actually not so much furiously (Vada was tricked into that by "pumping"—damned set phrases, seducing one into false witness) as placidly, like a cow in the field, if a cow in the field were priming a kegger. Lordy. Maybe set phrases are set for a reason. Wouldn't "furiously," accurate or not, have been better than that?

"Feeding the *other* face," repeated one of C. Bo's disciples, a biscuit-necked trailer-hitch salesman who'd earlier introduced himself as the Tripster. "*Ohhh*, yeah." The Tripster snorted, a laugh that had lots of wet-sounding *g*'s and *k*'s in it and made his jowls sway merrily above his collar, just like the hypnotic dugs of Cellblock DD.

Now Wyatt was thumbing the tap, filling a tilted cup for someone else before turning to his own—and still ignoring the idiocy in front of him. The guest of honor wasn't going to intervene. These weren't his friends, Vada knew; they were business partners and family acquaintances. Marriages might not be mergers, but weddings were. Unfortunately, there was no woman of action here like Latisha of Cellblock DD, who handled an ogling guard by shoving his face into her cleavage while kicking him in the cods with her prison-issue stilettos, and as she let him fall said, in a pitying whisper, "How'd you like your dark meat, peckerwood?"

No help coming . . . so what choice did Vada have, amid the detestable giggling that followed the gkkkkgghh of the Tripster? Sometimes, for the sake of decency, a man has to launch himself into the breach. Sometimes a man has to stand up and be counted.

But doing was never Vada's gift. He didn't grab the Tripster's head and tug it violently to his bosom. His unfearsome unstilettos would stay on the fake parquet of the Austerlitz Room. Which left only speech-making, a poor substitute even in ideal circumstances, which these were not. People had laughed at Latisha's dialogue, but oh, what Vada would have given to have his speech come out as well as hers did.

"Not," he burbled, "that I have anything against pie—only an idiot dislikes pie . . . I mean pie of some kind, whether it's strawberry rhubarb or pizza or whatever . . . different strokes for different folks—but it's a mystery to me how pie won naming rights for the safe. 'Cobbler safe,' 'strudel safe,' 'apple betty safe,' 'tiramisu safe'—just joking about that last one, guys—But 'cake safe' sounds just as good, and it's got assonance in its favor."

Vada gulped. Had he really said "assonance"? Dear Lord. Nobility sounds so much better in films. Where are the set phrases of nobility when you need them?

As the derisive laughter erupted, Wyatt turned, raised his cup, and gave Vada a smile. *Hello, old friend. Glad to see you're enjoying talking to my other guests. See, I told you it wouldn't be so bad.*

"Anyway," C. Bo said to his friends, "I was talking about my personal favorite kind of pie—fur. Now ol' Slurpy Smurf . . ."

"Tina," Vada said, and it killed him to recognize the eager-to-please tone, the apt pupil demonstrating that he'd been paying attention. He'd meant it as a vicious condemnation, a rebuke to C. Bo for demeaning this woman, calling her out of her name.

To Vada's surprise, C. Bo paused and glanced over at him—acknowl-edged his existence. *"Tina,"* he continued, a hint of grin tugging at his underlip, "is perfectly proportioned, pretty." A victory for Vada, this compliment. Doing the right thing had paid off, for once. "That's the difference between your high-class midget and some twisted-up freak. And a mouth soft as a bird dog's."

How did Vada announce his objection to C. Bo's sexism, sizeism, anti-cakeism, and general grossness? How did he react to his theft of that innocent phrase? Boldly, reader: he glanced at his watch and per-formed a child's pantomime of startlement, with open palms flung out from his cheeks—the same gesture, Vada couldn't help remembering, that had made Wyatt spew Dr Pepper through his nose during a senior-trip game of charades, when Vada used it and an open-mouthed smile as clue for the first word of "sunflower seeds."

No one was looking. The heads of C. Bo and his claqueurs were thrown back in laughter, and as Vada backed away the men on either side of him pressed forward and angled their shoulders, closing the circle. Time to exit in a way that would convey his disgust. Vada shoved his hands wrathfully into his pockets (take *that!*), pressed his tongue against the backs of his teeth with righteous fury, and tried to think of a line that might compare with "How'd you like your dark meat, peckerwood?" But nothing came, and his neighbors' shoulders continued to swivel and hips to encroach, crowding him out.

Vada huffed off to the food table to claim a deviled egg before the platter was empty and the offerings had dwindled to a truck-tire-sized bowl of Combos. There's something soothing about holding the cool, smooth semi-sphere of a deviled egg. It feels like victory, even if the victory is only that you're exempt, for a few seconds, from the vexations of party chat. But surely there was a larger triumph here, right? Surely his effort had not been in vain. And then he located it: *These* were two delicious egg, mustard, and paprika treats that would not be available for C. Bo Beckley when he finished his tale. And only two more on the plate, and those soon to be scooped up as well by the avenging angel. This was better, much better. *How do you like your official cheese-filled pretzel snack of Nascar, peckerwood?*

26

Flying the Coop de Grace

Vada's tired. Can he die already? Is there anybody out there with the power to snip his thread? Darla, come back inside the house. Open the glass-front cabinet over there, beyond the upland grouse. The key's in the lock, either because Wyatt doesn't care about firearm safety or because— marriage is a major step, and you need to consider the possibilities, unpleasant though they be—he may be trying, unconsciously, to make easy work for any wife-murdering psychopath who beats the alarm system and finds himself in the tropharium/arsenal. Anyway, load one of the shotguns with the shells in the drawer and *help*, please: Darla, put Vada out of his misery. Ask the Great White Hunter, your husband to be. Once you bloody the bull and festoon him with ribbons, you're obligated to finish him off. You are not allowed to fly the coop de grace. (Ask not for whom the corpse puns, love; he puns for thee.)

27

A Metaphor from the Theater, Vada's Main Experience of Which Is Playing Skate Punk #3 in One of Those High School Productions in Which the Bard Is Made Relevant by Having Mercutio Wear Painter's Pants

But as Augustine of Hippo said about celibacy, so says Vada of Grizzly about croaking: *Not yet, Lord. Not yet.*

Because Vada has a few things still to tell, reader. This is not to say he's been holding out on you. He has no tricks up his sleeve, no brilliance to offer, and the only shadowy ecclesiastical conspiracy he knows of (those are popular, right?) involves not Mary Magdalene and a priestly order of masochists but Reverend Rick, the hipster youth minister who one week in Vada's childhood—after a fellowship-hall slumber party, the Fun in the Son Teen Lockdown, from which he emerged in the Lord's new morning with Linda Plumb's lip gloss all over his face—disappeared, taking with him his lemon-lightened hair and his 280-Z and his mesh bag of volleyballs and his habit of calling Jesus "The Big Guy."

The things he has to tell aren't *those* kinds. Vada's time is short, his sleeves likewise . . . and not every book can end with Revelations, right?

What would be the point of holding out on you? He couldn't do it for drama's sake, as in his case there's only one trivial plot point left to be settled: How long till the Stage Manager in the Sky yanks down the curtain? The Old Man is napping at His cord despite impatient applause from the loges. The patrons are famished and bladder-plagued and need to make the 10:46 to New Canaan, the last one with a bar car, and wake up, Schmuck Backstage, bring up the lights already, there's only one kind of curtain call that's going to happen tonight.

28

The Last Half-Inch of Life

Whatever illusions he may have had (or even contributed to your having), Vada hasn't been in control thus far. He's been a pawn, people, just trying to bleat faster than he can bleed, to keep the words coming, the synapses firing, the soul from flatlining. The only question he's been able to muster has been a selfish one, when his life will end—and important though that seems to him, there's not much in it to interest *you*.

Nor any suspense. Because you have the edge on Vada—you can tell by the dwindling thickness at your right hand how much time is still allotted him. Ten pages? Fifty? A hundred? Forty-two thousand?

That last figure was a joke, intended to raise the blood to your ears. It also serves as a reminder that you're a demigod—Schmuck-Backstage Second Class—and may at any minute choose to end him, promptly, by casting the book aside. Forty-two thousand? Over your dead body, you say. And you're right. If it comes down to only one of you surviving, the corpse will be Vada. He's clear on that.

This might be a good time, then, for Vada to thank you for your sufferance so far and to wish you the best. Felicitations, friend. He humbly hopes there's no more than an inch remaining in his life—no, half an inch. Surely he can cap this off in half an inch, or maybe a speck beyond. He has no reliable way of measuring, so he asks please that you judge him by the spirit of his vow rather than its letter. He is a man of no depth and rapidly dwindling width.

29

Biography-Scotch

Sleepless Vic used to read fat biographies, and Vada would sometimes spread scores of them across the living room floor and play a version of hopscotch in which one might leap from hearth brick to Martin Bormann to John Muir to couch to Hedy Lamarr to Wilhelm Reich, all without touching carpet or breaking spines, including one's own. Vada would lay out the volumes in meticulous order, based on field of fame or century or cover color or alphabet—challenging himself, for instance, to find his way through a maze of villains without stepping on anyone but a Nazi or a New York Yankee. Wyatt took no interest in this element of the game. While Vada surveyed the phalanx and tugged his chin and then switched Fatty Arbuckle for Erwin Rommel, Wyatt lay listlessly on the couch, watching TV. But when the books were arrayed and the time came for leaping, he perked up. His favorite trick was to fly six or seven feet across the shag, bounce on the spineward side of one of the thinnest books (usually one of the Presidential Biographies for Boys Vic had bought Vada to get him started—little did he know—on being pinned to the mattress by the lives of those more consequential than he), and then quick-hop sideways to another volume, thus flipping Lyndon Johnson or James K. Polk onto his back. His precision and grace were amazing; if biography-scotch were an Olympic event (which seemed possible, once they'd seen curling), Wyatt would have taken the laurels. But his fondness for the game had less to do with glorying in his own skill than in watching Vada negotiate, badly, the twin dangers of injury and property damage . . . and in fact the game ended once and for all when Vada, attempting to set a personal best by springing from Carrie Nation to Bill Veeck in two strides, skidded on a book about the sepia-skinned lover Wyatt called Valentine-o, cut his knee on an end table (resulting in four stitches rather than the full Veeckian peg leg he deserved), and smashed one of his mother's lamps.

Some of these biographies were four inches thick, impenetrable as vault walls. Wyatt couldn't trouble himself to read even flap copy, and would have been hard pressed to distinguish between P. T. Barnum and PT 109, but girth was a measure he could understand. It stoked his competitiveness, made him prone to brag, "When I die, the book about me'll be fatter than Patton's or even Howard Cosell's. *This* high"—at which point he lifted his right leg a foot and a half, set his hands on his hips, twitched an imaginary mustache, and gazed into the middle distance, a recognizable mimicry of a photo they'd looked at a few minutes earlier when Vada, attempting a left-legged "Hall of Presidents," accidentally kicked Teddy Roosevelt open to the pictures in the middle.

Vada didn't doubt him even then. Someday, like TR, WAY would bag a prize biography. *Wyatt A. Yancey, colon, A Life.* And already Vada knew too that he would have to get by, perhaps not without a colon (though he was at an age when he thought wearing a colostomy bag on his hip, like San Diego Chargers' kicker Rolf Benirschke, might be cool), but without a life.

What Vada means to say is that he's long known that *his* biography is better suited to pamphlet than tome. He promises to bear that in mind. A word of warning, though, since he's determined not to mislead you again. There are trials ahead still. Half an inch, yes. But that's half an inch on cheap paper, as he knows he won't rate the heavy nonacidic stock that the dons of Oxford or Corleone get. (On the positive side, though, it won't be on the holy tissue the Gideons use, either. And Vada has no begats with which to pad it out. He will leave no issue, and only this one paltry survivor, on paper prone to brown and crumble over the years. It's in your hands.)

Half an inch more. Please.

30

Attestations of the Party of the First Part

A vigilant Lord would have squelched him by now, yet unsquelched he remains; ergo God has vamoosed. It shouldn't come as a surprise, His withdrawal to the vault of Heaven or vinyl banquette at Denny's or sleeping-chair amid snaking cords backstage. Jehovah's made folks wait beyond all patience before, after all. And can you blame Him for letting His attention wander? Are *you* so gripping? Human beings are a drag, with their Facebook quizzes about what kind of laundry detergent they'd be if they were a laundry detergent and their talking on their cellphones all the time about where the fuck they *are*. The raw end of being all-seeing, Vada presumes, is that you've always already seen it all.

Which leads to the happy news for you, reader. If God's not in charge anymore, and if you've forborne this far and thus proven that you either have no murderous intent or can control said intent, then Vada can relax into his task and tell his life straight or straightish, let you know what *happened*. It'll be like a regular story.

Feel free to consider this a contract.

31

The Last Leak

There is, as he's said, the story of Wyatt, of Darla, of Wyatt and Darla; plus he's got, what . . . eleven minutes of chronology to get through still. He's just about finished mowing now—tell you what, he *is* finished, has cut the motor and squeaked down the slope and . . . no, just for you he'll skip that too, and also the first ninety uneventful seconds inside the house (clomp, clomp, bang, motherfucking ow, clomp, clomp, clomp, etc., pisssssssssssssssssssssssssssssss, sputter, pisssss, sputter, hiss, flush, soap-squirt, rinse, dry [those last three dedicated to Celeste, a final tribute: your son died with clean hands], clomp, clomp, whirr), and now he finds himself standing in the open door of the refrigerator, nine minutes left in his life.

Farewell, last leak. Farewell, protruding board. (He counts on you, reader, to inform the coroner that the knot on his temple is unrelated to cause of death; you'll find DNA evidence on the underside of the motor oil and solvents shelf in Vic's workshop.)

Oh, and he hasn't said *how* his parents died, which he'll need to take care of . . . and he'll have to start with a few clarifications and corrections, since panic may have o'ercome him back when he wasn't in charge and made him fudge this or that, which lapses of judgment he's now put behind him, honest.

32

The Streep of Death by Canned Beer

Correction number one: Early on Vada may have left something out, a certain subtext—or supertext.

Where it says snow, read Darla. Where he said he was thinking of Great Dane scat or cursive script or honey-dipped hands or Mussolini in an elastic-waist jumpsuit, read Darla. Where it says anything besides Darla, read Darla. He didn't leave this out as part of any plan; he was just trying to be discreet. He hopes you will be, too. His mute mouth to your deaf ears, and throw away the key. Please. What good would it do now for her to know?

Besides, you could have figured this out for yourself. He's done his best to be aboveboard even while belowbeast. Vada left clues. For instance, you surely wondered why he was mowing at noon on a July Saturday, in sweltering heat and in defiance of public pleas to be a better Steward of the Earth. Better stewardship means mowing at dusk—wreaking one's usual havoc upon the ecosystem, but at off-hours, so as not to set off EPA meters and cost the county an ozone violation. (Environmentalism has become less satisfying, more dismal, since they promoted economics to a science. What's the cost-benefit ratio of a damselfly?)

What Vada means to get across here is that the earth is important to him. As he's said or hopes he's said, the way they came to live here is that back in 1971 his father was promoted to game warden in charge of

Lake Murray's southern coastline. Vic wore a dark-green uniform with epaulet-like buttons on the shoulders. He commuted to work in a motorboat, a fact that in later years would constitute Vada's closest brush with cool. Eventually, part of Vic's job was to give school assemblies about ecology alongside his friend Woodsy Owl, actually Wyatt's dad wearing a makeshift costume—the feet were swim-flippers painted into talons, and because the wings were too short, Reid wore brown Wildlife Department–issue socks to hide his hands. Part of the presentation about the dangers of litter featured waterfowl strangling themselves on the plastic honeycombs that held six-packs together. Reid Yancey had a genius for this part of the show; he was the Bernhardt or Streep of death by canned beer, and Woodsy would reel about sometimes for three or four minutes, making those socked hands *sing*, before he coughed his owlish last, fell, and turned up his tailfeather for the last time. One heard tell that his performance brought some kids to tears.

Vada's classmates weren't so soft-hearted—though, to be fair, they didn't get the benefit of Reid's thespian chops, as he was the sort of father who knew better than to appear in a bird costume at his own child's school. Instead, two kids took Vic's solo lecture as a how-to and invented a kind of duck-hunting that consisted of setting out six-pack dividers and waiting in the weeds for mallards to fly in and garrote themselves. "Your daddy's a fucking liar," said Freddy Firpa on the playground the next week, by way of explaining why he was grinding Vada's face into a trash can.

33

Lumpkin's Choice

When Vada was nine, his dad deputized him to use the grownup scissors and clip to confetti all the plastic six-pack rings they had in the house. Vic did this over the objections of Celeste, who declared herself no friend to the earth, if earth-friendship required her to watch her only son cut his fingers off: "You know what he's like," she said. "I know you haven't forgotten the time he tried to cut the clown picture out of his pajama shirt while he was wearing it. His chest looked like ground meat. He could've nicked an aorta." Vada's father ignored the fact that Vada had but one aorta, likewise the fact that his son would have to be ribless in order to nick his aorta with craft scissors: avenues of argument that seemed to Vada worth pursuing, given that he was equipped with the usual complement of ribs and aortas and his mom knew it and he would gladly have pulled up his shirt to prove it, and after six years the wounds from his clown-pajama misadventure were healed, almost scar-free, so they wouldn't have undercut the point much, and Vic answered, "Granted, but he's got to learn sometime, right? How to avoid amputation while performing simple tasks is a good first lesson. Do you want him living at home till he's fifty?"

Celeste gave in, and Vada's dad set him up at the kitchen table with a sack full of plastic. "Mind your fingers," he said in a confidential tone. "I'm trusting you not to bleed here, or you'll land me in divorce court.

Got me?" Vada said he did. "The birds that don't choke to death will thank you," Vic finished.

They never did, by the way, perhaps because they didn't know whom to credit; Celeste made him do the work inside, without the TV on, under a glaring gooseneck lamp and tight supervision. She had to admit, when it was over, that Vada had kept all his blood on the inside. He'd helped the ducks without hemorrhaging or wrecking his parents' marriage. Those shards of plastic marked a great victory. Vada asked to keep them as a souvenir, and into the back of his closet they went (sure enough, when he finally had need of them again the other day, they were still there).

Next Vada became a Junior Litter-Getter. For delivering ten big bags of roadside trash to the dump manager, he was issued a commemorative trash spike and yellow refuse bag along with a matching baseball cap that, during the next six months, he put on almost every time he went outdoors.

Vada was grossed out by food garbage, which tended to make him gag, so he decided to specialize in aluminum can tabs. They were unmessy, light, countable, doubloonlike. He toted his sack everywhere and collected booty from marinas, picnic areas, convenience-store lots. He imagined the tabs as mouths with obscene oversized tongues attached—mockeries that needed picking up.

Celeste didn't like his hobby. She'd see him along the main road to town, alone, rooting through Bahia grass for tabs flung from windows. She begged Vic to make him stop. "It's embarrassing. People will think he's a jailbird."

"Let him be. He's trying to help."

"It's dangerous."

"He's got a good-sized spike, honey."

"He's going to turn strange. He already is. His room's overflowing with aluminum bent into décor. Every morning he quotes scrap prices from the paper."

"All kids are strange, Celeste. Would you rather have him screwing sheep like that Lumpkin kid off Highway 6?"

"Shhhh! He's in the next room. He doesn't need to know such things. And you know how he loves animals."

Vic shrugged. "His way's better than how the Lumpkin kid loves animals. Given our choices . . ."

Celeste yielded again. If Vic made it a Lumpkin's choice, with the only two options being eccentric trash-collecting or the literal kind of animal husbandry—well, she could see her argument was going to need reframing.

Eventually, with an assist from packaging science, Celeste found a way to end Vada's obsession. One day, home after a trip to the grocery, she didn't even turn off the ignition or unload the bags; instead she scrambled in to drag Vada from his room and then sped back to Piggly Wiggly. There she made a beeline to the soda aisle, bought a six-pack of Coke, and just outside the store's threshold, so close that Vada could feel the pulse of AC every time the automatic door slid open, she stopped, yanked a can from the sleeve, and—snickered at by Girl Scouts hawking thin mints just inside and bagboys racing snakes of interlaced carts through the lot, by matrons wrestling sacks and offspring to the car—showed him the ingenious new lid that allowed you to poke down a mouth-shaped keyhole and drink without detaching the tab.

"Congratulations, honey. They've surrendered. You've broken the litterers' will. Now when we go to the park, you can play games with the other boys. Climb up in the cockpit. Ride the spinner. OK?"

"The spinner's a good spot," Vada said. "Kids get dared to drink soda on it all the time, so there's always tabs around the edges. Dad says that has to do with math. You've got to look out for vomit, though. That has to do with math, too. Except with barf it's called 'fluid dynamics.'"

"Do you hear me? I mean you can *ride* the spinner with Wyatt and them. Maybe play kickball. These tops are a miracle of design. No more waste." She handed him the can for inspection. "Look!"

Vada examined his new nemesis. The handle part looked like a fat zipperhead, and its bottom edge was just a hint sharp. You could press your thumb to it, hard, and possibly draw blood. Maybe there would be a recall?

Of course he'd understood her. How dumb did Mom think he was? He was buying time, adjusting to a world whose rules kept changing for no good reason. Vada had been content with the simple arrangement: *You litter, I getter.* It provided purpose in a childhood not otherwise overflowing with it. But could Celeste be right? Had he been too good at his job? The last thing he'd intended was to fuel innovation.

Vada lifted his eyes to the green, sweat-stained underside of his cap's bill, his name upside-down across it in his handwriting from two years ago, which did look immature now. The hat had faded to the color of pine pollen, and the adjustable back was stretched to its last knob. Also he'd melted his bag a little the month before when, because it stank and attracted yellowjackets, he'd put it through the wash.

But still. He looked back down at the can. It looked like you could worry the tab off if you wiggled it back and forth. Which he did, faster and faster, and when after fifteen seconds it snapped off in his hand and he looked up in triumph, his mother did not beam triumph back at him. Her eyes were wobbling in their sockets, and she was *shaking*. "Vada," she said. "Vada . . ."

Invulnerable Celeste, the woman who just a year before had been ready to carve out her own trachea at an intersection, was all set to blubber.

One of the zitty bagboys crashed his conga line of carts into a pillar because he was laughing so hard. He pressed his finger and thumb together and oscillated them frantically, mocking. It looked like small-scale masturbation, even Vada could see that. The whirring door, cold, hot, cold, hot; the intermittent chatter of the Girl Scouts in the foyer discussing whether "trefoil" is a word besides in cookies; Vada standing there before his mom with a room-temperature Coke in his left hand, a squat new miraculous tab, friction-warmed, in his right . . . and he knew it would from now on be *his* vomit around the edges of the spinner, there was no getting around it, and Wyatt and the others would laugh in his face as opposed to at a safe distance, behind his back where it didn't matter, and he'd be dizzy forever.

He thought for a moment of the braided garlands of pull-tabs that circled his room (twice!), suspended from the ceiling by hooks his father had installed at the corners and midpoint of every wall. He would never again hear them shiver and chime when a summer squall rumbled through. They would come down this afternoon, and he'd sell them to his friend Bilmo at the scrapyard for a nickel a pound.

"Yes, ma'am," said Vada. He wanted to please her. He wanted her voice to lose its waver. He wanted to see the clarity he saw that day when she held a ballpoint pen to her throat. He forked over his yellow cap, right there in the lot, like Lee at Appomattox, and they made their way back to the car through a ceremonial cordon of shopping carts and chortling morons.

34

Above Covenants

Lately, Wyatt has become fanatical about conservation, worse than Vada was in his Junior Litter Getter days. An example: this winter, after a backcountry Idaho trip to hunt loup-garous or passenger pigeons—yes, he flew three thousand miles, rented a pickup and a snowmobile, expended many rounds of ammunition, and constructed a piñon pyre every night for warmth, all in the name of a conservation better served by, say, sitting at home not killing things—Wyatt tried to carry on to his flight home a backpack full of recyclable cans. Denied by security, he backtracked to the airport post office, bought a box (blah-blah post-consumer blah-blah, Vada wasn't listening), and *mailed* the cans. Two days later—dramatic gestures go express, the extra three bucks be damned—the mailman made the mile-long trip up and down Wyatt's driveway, at the cost of gas and time and whatever else such things cost, to hand-deliver a parcel full of stomped beer cans and pork-and-beans tins. All this so Wyatt could have a tale of high principle to tell.

At Wyatt's behest—if "behest" means badgering, which Vada's pretty sure it does—Vada started composting last spring, and kept up with it until his pile attracted mice, one of Vada's phobias, at which point Vada submitted an anonymous complaint to the neighborhood association ("Vada Prickett has food garbage rotting in his yard, and it stinks awful and attracts rodents. Some kid's going to get the plague I bet, and

I'm pretty sure you can't give innocent kids the plague around here, that must be in the covenant"). They made him stop, and would have tried to intervene with Wyatt, too, but as scion of the original landowners here, Wyatt is exempt from rules. He is the grandson who's been grandfathered. He is above covenants.

Vada is not. And so he's aware that he has some explaining to do, as this erratum or whatever the singular of *errata* is has delocuted and self-circumstructed. The point of this chapter is to tell you that he surmised already twenty minutes ago that something odd was going on; he knew it when Wyatt rushed past in the cart and didn't stop to lecture him about mowing at noon. Vada should have mentioned that earlier. He's tried to be scrupulous about mentioning the things you need to know.

35

That Damned Lissomeness

Back to the tension and mystery that he thought were implicit in his mowing at noon—brazenly polluting, before God and the Council of Neighbors!—but that turned out, because of incompetence, not even to have been hinted at:

Among the plea-issuers Vada disobeyed was Darla. On Thursday's midday weathercast she announced what the graphic over her shoulder called an Ozone O-lert. There was a piping electronica fanfare, presumably supposed to sound like stagnant, noxious air—no easy task for a piping electronica fanfare—and Vada, to whom it sounded like the music used to introduce good-looking groovesters on the *Dating Game,* may have been the only viewer for whom it hit the right note of ominousness.

But the new production team didn't stop there. Gone suddenly was Darla's familiar pie-wedge map of South Carolina, replaced by a scowling cartoon O^3 molecule. The molecule had aggressive-looking covalent bonds, the kind that can only be built up in a prison weightroom, and a do-raggy sweatband thing around the atom at its head. It looked like scrubbing bubbles gone gangland. Ozone, the graphic suggested, was the kind of pollutant that would get all up in yo' bronchioles, yo, and exacerbate your asthma.

"Pop a cough in your ass," as Darla would later joke. But she wasn't joking now. As she pronounced the O-lert, Darla's smile displayed eight teeth that Vada could count, possibly a glint of a ninth (oh, she was a *pro*), but she was plainly furious. She, who never missed a mark or flubbed a line, drifted steadily forward and toward mid-screen, trying to block the graphic. But she was too slender. That damned lissomeness . . .

"Ozone is a significant problem this time of year," Darla intoned, and we could see the evidence behind her. It was three feet by three feet at least, this ozone problem, with muscles, a bandanna. And then the keyboard tootled it away, until the next newscast.

36

Where It Says the Heavy Head
of Pablo the Possum, Read . . .

Darla the Weather Girl, Darla the Divine. Until six weeks ago Vada
would have thought her unflusterable. Here was a woman who
commanded her clicker with a magician's invisible nimblesse: Goddess
of the Green Screen. The pinnacle of cool, if cool has a pinnacle. Peaks
always look like they're *trying*, which Darla never did until that once—
until her live interview with Pablo the Bible-Believing Possum, mascot
of a semipro baseball franchise in the farm country west of Columbia,
just ten miles from Vada's home on the lake.

The ballpark visit was part of a spring promotion called Up in Your
Grill. The TV station sent its weather-readers into the community—first
to backyard barbecues, later to even bigger infernos—to deliver the forecast while wearing a WIST apron and searing burgers. The message: We're
plain folks, only prettier. Often there were mesh trucker caps or T-shirts
to accept (Pengilly Reunion Welcomes the Weather), embroidered pillows
to exclaim over, or side dishes to taste. On Darla's first venture out, the
producer had her pause in mid-report to nosh on Aunt Pearlene Pengilly's
tater salad, which featured a secret spice called "turmurk."

"Ah, turmeric," said Darla. "That's great. Flavorful. Thank you, Mrs.
Pengilly. Tomorrow . . ."

"Turmurk," Aunt Pearlene interrupted, "is A-rab for zesty. But you
mix it with good American spuds, yeller mustard, and all it makes you

want to do is nap, like picnic food aims to. Reckon the starch cancels out the killin' urge. I been makin' it this way on forty years, and ain't none of my family started wearin' a turbine yet."

"Thanks, ma'am," said Darla. "It's good, all right."

"Maybe we should bomb I-rack with picnic grub. They'll be too logy to massacre Christians. My boys say my cupcakes like to make you jump up and thank Jesus."

Darla kept her composure. Her teeth glowed; her skin sang. Instantly a production assistant, responding to signals Darla made somehow using only her shoes, tugged Pearlene away by the elbow, and the cameraman moved in for a tight shot of the grill. Darla showed off her black-striped patties, then glided through the five-day forecast without even a hint of pique.

Her professionalism was held against her in some quarters. Some folks, lacking it, like to punish the cool for their cool; Darla could understand that. Still, she'd expressed no sympathy with Pearlene's politics. She'd said nothing untoward. What was she supposed to do? Tackle the old kook? Grind broccoli slaw into her face while shouting *Allahu akbar*?

No, Darla was not to blame. But it was she who in the next week received five envelopes containing indignant notes and a not-so-suspicious yellow powder. This experience with spice-rack jihad, two months before her venture to the ballpark, had left the off-camera Darla wary and irritable, and might have disillusioned her had she been naïve enough, six months into her on-air career, to hang on to any illusions. The threats were too well-spelled to be the work of anyone with balls enough to actually hurt her, she figured—one used the word "nonplussed" correctly, and another alluded to the Spice Wars, and didn't mean bickering amongst some tarty 1990s girl group. Still, for her safety Darla begged to be excused from Up in Your Grill.

But the controversy had been a ratings-grabber, vaulted the newscast to the top of Arbitron for the first time in years, and she was stuck. WIST capitalized during May sweeps with days of crowd-pleasing Beautiful-Weathergirl-Is-Victim-of-Liberal-Terrorists stories, including one in which a lab-coated "chemist" (the producer's cousin, a part-time instructor at the technical college) divulged that one letter contained, "according to my analysis," not turmeric but cumin.

The reporter's segment, "Jody Bates Investigates," was usually devoted to body-shop ripoffs and, during heat waves, investigating whether you could literally fry an egg on the sidewalk. This was his big chance, and he was going to milk it. Speaking in a staccato lifted from 1930s noir, Bates then asked a local Bible-college professor: "Prof? Your take on the perps. Their deadly game—what is it?" The sash of his signature trench-coat trembled with every finger-jab.

The professor could be identified as such by his owlish specs and the fact that he stood against a backdrop of books—though the backdrop appeared to be wallpaper. "Mr. Bates," he said, "this is exactly the kind of imprecise vengeance you'd expect from people who took Jesus for a mere prophet."

Bates glared into the camera. "Scumbags, we're on your heels. The jig is up." He paused. "No calls, please—I don't mean that in a racial way."

All this made Darla, just twenty-six, a regional celebrity. "Yeah, the celebrity *victim*," she scoffed. "Like the Black Dahlia, but with my head still on." Beneath the complaints, though, one could glimpse a hint of pleasure: As she spoke, her hand went up to her hair, probed above the ear as if checking for a flower. Then her hand came down and her tone hardened. "More or less on."

Perhaps the most distressing part was political. Darla found her-self beloved, as she'd always imagined she would be, but by the wrong people and for the wrong reasons. She, a fire-breathing liberal from Maryland, miscast as the offspring of Margaret Mitchell and the Moral Majority. Everywhere she went to grill, the crazies teemed and flocked. There were hand-painted vans from splinter churches; guys in fatigues carrying flags, Confederate and DON'T TREAD ON ME and the state's crescent moon and palmetto; color shots of aborted fetuses on foam-core, mounted like heads on pikes; a booth manned by partisans of a barbecue king who gave out samples of his "certified turmeric-free 100% American sauce" along with brochures explaining how the myth of the happy darkie wasn't a myth at all, that West African slaves blessed the Lord for his bounteous goodness in delivering them to mild Christian owners and a climate that suited their complexions. There was also a florid rotundity in full Rebel uniform and sidewhiskers who carried a sign reading, "Remember When Salt and Pepper Were Spice Enough? And We Kept 'Em in Separate Shakers?" Darla couldn't help noticing that the flags were mounted on stout sticks that could double as truncheons, in the lucky eventuality of a riot.

Darla was adored by these people, and her bosses—though they didn't go so far as to make her *embrace* her fans—asked her not to rebuke them, either. "We've got a good thing going," said the station director. "Let it ride."

"More like night-ride," Darla complained—but only to Vada, and only later. "There's one guy out there whose van says he's from the Church of the Blood of the Lamp. Are there seriously people out there who can't spell 'lamb'?"

Vada thought of his mother's shattered chicken lamp, of the surprisingly intestinal-looking cord that had been threaded through its hollow body cavity. The Blood of the Lamp: it sounded almost plausible. "Maybe he's an Aladdinist. God is the light and the way. Or else it's some weird vertical-plane dyslexia."

"Sounds dangerous for a Christian. Stakes are high if you confuse down and up."

There was the sex-symbol stuff, too, a flame fanned by the station. Usually she was costumed as a combination of ingenue and minx that Darla called Catholic-School Call-Girl, and her report featured inexplicable midrange shots of her tartan-plaid miniskirt, held together with a gold safety pin the size of a padlock. Now the station issued her a grilling apron that fit as snugly as a wrestling singlet. It offered no protection against burns or splatter; it did little but lift and separate. And they started sending her out every Friday, always to majority-white suburban or rural events. (The station did air an occasional Diversity Barbeque, an event always given the uppercase letters of self-congratulation, but these were presided over by Nykesha Davenport, one of the weekend meteorologists. She was beloved around the station for the time when, advised to "dress more ethnic," she shuffle-bowed into the studio one day in full kabuki makeup.)

Darla told Vada she was ashamed by the attention, but she was clearly flattered by it, too. She'd made the calculations that ambition bade her make. Vada didn't hold this against her; nor, he believes, should you. In fact he found it thrilling, her quiddity of need. That someone like her could suffer that way. People with actual needs fascinated him: *needs,* not halfhearted impulses to be jettisoned at the first resistance, like his, or whims like Wyatt's that were so quickly granted by fate, that brown-noser, that they never got chafed or worried or obsessed into need. Darla was a woman who knew what she wanted and pursued it, not blindly but in full knowledge that her goal might be unworthy, and therefore she unworthy too by the associative property of unworthiness. She would (lovably) be chastened by this but (also lovably) not deterred. The heart wants what the heart wants, they say. That had always sounded to Vada too glib—how were you supposed to tell what the heart wanted, and what if the brain or the spleen or the ileum wanted something else entirely, as brain or spleen or ileum was wont to want?—but Darla seemed the *embodiment* of the principle.

Her calculations, as reported to Vada: For now, as long as it stayed discreet, the adulation would do her no harm. Most viewers would have no idea what a cult figure she'd become to the right wing, because by design the hullabaloo played out offscreen. She'd warned the station manager that if they did anything to identify her with the cause of the downtrodden white Southerner, bereft of his "sacred hurtage," she'd bayonet an effigy of General Lee on camera, then squat and pee on his beard.

Her boss, Bruce, acquiesced. Management was dancing the same razor's edge she was. At the carnivals that began to surround Darla's grill-outs, interns dispensed trinkets to WIST's new constituency, and each week the brass sprang for a truck with drinking water to make sure the righteously rageful remained hydrated. But the gestures could go no further; balloons and change purses and paper cones would have to suffice as tokens of friendship. The owners couldn't afford to alienate other viewers, so every week they finessed the camera angles and banked her in with rows of children whose job it was to wave and smile and prop up the dry-erase board on which were printed the day's weather statistics. Darla began to refer to the kids as her human shield.

*   *   *   *   *

Up in Your Grill at the Ballpark was an especially nervous-making gig, and Darla would say later that she knew all along it would go south and sour. The franchise was owned by two evangelical brothers who operated it as missionary outreach. They'd conceived of small-time minor league baseball as a new way of proselytizing: Hitting the Eternal

Cut-Off Man, Dropping in the 3&2 Gakker for Christ When Satan's Sacks Are Juiced. Gilyard, twenty miles west of Columbia, was one of those formerly rural towns turning quickly exurban, with incursions from the capital's upper middle class, who brought along their wrought-iron gates and security-guard cabanas and dragged behind them a train of Applebee's and Target and TGI Ruby Bennigan's, and also from Hispanic farmworkers, former migrants now setting down their roots and their signage, replacing the abandoned wig shops and appliance stores downtown with *lavaterías* and *taquerías*.

The brothers' idea wasn't bad; it was even ingenious. Independent-league baseball had begun to thrive again, in towns otherwise too dinky and sleepy for the minors and in need of an infusion of civic pride and family-friendly entertainment. Plaster "Pelion" or "Edgefield" or "Gilyard" across a throwback buttoned-front jersey, and people would come. The allure would be all the greater if the fans—and South Carolina's Midlands are Belt High in the Bible Strike-Zone—could conceive of going to the game as a boon to their souls, as a way of augmenting or even replacing their churchgoing. Show St. Peter your ticket stubs, my child, and all will be forgiven.

Two weeks before her ballpark appearance, Darla read an article about the franchise in *Sandhills Business*. The Shealy brothers came across as perfectly sincere. Vern Shealy cited as his inspiration a troupe of Lycra-clad soul-savers who'd been touring the state bringing sinners to Christ through weightlifting; they were called Spot Me, Jesus. The epiphany, as Vern described it, was banal and businesslike, less Saul-on-the-road-to-Damascus than Bugsy-on-the-road-to-Las-Vegas. But the Lord helps those who help themselves, and if a troupe of steroidals in cheerleading gear could make a living bench-pressing for the Lord in high school gyms, then surely . . . yes, praise God and pass the fungo bat.

According to the article, the Shealys figured their customers at first would be local church groups and families in search of wholesome outings, and for almost every home game they dreamt up a promotion, a task for which Bill Shealy turned out to have a talent that verged on mania. He arranged giveaways (Gideons' Pocket New Testament Night; Lazarus Arise-and-Bobblehead Day; the controversial Inglenook Feast of Cana Night, where fans of age who brought in a sealed bottle of water to be donated to charity could exchange it for a plastic cup of white, red, or blush wine; Dr. Scholl's Least-Among-You Sandal Night, featuring free flip-flops for the first six hundred fans, and also foot-washings by volunteer penitents—an event that went awry when the penitents got infiltrated by foot-fetishists, who were slow about relinquishing their turns). There were visiting evangelists: Baptismal Font Night was a big one, with wildly cheered dunkings after every half-inning in an aboveground pool installed in the visitors' bullpen, a pool donated for promotional considerations and thus carrying ads for Flip Fersner Swimming-Holes-to-Go. Before long the region's TV preachers, having absorbed the Gospel of Cross-Promotion, began vying for spots.

There were also political nights, exploiting the target audience's xenophobia (Osama Night, when the Shealys let in all men wearing beards and homemade head-wraps for half-price and offered free admission to the first seven hundred virgins, signed pledge required) or prejudice (on Homosexual Shame Night, their answer to Gay Pride, they flew in G. Gordon Liddy to throw out a first pitch—and had a local guy who professed himself a "recovering fag" catch it after a short, ugly tiff that had to do with the man's insistence that, as what he called a "former power-top," he should be on the mound rather than behind the plate. "I wasn't *that* kind," he kept saying. "What will people think?").

God smiled upon the venture with big crowds and regional, even national, publicity. Buttering up Liddy won them a following on talk radio, and some TV reverends who wrangled gigs in Gilyard showed video packages of their trips when they got back to the pulpit. In June, Jerry Falwell was photographed wearing the purple Gilyard cap, the logo an effulgent golden G in a black background with a pale circle partially superimposed to the right—the Shealys' version of the empty tomb and rolled-aside stone. Soon folks started making pilgrimages from across the South, and the brothers had to haul in new aluminum risers and deploy them down the foul lines.

All this, too, contributed to Darla's anxiety. The team's church affiliation was well known, and if the station was seen to have scheduled this weathercast to curry favor with the religious right or to give the Shealys a platform, her reputation would be cemented, and good-bye forever to more sophisticated markets up east. She'd find herself, at forty, singing praisesongs to frito chili pie on *Good Morning Phenix City*.

Also, the event was by a factor of ten the biggest WIST had yet attempted. The Pengilly barbecue had taken place in a fenced backyard in a split-level suburb; guests had been limited to thirty. But the events had grown steadily larger and more public, and now Darla found herself occupying an astroturf platform outside Jesus of Nazareth Field, home of the Gilyard Risen.

It was a gruesome vision that she conjured for Vada later that night: Darla, her determinedly vacant smile making her cheeks ache as if someone had implanted bolts just above her eyeteeth; Darla, avoiding her public by touching a finger to her nonexistent earpiece and doing a pantomime of hearkening to invisible voices; Darla bobbing amid a maelstrom of yahoos.

They'd set up, as always, by 5:45—to give her an hour to mingle before preparing for the broadcast. She wandered, shaking hands, waving at the wolf-whistlers rather than flipping them off. She turned down countless offers of junk food and soft drinks, including one (nearly irresistible, she said) from a rainbow-wigged ectomorph sipping cola from a Tupperware bowl he said had been blessed by Elvis's personal minister.

The stadium was an old American Legion field with the power alleys expanded, extra bleachers plugged in, and the whole enclosed by an aluminum fence sheathed in the green mesh that cuts wind around tennis courts. Stated capacity was 1,500, but by 6:30 at least twice that many people had assembled, and the Shealy brothers were determined to have each and every one pass, like camels through the eye of a needle, the three grimy turnstiles that led into the park. It would take extra time, they warned, and sent a couple of kids up and down the line to cry out Bible verses: "Let patience have her perfect work," yelled the boys in purple satin Risen jackets, "that ye may be perfect and entire, wanting nothing." Darla noticed that the Shealys, canny operators who understood human frailty, also equipped these criers with keychains, superballs, and promotional sponges to assuage those fans who'd let patience have only imperfect work and were thus unentire and wanted something. The sponges were especially sought after—each was a flat blob of about palm size that, wetted, inflated into the stone that sealed Christ's tomb, if the stone that sealed Christ's tomb could swab away dish crust and had the name of a certain carwash sponsor on its Savior-facing inward side.

All this made for a dicey situation, community-relations-wise. By dispatching the Up in Your Grill crew, WIST's brass wanted to send the message to the Shealys and their flock that the station approved . . . but couldn't afford the appearance of endorsement. Darla was instructed to make clear on air her delight at being on hand for this *exciting* event, but not to indicate what said event was, beyond a baseball game.

This was difficult, given the atmosphere. Tonight was the first of a two-game set against the Chester Red Devils, and the Shealys, playing off the opposing mascot, had declared it Armageddon Night. Besides the usual suspects who haunted Darla's Up in Your Grill forecasts, millennialists from as far as Tennessee and central Florida had come to celebrate the end times and eat dollar franks. Two dozen Operation Rescue activists had bused in from Mississippi, and they were jostling with cops at the barricades around the WIST platform, presumably because God's plan was to defeat abortion once and for all by getting their picket photos into a corner of the weather report. At 6:33 a shout went up from them, a cheer. A tiny plane chugged high overhead, trailing a banner with the legend THIS IS *ROE V. WADE* and an illustration that looked from this range like maybe a DeKooning, or one of those classroom Maps of the World with the colors gone lurid. At 6:35 Darla went to test the microphones, and three protesters surged after her. When a chubby cop barked, "Back across that rope, chief!" one antiabortionist turned to him and hissed, "Brother, there ain't no doughnuts in *hell*."

WIST's platform was set up along the left-field fence, just beyond third base, and through the narrow lane between two bleachers Darla could make out—when she grew tired of Cameraman Joe's entreaties and gave in—what she was told were the armies of Megiddo, massing behind the shoulder-high outfield wall into the battalions of the earth's four corners. Two hundred people, mostly teenagers, milled there, divided into more or less equal squads. Cameraman Joe, who had his lens trained on them, said they were responding to the prompt of an end-of-days website called beammeup.org. Darla could see only the yellow T-shirts in right, blue in right-center, but Joe told her that a scraggly white army was encamped behind the Dairy-O sign in left center, and a slightly skimpier group in red clustered around the foul pole in left. (The skimpiness of the red army, Joe suggested, was because "No one in this crowd wants to be called a communist." Joe was an ex-hippie who gave it up, he said, when his ex-girlfriend Starfire became a periodontist. Over the years he'd made his peace with the straight world, but if you asked him—few did, Darla would guess—gum care would always and forever be counterrevolutionary. He claimed still to be an ex-radical— but that was out of nostalgia, he said, and for the music, a sentiment that made him sound to Darla like many an Episcopalian. Meanwhile it was his sorry lot to be "shooting weather and griddle meat at some kind of Rapture freakshow.")

6:42, and Darla's nerves were jangling. There was for one thing the difficulty of getting through these next forty minutes without offending the ideologues of hin or yon, Gog or Magog. Joe's not-quite-whispered diatribe might spark a melee at any moment. Already there were those who'd seen his camera and detected his disdain. One woman in a sack dress asked Darla's producer whether they as representatives of the MSM (mainstream media, Darla had to be told) were there to spy for the satanist left.

Then there were the antiabortion activists, who lacked both the local picketers' politeness and their reverence for the MegaDoppler Power of 10 Radar Weatherteam. Most nights when the spotlight came on, Darla was amazed that the shouts ceased instantly, the signs quit bobbing and the hands that held them fell limply to sides, and people stood mesmerized—silenced by the cathode glow of celebrity. But these Mississippians were professional disrupters, immune to the spell of Darla's face bathed in white light. They might interrupt.

And the heat. No surprise that South Carolina in summer would set folks to imagining molten pools and brimstone. It was still ninety-five, and humid enough that Darla's makeup felt like a melting mask, deforming her, un-forming her. She had the idea that a sculptor, if a sculptor happened by, could remake her face with a few expert pinches, give her the shape of crone or monkey, and she'd go on air and scold or gibber. She didn't feel *herself.* Anyone could come along now and *mold* her, and she didn't like the available sculptors.

But mostly she worried about timing. At 7:18 the airwaves would be turned over to her for four minutes, no less and no more. The plan was to have her report five minutes after first pitch, by which time the hubbub outside the stadium would have subsided. She'd be encircled by cute kids in choir robes, representatives of a safe denomination and a church with

"First" in its name. Bruce considered this to be clever stagecraft, a way to indicate friendliness to Christianity without endorsing the Shealys' plague-of-boils-and-popping-eyeballs version. To palliate the brothers, Bruce had consented to a brief on-air "interview" with their mascot—an even wilier move, he thought, as the mascot was a cartoon mute with a head the size of a microwave oven, and silent by costume design, sacred vow, and league bylaws.

The broadcast was planned like Operation Overlord. The first fifteen seconds would be devoted to interanchor patter. Then there would be seventy-five seconds of back-but-not-forth with the mascot, Pablo the Bible-Believing Possum (who would, for Darla's purposes, be just plain Pablo; viewers would be left to their own devices to figure out his species and, should the Lord grant a revelation, his Bible-believing). After the interview would come a quick shot of the grilling meats. A test run was just now being laid out to sizzle by the production assistant, Meg, a squeamish vegetarian who was handling the dogs and patties with surgical latex and averting her eyes from the carnage—an example of which would at 7:20, thirty-six minutes from now, be hustled into a bun, squiggled with mustard, and given to a grateful youngster as the camera rolled. That would leave Darla two minutes in which to present the same forecast she gave every summer day: sweltering, 30 percent chance of pop-up afternoon showers. Cake.

Except that the hubbub had not yet subsided and gave no sign of doing so soon. The choir kids too had been made cranky by the heat, and were squawking at stage left. Many of the cream robes with purple velvet at the neck were smirched by condiments and drenched with sweat, and mothers were attacking these as if they were the taints of sin, using stain sticks and Christ's-tomb sponges and even parchment-colored liquid paper. Several mothers had out powder puffs and hairspray, and their children squirmed and shied from beautification. Why couldn't fame, like heaven, be come as you are?

At 6:46, almost twenty-five minutes early, the mascot arrived. Darla was standing behind Cameraman Joe, half-listening to him and half-trying to screen him from the antiabortion guys twenty feet away, who thought he'd laughed too uproariously at the "no doughnuts in hell" line and who were threatening to rush the stage and give him a foretaste of the torments to come.

Pablo's shoulder-tap caught Darla off guard. She whirled and discovered problem number one. He was carrying, or had been carrying until she startled him, a huge book—it landed on the podium with a sound like a rifle crack. She recognized it as a dictionary, but a dictionary disguised and caparisoned: sprayed black, HOLY BIBLE stenciled on its cover in gold block letters. They'd even dusted the deckle edges with glitter.

She looked from the floor to the mascot. No wonder he'd dropped the book. In a misguided attempt at truth to nature, the costume designer had given Pablo short forelegs. He looked like a thalidomide possum. The kid had to keep his elbows locked against his ribcage, she guessed, which made it nearly impossible to carry the book, much less carry it while freeing a finger—an oddly delicate pink rubberized finger, like the nipple of a baby bottle—for tapping Darla's shoulder.

Darla pointed to Webster's Third Holy Bible. "Shealys' idea?"

The kid made a palms-up shrug, cocked his head. Staying in character. It looked like it pained him even to turn his palms up. His triceps must be duct-taped to his chest.

"You can talk to me. You have to, in fact, or you can't go on air. This book the Shealys' idea?" This would mark her first venture into live interviewing since the Pearlene debacle, and Darla was determined to gauge him—mute cartoon rodent or not—with a chat beforehand. The prop Bible only fed her resolve. If he pretended during the interview that God had spontaneously granted him—miracle!—the ability to speak, she'd be a laughingstock, and the clip would enliven blooper reels forever. No way. She would not suffer the good-natured jabs of a hundred-and-twenty-year-old Dick Clark.

The snout swung down. The kid was looking at the fallen Bible for guidance, or maybe waiting for feeling to return to his forearms. He brought his hands together, bounced the eight pink bottle nipples together in a parody of contemplation. "Yes, ma'am," he said at last. The sound zizzed through a silver grate at the possum's neck.

"You can't bring that book on air," she lied. "FCC regulations." He'd dropped to his knees to pick it up.

"Yes, ma'am," he said.

"You can just leave it there for now. It's fine where it is."

"No, ma'am. The Shealys wouldn't like that. It's sanctified." The last word had a tired, sardonic edge.

"It's a dictionary."

"But it's a sanctified dictionary."

In sunlight the costume looked grubby. The possum is a nocturnal creature, and the suit too was built for after dark. There were patches on the thighs, and the long curlicue of tail was soiled with parking-lot gunk and looked like it had been stepped on countless times. Nor did the costume allow for much display of fine motor skills, Darla noticed as he tried to corral the dictionary. Ten seconds passed as he scrabbled at it with his pink nubbins and tried to hold up his heavy head. How *hot* must it be in there?

"Why didn't they hollow out the dictionary?" Darla asked. "Or just make one out of a cardboard box? How are you supposed to engage in, you know, hijinks in the stands while you're hauling a holy . . .

"Cinderblock?" offered Cameraman Joe over his shoulder. "Ingot?"

Darla left it at that.

From twenty feet away, one of the Operation Rescue guys yelled, "Is that creature salaaming? Is that possum praying to the whoremaster Mohammed?" Darla saw the crowd-control cop roll his eyes, put one hand on his billy club; a smile creased his face. He looked like a man who wouldn't mind a beat-down, were the chance to present itself.

"They didn't think about the weight till after they'd painted it," mumbled the kid, still on his knees. He started to turn to her, then abandoned that lost cause. The head was big as an oil drum and no easier to wield. The costume's feet were flat and dusty, shaped like baseball gloves; it seemed to Darla a strange intimacy to see his soles, and the tail draped between them, umbilicuslike. "And then it was too late. Vern said it might have been consecrated by the stencil. The brothers told me they were sorry, but they said to buck up and think of Christ at Calvary. Pablo returned to his flipperish digging and batting. This was hard to watch . . . but damned if she was getting down there. She'd *told* him to leave it.

"But do *you* get to sit at the right hand of God when you get home tonight?"

The kid lost patience at last. "Yes, ma'am. I should have held out for divinity. Do you think I don't know it's a shitty job?"

Darla suddenly liked the kid. Shitty job? She knew all about those. She bent and put a hand on his shoulder. "Maybe I could stand on the book, for the interview. It would help, heightwise. I'd consider it a favor."

"Yes, ma'am?" said the kid, restored to his former deference and diffidence. He seemed distrait, a hostage not quite sure help had arrived. Or maybe it was just the heat. The tar beneath the plywood seemed almost to be pulsing now.

"I'm not the synod, but I am short. And I rule it's not sanctified."

"Your funeral. Your eternal-boiling-in-hell after the funeral."

"I'll take the heat." Darla squatted, flipped the book shut, turned it to the secular side so as not to taunt the devout with an out-facing spine. Then she helped the boy to his feet. "No need to be hauling that in this sun, Pablo. *No es justo.*"

Naming the mascot Pablo had been the Shealys' idea of ethnic outreach, and it was the rare ploy that hadn't paid off at the gate. In the *Sandhills Business* article, the brothers pronounced themselves disappointed when their "gesture of inclusion" didn't bring a stream of Mexican migrants from outlying farms. Here was proof, if proof were needed, that "diversity" was bunk. They'd come halfway, given the Hispanic community a stake in the franchise, a flyspecked patch-assed secondhand rodent to call their own (elsewhere in the article, as an illustration of their shoestring budget, they explained that they'd bought the getup at auction for twenty bucks, *cap a pie,* from a folded franchise in south Alabama, the Opp Possums). Darla remembered wondering: Were the grateful Hispanics to come on foot? Crammed into slat-bed trucks that smelled of the peaches or strawberries they'd picked all day? Driving the Lexuses of talk-radio myth? At an hour's wage a head, at the end of a twelve-hour day, to watch bad baseball among gawking peckerwoods and be brought by gringo businessmen to a proper English-speaking Jesus?

"The Lord gives us all tribulations," Bill told *Sandhills Business.* "But let me assure investors that this particular tribulation won't affect attendance projections. God is good, and possums are survivors."

The interview plan was simple, and Darla—relieved to have a task that would allow her to ignore Joe and his antagonists—prepped Pablo. They walked to the side of the production truck that faced the bleacher-backs and stood, sinking, in the searing tar lot. She would ask four questions that could be answered in pantomime. She ran through them, and he had ready answers. Cute, short, silent. He'd be fine.

Afterward they chatted. Chuck turned out to be a nice kid, and voluble for a mute. He was seventeen, headed to Duke come fall. A schoolboy thespian in a town stingy with opportunities for schoolboy thespians, he'd been desperate enough for this gig that he'd signed a contract stipulating that he'd never lain with man and would avoid abomination in all its forms (except, he noted, the contractually obligated abomination of wearing a possum suit and glad-handing people wearing God Hates Fags T-shirts. "And the vicious ones aren't the worst," he said. "You can't imagine how weird it is to have people turn to their kids and say, in all seriousness, 'Why look, Cody and Briana, it's one of God's creatures. Praise the Lord.'")

He'd been instructed by the Shealys to be mischievous, but in a way befitting a Christian gentleman of a possum—only the kind of mischief that would be sanctioned upstairs, in the owners' box and beyond.

"Specifically," Darla asked, "what's OK?"

"Commandments tend to be negative," piped Chuck/Pablo through his confessional grate. "They gave me a much better sense of what *won't* go. No goosing, for instance. Possums don't goose. None of that cross-species stuff. But I can let you in on this. The chosen love a good whoopee-cushion gag."

"What's with your name? They didn't really choose it to draw fruit-pickers."

Now Chuck turned analytical: the Possum Sage. He figured it for a bit of creative blame-diverting. Give the Shealys credit: It was chancy to give a team nicknamed the Risen a possum mascot, and he said the possum wasn't their first choice. The Shealys had already lined up a local flour company as their major sponsor and offered to name the mascot after the company when they learned that their intended mascot, a buttermilk biscuit, had been claimed, butter pat and all, by an upstart club farther south and west. When the Shealys argued that the biscuits down that way were mere hardtack, as kin to real biscuits as they were to rocks, and what they wanted was a big, fluffy South Carolina sort and therefore not copyright infringement, they were rejected by league officials—"an unleavened-bread sort of crowd," Bill Shealy told Chuck. Their dreams of Buttermilk the Bible-Believing Biscuit squelched, the company had settled for a big sign on the centerfield wall that read FLOUR CAN SELF-RISE. THE REST OF US NEED JESUS.

Anyway, Chuck went on, the second-choice mascot was a cleverness, and therefore a risk. People could think it sacrilegious—the possum's fake resurrection a burlesque of Christ's real one. Which is where Pablo came in. *Now* if the public judged it amiss, you could put it off to cultural differences. Sacrilegious, sure, but in just the ways Catholicism was. The customs of fast-talking, bead-pulling, tortilla-making brown peoples are strange, and they're going to hell of course, but they're *trying* to do the right things and worship the right God, it's just that His Grace is easily mistranslated.

The Shealys told Chuck that he *could* use Hispanic gestures, if there were Hispanic gestures that weren't gang-related. Stuff from *Westside Story* was probably OK, but he wasn't to push it. They might even get him a sombrero, if they could locate one of sufficient size and figure a way to secure it; they'd been in touch with the folks up in Dillon at South of the Border. But in general he was to be an unimpeachably American possum. "Which means we need to dial down the macho," said Bill Shealy. "Or take that back. Macho's not going to be much of a problem with you, I sense."

As he spoke, Chuck seemed to melt in the heat. He leaned back against the station's truck, and his plastic head made a solid thunk against a metal panel. His posture crumpled. He began to slur, and his wrists and forearms slumped. Darla's feet felt like they might combust.

"Do you need water? I've got a parasol I use to keep the sun from cracking my makeup. You want that? Some shade?"

"Yes'm, I need water . . . but I can't get it till first pitch, and then it has to be in the locker room. But I guess you could splash some through my mesh."

"What?"

Chuck mumbled that management wouldn't let him doff his head or sit down on the premises. It was partly his fault, he said. The suit allowed no peripheral vision, and a week earlier Chuck had found an apparently deserted spot in the rightfield stands—the Risen were up 8-1 in the home half of the seventh, and he thought a conspicuous nap might look like a gag, count as entertainment—and he sat on a child who was out there playing with the Old Testament paper dolls the club had given away that night. It was bad enough that a reeking beast startled her and that Delilah and Ruth, fast friends, had fluttered down through the bleachers, lost forever. But the little girl *really* freaked out when Pablo/Chuck yanked off his head to make sure she had no injuries. She was just shaken up, not hurt, but the Shealys issued an ultimatum. Chuck would keep his feet, and his head would stay on. He represented the Gilyard Risen, and he would not squash children and terrify them into thinking he was wearing the mask of the Antichrist.

Chuck fell silent, and Darla scurried to the water truck and brought back four complimentary cones. "Don't be a martyr," she pleaded when she got back. Chuck/Pablo was slumped against the wheel well, panting. "Take off that head and *drink*. It's 150 degrees on this asphalt. You're going to monkey from the heat, and I'd guess that monkeying is as grave an offense as goosing. What will people think if you collapse?"

"They'll think . . . playing possum," explained Chuck, thickly but—Darla had to admit—reasonably.

"Please."

"Mmmmf," he said, in a tone that conveyed no. Darla could see that the fabric parts of the costume were soaked through, and he gave off a sour odor, not unlike the possums she saw on the road as they underwent the sun's steady subtraction from three dimensions to two.

Darla put one hand behind his head, right at the neck seam. "Mmmmf," said Chuck again. She tossed the cones of water into the possum neck one by one. The metal mesh, impregnable as a fencing mask's, seemed to repel most of the liquid, but it must have helped some, because Chuck revived. He thanked her and asked for another round, and she did as she was asked; this time she risked hauling six cones. She'd once waitressed at a *Biergarten* in Baltimore, she told Vada that night, and she was getting the hang of it again.

And then Chuck seemed better, even jovial. "This head weighs twenty pounds," he babbled. "I'm like Mayor McCheese. I'm a combination of Mayor McCheese and a nine-hundred-foot Jesus. A nine-hundred-foot Mayor McChesus. I'm getting killer neck muscles, like Herschel Walker. I have his poster in my room. His traps? Awesome. Looked like he'd swallowed a pool rack. Man, it's hot out here. In here." He grunted and rocked to his knees, then braced a shoulder against the van and shimmied to full height again.

Darla didn't know what to say to all this. She'd liked him better when he was mute, a martyr, when his shimmying looked like bad comedy rather than good tragedy. She glanced at the stack of empty cups in her hand and—she couldn't say why—held them out to him like a bouquet.

"No," said Pablo/Chuck grandly, as if turning down an ambassador-ship, "but thank you for the offer of your cones, kind lady." The suit's chest glistened. He bowed and seemed almost to pitch over. "You go on now," he continued. "I need to make one quick lap of the stadium, but I'll be back on time. OK?" He didn't look steady, but he was already bounce-shuffling off, the gait oddly possumlike for a creature on two feet. Behind him Darla nodded, and hoped his dragging tail wouldn't get tangled in power cords and trip him.

Her watch read 7:02—the newscast had begun. Darla returned to the stage, where the scene had grown even tenser, stranger. The pro-life Piper Cub buzzed the stadium, clearing the light standards by no more than two hundred feet, its banner snapping smartly behind, a Technicolor close-up of what turned out not to be a world map. ABORTION AT TEN WEEKS read the caption. A toll-free number was listed below.

"Sweet Jesus!" yelled Joe the Cameraman, affecting wide-eyed ear-nestness, as the roar faded. "The babykillers have joined forces with the pilots, and now they're doing midair abortions so they can piss God off at closer range? And they're *advertising*! What blasphemy will they think of next?"

From the Operation Rescuers rose a murmur of . . . puzzlement? rage? Or was it anxiety? They'd chased abortion out of the South, confined the practice to a handful of windowless, cyclone-fenced clinics in dead city cores, and outside these last remnants had established permanent pick-eting missions, at the very least a Panama-hatted oldster napping in a chair alongside a copse of sonograms on sticks and a sign urging drivers-by to honk forth their righteousness. They were *winning;* you could see it. The misguided women now had to be hustled down the parking-lot gauntlet under burqalike coats and under escort, and if you glimpsed their eyes you couldn't but recognize the wet gleam of fear. Inside, before the so-called doctors donned their killing bibs, they had to burden their coatracks with Kevlar vests. The things must hang there all day waiting, wings spread, like buzzards on winter trees. *Judgment awaits.*

But Satan's wiles, they knew, were low and ceaseless. Had they left a loophole that allowed for abortions overhead . . . tauntingly overhead, in God's blue heaven? Was this plane above not a friend but a foe?

Joe kept needling. "Hell in a handbasket. Chuck Yeager wouldn't have done this—God was *his* co-pilot, and the Lord was Alan's Shepard.

High-altitude baby-snuffing. Soon it'll be an event in those X Games, where the freaks fly their bikes upside down. Used to be kids rode their bikes right side up, and didn't put their dingwillies in sock puppets and wave them in front of snakes so they could show the fang marks on TV. And didn't murder children in the skies."

"Joe!" whispered Darla. "Please! This isn't a joke to them."

"To me, either," said Joe, looking her in the face. There was a ferocity she hadn't seen in him before; the silver soul-patch below his underlip looked electrified. "If you think I'm joking, you read me wrong."

She was rescued by the renewed roar of the plane making another pass, so close this time that they could hear the crackle of the banner. Seen close up, the picture was gruesome: all reds and purples, at the center a translucent amphibious hand. This even worse carnage snapped Meg the Vegetarian's head back down to the grill, a horror she could at least flip shut, and Darla caught herself wincing away. The flapping sound trailed by about fifty feet the banner she could see, which made sense. Time is a warp. It deforms all who enter it.

The task at hand, she thought. The task at hand, the task at hand. Darla took a microphone stand and shuffleboarded the dictionary to the proper spot for the interview. Then she withdrew to the van to pat herself dry and apply a final touch-up.

37

Sorry for the Interruption, Which Only Serves to Prove That Philosophy Is the Last Refuge of the Sphincter-Loosened and That Vada Can't Bear to Yield the Spotlight, Even to His Beloved

At that moment, Vada is certain, another biplane must have burped and buzzed across the sky above the stadium hauling a banner—but a banner too big and too taut with wind, so that the plane seemed like a housecat trying to plow in an ox's yoke. The banner was an advertisement for Spot Me, Jesus, and it featured the Bible verse that, said the *Sandhills Business* article, was the creed of all God's dead-lifters and clean-and-jerkists—Job 17:9: "The righteous also shall hold on his way, and he that hath clean hands shall be stronger and stronger."

Darla glanced up at it—OK, right, she was in the van, and a glance up would have yielded only scarred steel, maybe a deposit of chewing gum . . . Darla happened, while looking at herself in the passenger-seat vanity, to look sideways, and in the up-tipped outside mirror (up-tipped *who knows how,* skeptical reader: perhaps by God himself, or by Pablo the Bible-Believing Possum's ungainly sideswiping retreat?) she saw the snapping legend, nineteen words long, a football-field's length of wisdom pinned to a butterfly that couldn't shake it.

*   *   *   *   *

Vada feels for you, Lord. Omniscience ain't as easy as it looks. How you contrive the fancy stuff more or less believably—protective coloration, say, or that sticky bun that looked so much like Mother Teresa, warty chin and all, or the charmed life of someone like Wyatt Yancey—is beyond him. He's not sure how Darla learned to read backwards, at a glance. She just *can*. And *did*.

The righteous also shall hold on his way, and he that hath clean hands shall be stronger and stronger. Vada could have told Darla, as she sat there, lipstick poised before her mouth, watching the plane try to shake its heavy tail. Or couldn't have told her *then*, as he was not yet Permanently Recumbent Man, and prone (for the sake of accuracy, supine), as Permanently Recumbent Man is, to philosophy. But *now*, armed with his experience of the last few hundredths of a second, he could and does.

Does what? Sorry: does *tell her*.

Darla: righteous or not, there can be no holding on one's way. One's way is to be trodden, and will raise its dust behind you as applause. But if you stop, it stops. Take the advice of one now as still as still gets, pinned to the mat while God the Referee, taking His sweet time, pounds three and raises the Reaper's hand. Stillness is an option you choose just once and forevermore. We know from the start where our way leads, and it's our nature—our duty—to err, stray, stall, linger. Time is a leash we yearn to slip. We're never more human than when we waste it.

What good did time ever do for *you*? Remember your mom's diagnosis, Darla? The doctors pointed you to a catalog that featured odor-dampening bedpans, pill organizers, rubberized sheets. They said she'd get "progressively weaker." What kind of progress is that? The kind that belongs to tick-tick-tick, that mindless linearity.

Vada's eyes have flickered shut for the last time. He's lost his body now for good. *For good:* another of lying time's lying phrases. Don't let anyone fool you: he has lost it for bad. And he'll stave off that loss for as long as the Lord permits, until the last neuron squibs, fizzles. Dies.

Vada loves Darla, and she'll never know it. Or if she does, thanks to the contents of his father's barn, contents that will be discovered in the next few hours and then gossiped about at the wedding banquet, it will appear to be a pathetic, stalkerish love. Without Vada to serve as docent to the museum of his adoration for Darla—which was, he admits, his not-so-hot plan for this afternoon, to woo her from Wyatt with a guided tour of a corrugated-aluminum barn that smells of flypaper—that museum will go down in communal memory as a psycho's shrine, and his death will be the blessing that spared poor Darla, assailed on all sides by wackos, a fate not to be borne.

38

Armageddon on with It

Using the weak vanity light of the passenger-seat visor, Darla patted herself dry, applied a final touch-up, retrieved her sunshade so as to keep the makeup from annealing. She checked her watch again: 7:05. The choir kids kept wailing as they were fussed over by their mothers—and a lone father, whose dexterity with the powder puff set rival moms to whispering about the unfair edge of sin. Humidity made the hairspray's aerosol reek linger in place, a poison cloud that mingled with hickory grill-smoke and caused her stomach to lurch. The sun seemed a steady pressure, a hand holding them remorselessly down. The Operation Rescue protesters serenaded Joe with a ditty not quite in the Cole Porter mode. Its refrain was "It's a child not a choice,/Kill them all and rejoice./And abortionists' blood in the streets."

It was a scene, she'd tell Vada later, from those Renaissance paintings they used to show in Vacation Bible School to scare you straight, though you were straight already and mainly used them to get ideas— out-of-date and allegorical ideas, but such were the only ones available to a goody two-shoes in a sheltered D.C. suburb. The mortal sins of sixteenth-century Middle Europe—hard to tell from the paintings what they were (being impaled on a giant protractor? falling into a mandolin?)—seemed to her as likely then as smoking wacky weed or defying curfew in a car in which someone was drinking. Snorting at a flagon and

having your jaws stained carmine as a cannibal's seemed more tempting and more plausible than sipping demon wine cooler in a girlfriend's
Caprice in a cul-de-sac they hadn't built back to yet. Second base? She
would *never* . . . but her parents hadn't specifically forbidden, say, being
rogered by a satyr with cloven hooves.

At 7:07 the PA blared out several explosions of bass and static,
pronouncements from on high that were, as usual, unintelligible.
Cameraman Joe, looking through his lensfinder again, kept up his play-
by-play: "They got the vials of wrath lined up on a flatbed—and they're
massive, more like fifty-five-gallon drums of wrath. The armies look
ready to rumble. And oh, man! In the bullpen there's a stripper on an
Urban Cowboy bull, only the stripper's wearing like a flesh-colored leo-
tard with a black line down the front to simulate cleavage. Is that the
Whore of Babylon? It *is*, it is! Ho-lee Cow."

Meanwhile the fans in the bleachers chanted "Ris-en, Ris-en, Ris-en,"
and behind the visitors' dugout a busload of buglers up from Valdosta
laid on their horns, heralding the end of time until Darla began almost
to wish for it. 7:07 passed this way; 7:08; 7:09; 7:10. Eight minutes to
airtime.

Still no first pitch. The umpires lined up in front of the visitors' dugout, protecting the Chester players from the raving faithful. Someone
had unleashed into the habitation of devils a gunnysack full of pigeons.
Cameraman Joe reported from his lens that it looked out there like a
park bench at feeding time, lots of head-high flapping and shitting. One
Red Devil had to be restrained from going after the pigeons with a bat.
The home-plate umpire turned the angry player back, and from above,
for his trouble, absorbed a runny dunging. The evidence shone white
against his chest protector.

Where was the crowd control? It turned out, Darla discovered later,
that every employee not assigned to concessions, the Shealys included,
was collecting cash and trying to usher in the last few hundred fans.
The brothers had asked the umps to delay the start. At 7:11, "The Star-
Spangled Banner" was finally performed, by a Shriner who held his fez
over his heart like a conical pasty and warbled the song feelingly; the
crowd hushed. After that, Kate Smith belted out "God Bless America"
from beyond the grave, on a suitcase-sized reel-to-reel player held to
the microphone by the Shriner. That went smoothly, and for a minute it

seemed like those assembled had remembered that this was after all the fruited plain, not the plain of Jezreel.

7:15. The Shriner strode off, tape machine under his arm like a hen secured by a thief. The Gilyard players took their positions, and applause went up that sounded polite, uncrazed, normal. Darla allowed herself a sigh. Now there'd be baseball. God's judgment would be staved off for another day, the world made safe again for weather reporting. Her segment would go smoothly. Minutes from now Darla would ask Pablo—who'd arrived during the anthems, bedraggled but present, another source of her rising cheer—whether he was happy as a possum in a yam patch about the team's 29-17 record so far (her viewers *ate up* shit like this, so Bruce had presented her a pocket dictionary of Dixieisms, the better to pone it up with). Pablo would give a thumbs-up, a flurry of nods. Then a towheaded cutie in a pleated robe would scarf a wienie, and Darla would pat her head and give the unsurprising forecast. By 8:30, God be praised, she'd have her deliverance, an extra-dirty martini with Wyatt at the Summit Club downtown.

But the Chester manager refused to send out his leadoff hitter. He'd explain to the press later that during warmups the home fans had been consigning his players to hell, which was hurtful, and dumping winged rats into the dugout, which was unsanitary. And those bugles needed confiscating, or tomorrow night he'd hark some heralds up around their brainpans with a thirty-six-ounce club made of ash. "Our boys are Christian, too, goddamn it," he'd insist. "We expect some razzing on the road, but them people wanted us chomped in the devil's jaws like we was Judas H. Chariot."

7:17. Joe the Cameraman abandoned his vigil and prepared for the telecast. "The world's not out of the woods yet," he said. "I'd still bet that end-times win out over pastime. Takers?"

Darla laid no wagers, but she did cling to hope. The national anthem had mollified the crowd, snatched them back to the everyday. The buglers were taking a respite, maybe swabbing out spit valves. The pigeons flapped off to the concourse to peck at fallen popcorn. The abortion plane had chugged toward the airfield, followed soon by the Operation Rescuers, who had an early-morning protest in Tampa and an all-night drive ahead. The choir kids had cleaned up nicely; their complexions shone. Meg the Vegetarian had mastered her disgust and done a beautiful job with the franks. The heat hadn't ebbed, but it had been subsumed into the flush that always burned beneath Darla's skin as airtime approached. Now it was *her* heat, fully owned and operated.

Chuck/Pablo stood alongside Darla, though he'd retreated into what was either character or stupor—*Think positively,* she reminded herself: character, definitely character—and refused to answer her queries about his health, thirst, readiness. But his head was on straight; his stance was wide and stable; he wore a bright purple cap sideways, like the fungo artist Darla's dad had taken her to see at Memorial Stadium when she was little. The Clown Possum of Baseball. It was going to work. Joe, returned to professionalism, gave the OK sign and began counting down: five, four . . .

But optimism is fragile, and by the time Darla stepped onto the dictiobible and flipped away her WIST sunbrella, it had gone poof. A renewed roar from the stadium threatened to drown her out, and the buglers began a frightening, discordant stew of "A-Hunting, A-Hunting, A-Hunting" and "Onward, Christian Soldiers."

Worse, she could see that the heat was getting, had gotten, to Chuck. He'd gone gooey in the brain. Sure enough, after the first question and listless answer—"It's a great night for baseball here in Gilyard, huh, Pablo?" was answered not with a vigorous fist-pump but with a 360-degree wobble of the head and a loose grip raised from thigh to waist level, a drunk hoisting a phantom pint—Darla heard a sigh, and Chuck/Pablo spoke, saying, "Green glow. Who turned up, gleen grow?" Then he crumpled straight back. The fall was hard enough that his head tottered and threatened to roll away.

Joe, the bastard, caught it all. He moved smoothly from Darla to Chuck and perfectly framed the fall—including the head-bounce, the almost comical postconcussive shiver of the snout. He jerked the camera rightward just in time to see Meg, rushing to help, trip over a mike cord and topple the grill, the hot coals and sausages spilling across the stage toward the helpless children, who sang "Oooh" in lovely chorus, their mouths like those of hymn-singers in Christmas books, a row of perfect O's. Vern Shealy, ever the opportunist, had rushed from the box office to watch the live shot and could be heard off-camera—Darla gave him credit for evangelism under fire—shouting, "He spoke! In tongues! Pablo the Bible-Believing Possum *spoke in tongues!* Praise God!"

Trusting that there would be time enough yet to save Chuck, leaving until later the weird pietá of weathergirl and purblind Hispanic rodent that would appear above the fold on tomorrow's front page, Darla had been a pro. She hopped off the book, strode to the camera, took the lens in hand, and—in tight close-up—forced a smile and pretended that Pablo was acting: "Those possums!" Vern Shealy kept yelling about the miracle, and several choir moms picked up the chant. "As for the weather," Darla went on, raising her voice, but with no sign of shrillness, "you know the drill. More of the same through your weekend, more of the same beyond. That's all from Gilyard. Back to you, Hannah and Rick."

So smooth. Even in close-up, she bore no taint of pores. Her teeth looked invincibly happy, and her eyelashes were sable brushes that lapped almost at her brows. She was a vision. Yet in her eyes there was nothing short of fury.

And that was the end, if not of the world, then of Up in Your Grill.

39

You Are Here

Vada remembers a time from the dawn of megamalls when his mom took him to the new extravaganza on the other side of Columbia, Eastmastre Centre. It was a bewildering place, frightfully out of scale with the world Vada knew. The Centre could not hold, and its widening gyre had gobbled a hundred acres of scrub pine, pasture, and a country store Celeste had loved. People used to drink phosphates there, she said, back when people drank phosphates. There was a stove with crispy socks laid over its fender.

Eastmastre's lot was airfield-sized, and every two hundred yards around the mall's circumference stood a leafless twelve-foot wayfinding tree made of metal—peach, lavender, powder blue, and on and on—to remind you either of where you'd parked or of what nuclear winter would look like in a pastel world.

It was an April Saturday. Vada must have been eight. On the way into the mall, Celeste and he had to squeeze past a small band of protestors. The designers had provided sidewalks too skimpy to allow for a circle, so the picketers were striding in a furious flattened rhombus and holding signs that objurgated against the mall's spelling. Most were schoolteachers, recognizable even to Vada by their union pins and scarred shoes and that already-defeated-but-going-down-in-the-last-trench-for-a-pointless-distinction look that schoolteachers specialize in. They were singing

"We Shall Overcome," but with no hint of soul: *Someday-ay-ay-ay-ay* seemed far away indeed. A few carried placards reading WE'D RATHRE BE TEACHRES THAN PICKETRES, and one oddball in a bunny suit was trying to hand out home-dyed eggs with HAPPY EASTRE lettered on the shells. Near the door, in the shade, a grouchy-looking double-amputee of around twenty—clearly protesting under protest—had a sign propped in his lap that read FERE EASTMASTRE.

Fere it Vada did. The building was so massive. He hung behind his mom at the automatic door as she shrugged into her shopping wind-breaker (an eccentricity of hers that embarrassed him) in preparation for being buffeted by the air-con—a bit of theater, like a knight flipping down his visor before storming a citadel, that didn't allay Vada's sense of this as a place of foreboding.

He found himself staring at the safety pins just below the amputee's knees. There's something unaccountably cheerful about safety pins, especially big ones, and their tone seemed to Vada cruel in a way that his staring was not.

"Dipshits," whispered the amputee as Vada waited. Celeste was having trouble with her zipper. "Spring break, so the old campus revolutionaries have time to give their principles a workout. If they don't get a good rage on once a year, they've officially sold out. In the ghetto we could find a thousand better injustices than this in like five seconds, but there's no food court in Blacktown, and some punk might key their Buicks. Jesus. Kid, send security out here to crack some heads. And tell 'em to bring the cripple an Orange Julius while they're at it. The cripple requires an Orange Julius for turning mall's evidence." Vada nodded as if he understood, though he didn't, except that he began to feel an itch build for a Julius. Delicious chalky fruit shake. Mmm.

"Vada," said Celeste, suited up and ready to brave the chill. "Come on. Leave the nice man alone." Vada waved to the nice man's safety pins and followed her in.

Eastmastre was a throwing-star-shaped thing full of atria and flecked orange marble. There were two-story indoor palmettos under which, on benches bolted into place, lolled codgers who looked like they'd been there since WWII, working jumbles and chipping away at bags of caramel corn. The mall must have been built around them.

Celeste stopped at the end of the first corridor, past the video arcade, a haircutter (cuttre?), and an emporium of sports hats, to comb the directory for a likely place to buy scented candles.

"Shh," she said. "Enough with Spencer's. I don't need musk candles in the shape of peepees. I want plain tapers of plain sandalwood. It's not *that* kind of party. Now shh."

Vada did quit militating for a trip to see the naughty bric-a-brac, but it wasn't obedience that stilled his tongue so much as fere. There on the schematic he'd spotted a big red dot like the one that marked the cinder-block exterior walls of liquor stores, and alongside it the legend YOU ARE HERE. Panic constricted his throat. Were the old men spies? Were there cameras among the palm fronds? You are here.

Celeste finished running her finger down the "Homewares" list and tapped with her nail, a surprisingly dull sound against what turned out to be not glass but plastic. "There you go," she said.

There I go? thought Vada. *You Are Here?* Was the big red dot *invisible* to Celeste? Did adults lose the ability to see such things, to understand their implications?

"Vada. Quit shivering. Why must they keep it so *arctic* in here? I've got a sweater in the car if you need it."

He shook his head.

"Did that boy in the wheelchair scare you?" Another head-shake.

"Mom," Vada asked finally, pointing to the red dot, "how do they *know?*"

40

Isn't It Ironic? Don't You Think?

In years to come, Celeste would tell that anecdote a dozen times, a dozen dozen. "Oh, the things kids say."

And it *is* dumb to think you're under surveillance. This is something Vada has been figuring out this last second. The so-called erosion of privacy: sure, the technology exists now to eavesdrop on anyone anywhere, to mock their foibles and even plumb their thoughts . . . but *what are you up to that anyone will want to watch*? Where do you intend to find someone who cares enough to surveil *you*?

Ever notice that paranoiacs are basically happy? They occupy the center of the universe. But they're nuts. Despite new technologies and crumbling personal boundaries, for most people privacy hasn't shrunk; it's expanded. Go ahead and write your blog. Post photos of your cat, of your genitals. Perform a scene from the Three Stooges or Tom Stoppard for an ATM camera. Everyone *can* look, but no one is looking. There are far more things to attend than attention to go around. Other people have their own cameras to perform for.

The truth is that no one *cares* where you are. Not mall security, not the government, not even God—and assuming they do is just another vanity that needs exposing, so that you understand once and for all your insignificance.

He gets it. He got it. He will get it. He shall have always been getting it.

41

Charity Begins at the Top of the Cup, Little Dude

Which, reader, leaves you . . . where? A reasonable question, and Celeste is no longer here to reassure the disoriented one with a laugh, a hand on the cheek, and, later, a massive Orange Julius that he'll try on the way out to share with the legless picketer.

Turns out it's dangerous to allow charity to bubble up, like a burp, out of satiety. Fisticuffs between the mothers, Vada's and the schoolmarm mom of the amputee, will narrowly be averted after he barks at Vada, "The bottom of a Julius is *froth*, little dude. You think I want your froth?"

Sir: Vada knows you do not want his froth. Charity begins at the top of the cup.

42

Your 20, His 30

Celeste is in no shape anymore to read mall maps . . . which leaves the
You-Are-Hereing to Vada.

So what's your 20, as CB enthusiasts used to say? Vada's dad was
one of them for a spell, ten years after the vogue had ended. Vic's idea
of humor, adopting a long-dead fad; it was his way of making fun of
the white suit and Wayfarer sunglasses Wyatt's dad bought in Miami
in 1986. That summer, Vic grated on Celeste by installing a radio in
his truck and talking endlessly in a gravelly baritone about smokeys and
bubblegum machines, not only in the car but at home, pausing at the
bathroom door to say that he felt "a mighty urge to 10–100 number 2"
and might be off channel a while, and responding to her groans by turning to Vada and saying, "I'm not sure why the first sergeant has to be
such a dead pedal, come on."

"30" is journalists' code for the end of a story. Darla uses it on her
weather scripts, a link to the days of Edward R. Murrow that she claims
is her way of ridiculing the idea that TV is journalism, but is actually
sincere—a sweet little affectation that makes Vada love her all the more.

Reader, your 20 is Vada's 30, or just-about-30.

But that's no help, and Vada is determined to be of help now. He's
tired of tempting God the Smokey, is ready now to abide by the rules.
From here out, it's double nickels all the way. "Keep the big rig between

128

the ditches," as his father said that summer, "and the little rig in your britches." Amen, Pop. So, your 20: Please recall that before it stretched on and on, the tale of Apocalypse Night began as a digression from the first of a projected series of errata.

Whew.

Yet this will have to be one time when Vada refuses to apologize for intention having gone astray. It may seem odd in a narrative like this (biography? autobiography? help him out, God the Kevorkian: assisted autobiographicide?) that the scene most vivid to Vada should be one he wasn't present for. But that evening at a ballpark he's never been to, carrying cones of water for succor like the beer-garden girl he never was, dodging barbecue coals that were to him only pixels on the kitchen TV, cradling the giant secondhand rodent head he's never touched in the lovely lap he doesn't have, is perhaps the moment of his life that seems most real to Vada, up to now.

He found it liberating to be rid of himself for a while—a rehearsal for what's next, perhaps, when he'll be permanently free of himself, and when you, too, will be free of him. You may be Here (and bless you, sir or madam, if you are) . . . but you will not be There. Death is a mall we walk alone. Somebody write that down.

To make it up to you, he'll bag the errata. They were a ploy dreamt up when time-wasting seemed his only chance at survival. But the Being Upstairs seems disinclined to call him home for following his thoughts where they lead, which means Vada can concentrate not on himself but on the people who are more important: Darla. His parents. Wyatt. And if the price of narrative is death, he will at least have died in a less sorry cause than before. He has stories to tell. For instance: Did Vada mention that Armageddon Night would turn out to be the greatest night of his life? It would. It did.

43

Death and All Its Serifs and Portals and Butterscotches

On their weekly trip to the dump, nine years ago last month, Celeste and Vic were broadsided by a poultry truck. The next morning *The State* printed a picture of the aftermath, and as Vada waited outside the mortician's office in an absurdly large leather wingback—built, it seemed, in the belief that mourners were magnified by grief, their bodies as grotesque and outsized as their emotions—he'd made the mistake of looking at it. Billboards against taxes and for realty loomed above the accident site on 378, and he could see a corner of Snelgrove's peach stand and the turkey-shoot Quonset behind it; beyond that, espaliered trees stretched endlessly. In the left foreground, his parents' sacks of garbage had exploded. Stunned chickens reeled about, pecking at slaw and sausage rinds and detergent boxes—his mother's cheapo store brand, a detail it would have mortified her to have in the public sphere—and Vada imagined he could recognize the celery seeds that were her slaw's "secret ingredient." He didn't dare investigate the crumpled metal hulk that occupied the right half of the frame. Instead he let his eyes blur and slide to the page's gutter. His head lolled against the side of the wingback chair, which projected far enough forward that it seemed a proscenium. All the world a stage, and even sorrow soon ruined by self-consciousness. *Hello, grief old boy.*

Vada's eyes ached to look again, but he refused to give in to them. Instead he stuffed the newspaper beside the cushion and scanned

Unglesby & Rowe's wall of diplomas in fancy fonts. Death, that fucking ham, does adore its serifs.

The paper itched at his hip. *Don't look.*

Look: A side table, heavy and ornate. A dusty fern. A wire-clip bouquet of florists' business cards. A small cut-glass bowl. The bowl was pretty, in an old-lady way, and Vada tried to block out everything else by thinking of facets. A top-notch word, a word of the highest water. The bowl contained many facets, which meant it had death outfaceted by a long shot, actually by n-minus-1 facets, if n was the number of facets the bowl contained. Death was a dull thing, poor in facets.

The bowl held hard candy in cellophane. What kind of machine did the wrapping, do you think? Look at those neat triangular tails, like fans. Now *that* was a pretty bit of engineering. Maybe Vada should have been an engineer. Was it lore or market research that said the bereaved would really go for bowls of butterscotch?

Lore or market research was right, it turned out, and Vada, sucking with eyes closed, had to shift the yellow lozenge under his tongue when he heard Mr. Unglesby's door glide open, startling him like an abrupt rent in the clouds on an overcast day—too much light from on high. The door was a ceiling-scraper, a twelve-footer. The funeral home, not content with doors of human scale, had replaced them with portals. Portals!

Mr. Unglesby closed the portal behind them, and Vada couldn't help reflecting that he'd encountered more high-quality hinges in one day of orphanhood than in the rest of his life altogether.

"Let me be the first to condole with you, Mr. Prickett. This is a terrible loss." Unglesby extended a hand that Vada could tell would be dryly warm and papery, comforting; he wouldn't put it past Mr. Unglesby to have been holding it under a lamp just now.

Vada tried to speak, but the butterscotch had expanded, grown into a giant spud in his windpipe, his tailpipe.

"Mr. Prickett. Are you all right? Might I get you a beverage? Chamomile tea? My very own blend." Condole with you! Chamomile tea! An eighteenth-century man, Mr. Unglesby, but one with doughnut jizz on his tie and larceny in his heart.

Vada would not accept handout beverages or handout hands. He wasn't going to let this creep inveigle him with his dulcet voice and his tall walnut doors with well-oiled works, with his mighty wing chairs and well-wrapped candies. Fuck death and all its serifs and portals and butterscotches. He might be an orphan, but he wasn't a tramp; he wouldn't go on the condole. Vada clamped his hands under his biceps so they couldn't disobey him and shake the proffered hand.

"Yes, yes, a terrible day," said Mr. Unglesby, and seemed to mean it. He brought his hand back, placed it palm to palm with his left in an attitude of prayer.

"Yes," Vada finally said. "It is." Then the first act of what he hoped would turn out to be adulthood: Vada swallowed the butterscotch. It lodged behind his sternum—he could feel it—but left his tongue free. "Their organs have been harvested, and they want their remains burned. Give me one pewter urn"—this his sole nod to sentiment; Bakelite would have done as well, or Styrofoam, but Celeste had always loved the word "pewter." "One pewter urn and . . . what's the word? *Mingle* them, Mr. Unglesby. Good day."

44

Unglesby and the Caramel Corn

It was a good start. Vada didn't fall down as he made his exit, despite the presence of perilous carpet runners, and this too was a stride; adults didn't fall down when making their exits from the adult places where they'd done adult things like spurning the waxwork hands of professional condolers and having their parents mingled. Portals were for putting behind you.

But by the time he reached his car Vada's purpose had begun to ebb, his pride to pall. That butterscotch seemed like it might be stuck in his craw forever, and he felt sorry. Unglesby probably wasn't a creep, and there wasn't larceny in his heart, or no more than in anybody else's. He was just a tall saturnine guy who comforted the hurting for a living, and if the tools of that trade were quaint talk and hard candy and hand-warming lamps and herb tea, what made those more blameworthy than the items in Vada's dreamt-of vet bag? It was death that had only one facet, not Mr. Unglesby, who had as many facets as the next guy. He was likely still tall in his daily life, but who's to say he was saturnine? Smiling Unglesby might have tan legs and a twenty-eight-year-old girlfriend, a redhead to whom he hand-fed popcorn at the movies, and she loved it all the more because his fingers were warm and damp and tasted not of death, as you might think, but of delicious butter. Vada had an urge to go back in and apologize, but he squelched it. Instead he scraped his tongue with his upper teeth, opened the car door a few inches, and spat onto the asphalt. Butterscotch always started out great and then turned cloying, and by the next time he encountered it, he'd forgotten that.

He drove the back way, avoiding 378, and waited until he was safely home to cry. But then he fell on the kitchen floor between barstools, pressing his nose to the floor, his fingers meshed behind his neck and his elbows locked hard over his ears. He wobbled back and forth like a badly designed rocking horse. He wanted to find this scene laughable, childish, but when he amped up his cries to wailing—in an attempt to stop by making the display seem theatrical and therefore false—the effect was too near sincerity.

The good start on adulthood had faded. Now he was just a lost boy, twenty years old, on the floor of his parents' kitchen, clutching at the legs of stools. His collar was wet. His shoulders quivered. Something behind his breastplate ached, perhaps the remnant of butterscotch. What was he supposed to do now? Grief was a show, and he was alone now, no one to perform for, and shouldn't that exempt him? This seemed logical, but there must be a flaw in there somewhere.

The floor was lemony fresh and crumb-free—that was so like Celeste. Even the chrome cross-rails of the stools were clean enough that Vada could see his foreshortened reflection. He stayed on the floor for an eternity, though it was an eternity that the stove clock, when he gathered himself and climbed to his feet, cruelly diminished to eight minutes. All afternoon he ignored the bell, though he conducted periodic casserole sweeps of the stoop. Every time the phone rang it was answered, eventually, by his father's placid voice on the machine, and every time, Vada's fool of a heart leapt.

45

The Hexagon of Friend-Having

Vada had recently seemed, for the first time, surrounded by friends. Or if not surrounded, flanked—and flanked not just from two sides but from more like four, even six if you counted generously. Vada was like a hexagon when it came to friend-having. Which was pretty good for someone who wasn't a mixer and was a geek. Flanking wasn't encirclement, true, and couldn't approach the seething vortex of friendship at whose center Wyatt could be found, but it was an improvement.

School was the one thing that had always come easily to him, the one success he seemed marked for, and he'd been determined to make Celeste and Vic proud in the limited way he could. The best thing about college was that you didn't immediately get razzed or vandalized if you read the assignments, even if you betrayed some twisted enthusiasm for learning. The liberal attendance policy was a stroke of genius. The people who in high school would have done the dishonors were not in class but home asleep, and thus couldn't even identify you, much less trouble to throw you into a dumpster. They had joined frats, now, and turned their torturing skills on kids who were *like them*. College offered such a wealth of niches that even those who didn't fit the standard-sized niches could find someone.

But as Vada had lately discovered, college friends are friends of opportunity. If you're no longer there to be bumped into, you cease to exist. There are plenty of other people to throw the Frisbee or to drink schooners with in Five Points or to quiz you late at night on the difference in shape and function between a horse's front-hoof coffin bone and rear-hoof coffin bone. You will not be missed.

Already, three weeks into his new life, Vada felt like a man no longer flanked, no longer niched. Or like one niched in a different way—in a catacomb. His friends had moved on to other friends, other beers, other hoof bones (the navicular, the pastern). And really, who could blame twenty-year-olds, at the moment when mortality seems remotest, if they didn't want to drive forty minutes off campus to hang out amid dead people's detritus with some mopey tragic dude they used to know at school? The last holdout had been the girl he'd been dating a little just before his parents' death. But Phoebe, too, cut him loose. "I'm sorry for your loss," she said in the rote way of TV cops. "I know you need someone to talk to right now. But I'm afraid I can't be that person."

For years, he meanly edited or misremembered Phoebe's kiss-off to make it crueler. *Sorry, Phoebe. What you said made perfect sense, and even the hitch in its middle made perfect sense: "I am afraid. I can't be that person." You said you couldn't be that person, so he made you into another one. Vada's bad.*

46

Sackcloth and Ashcans

For years now Vada has been introduced to people who say, "Your parents, lovely folks. I'm sorry for your loss. I think of them every Wednesday night." Why would that be? Because the news photo incited lakeside residents to revolt. What an outrage, people kept saying, that decent, God-fearing people couldn't even take out the trash without being T-boned. Taxpayers didn't deserve such a fate. It would be an insult to the Pricketts' memory if the county didn't immediately institute curbside pickup. And, after a crusade led by one Reid Yancey, that's exactly what happened.

One can never know the shape of one's legacy, and maybe the Vic and Celeste Prickett Memorial Fleet of Trash Haulers wouldn't have seemed to them glamour's pinnacle. No doubt Vic and Celeste wouldn't give much credit for the silent, ceremonious way Vada rinses his cans of Veg-All and Spam with scalding water and a brush and, careful to dampen any joyous clinks, lays empty bottles into the recycling bin. But it's the only tribute he seems capable of, these days.

The solemnities of sorting day. Sackcloth and ashcans.

47

Tintinnabulation

What would Celeste and Vic think now if they saw the homestead into which, for the last fifteen years of their lives, they poured all they had? What would they make of the whining faucets, the burn-pocked counters, the mildewed and carious deck, the crooked, storm-sprung pier?

All a fix would take, no doubt, is a twist of tool, a dollop of bear-grease, WD-40 with its jaunty red straw. But when they died, Vada was still in competency's waiting room, shuffling months-old magazines, rooting for coins in the couch cushions. Waiting, he thought, for his life to start. Waiting for the doctor to call him in.

And then she did. This was two floors above and two hours before his venture into the morgue, eighteen hours before he'd see that news photo from Unglesby's chair. In the emergency room, the doors had panes with wire woven through. Privacy curtains swished unnervingly. Vada was conducted to a ghastly blue corridor, and the surgeon on call came out to speak to him. She opened the door only enough to slip out, closed it behind her without looking. *Minimally invasive,* he thought. Her eyes were high at their outer corners, which made her pretty but hard to read.

"I'm very, very sorry," she said. She didn't touch him. He was glad she didn't, though he found that he'd expected she would. Was that because she was a doctor? A woman? She wasn't wearing latex gloves, or holding them, and there was no sign of blood. Vada figured she hadn't touched Celeste or Vic either, hadn't had to.

She kept talking, but Vada didn't hear. He could see the doctor's mouth moving. He could see her take off her blue skullcap, could take in the surprise of how much glossy hair was underneath it, naturally curly, could even recognize that it reminded him of the scene in the credits to *Charlie's Angels* where Jaclyn Smith pulls off a motorcycle helmet and tosses her fetching locks fetchingly back. But the doctor didn't toss hers, and she strangled the cap in her hands as she kept talking. Jaclyn Smith kept talking, the curly-haired hat-strangling not-Jaclyn-Smith Jaclyn Smith. The corridor kept pulsing blue. The doctor's rhetoric, too, was minimally invasive. All Vada heard, louder and louder, was the pealing of bells, bearing down on him, borne down already on them to whom he'd been born. Down already.

48

How Droll!

By the way, his parents' death was Vada's fault.

The weekend before, to celebrate the end of school and the coming of summer, Vada had a couple of college buddies over—Wyatt, too, and Phoebe had been invited but demurred—for beers and a night-swim across the cove. His parents cleared out, went to the movies in town. They didn't say so, but Vada knew they did this because they were elated (relieved) to see their son at last amass friends enough to populate their living room couch.

As they prepared to "vamoose," Celeste kept reminding Vada where to find ice tongs and jiggers and silver salvers—items she associated with cocktail parties circa 1975, but which he refused to set out in advance. Earlier in the day she'd exclaimed, "We ought to bring out the fondue pot! Wouldn't that be fun?" Vada would have liked to think it was his shudder of revulsion that brought her back from that brink, but it was his father's barking laugh. "And leave *him* in charge of a vat of molten cheese?" Then he'd reminded Celeste, for the hundredth time, of Vada's lone stab at turkey carving a few years before. The old man had watched him saw and scowl for thirty interminable seconds and then said, "Son, what kind of vet do you intend to *be*? The bird comes *pre*-disemboweled. Gimme the goddamn knife. Old Tom has suffered enough."

Points taken—Celeste let the fondue pot lie, also confiscated the skewer that Vada was using for imaginary swordplay. "Won't be worth anything if we don't keep the set together," she warned.

As Vic's truck chugged up the driveway at five till seven, Vada rushed to collect the *New Yorker* cartoon napkins Celeste had strewn on end tables and countertops. One featured a pearl-necklaced matron at a restaurant table, saying, "Don't contradict me for sport, Harlan. My guess is they don't *have* antisecco." Up in Connecticut, Vada mused, that might be droll. Or "dry," which when you said it down here meant plain Not Funny. Harlan wore an ascot and a constipated look. What was Prosecco anyway? Dry wit, dry county, dry socket—none of them funny. "Droll" was when you talked slow.

On the plus side, though, Celeste had provisioned him with a cooler full of good Dutch lager. He and Beaker and Hobes and Wyatt drained four six-packs, plus two pizzas delivered in bulky, unfoldable boxes . . . which is why, two days later, Celeste and Vic drove to the dump twenty-four hours earlier than was their schedule and habit.

What good did it do to blame himself, you may ask? You might as well point to the guy who poured the driveway, who'd swindled them out of five linear feet of pad and therefore made it necessary to waste thirty seconds, as you left the carport, in backing up and going forward and backing up and going forward. You might, like the Pricketts' loyal neighbors, blame the town for refusing to collect their garbage. You might pin it on the trash-can manufacturer, which screwed them out of a full cubic foot of space by the way they designed the wheel assembly. That extra cubic foot would have carried them through the next day's breakfast, at least. You might even blame Wyatt, who as part of an Eagle Scout community-service project had demanded a caution light be installed where the subdivision met Highway 378. That light was just enough to slow them, to hold them up to be broadsided by fate. Wyatt's fault. Now *there* was an angle worth considering.

But it wasn't Wyatt left in the empty house after they died; Wyatt had left hours before for his summer job leading bike tours through the former Soviet Bloc. It wasn't Wyatt who sat listening to his dead father's voice answer the phone again and again, wasn't Wyatt who refused ever to throw out that tape or record over it (#176 in your barn-exhibit catalog, inside the microcassette player and cued up. The watchword in museum design, these days, is "interactivity").

Nor was it Wyatt who promised his parents *he'd* make the dump run that day but forgot because, well, because he sort of figured forgetting was his *role* in the family.

49

The Pocket-Pool Talisman

When Vada spoke to Mr. Unglesby, he had the tracheotomy pen in his pocket, and he was clicking the nib in and out so furiously that he busted the spring. The pen is item #1 in the nonexistent, or only mental and therefore soon-to-be-nonexistent, catalog of Vada's barn exhibition. Mixed media, plastic and aluminum, length 5.5 inches, width (including clip) 0.6 inch, two-part construction, two-tone (green over white), with a metallic band between. The plant manager may have paid extra for the unneeded hyphen in "Meat Inspector On-Site," a detail the spelling champoin would surely have noted.

50

Ollie the Punt Returner

"Man is like to vanity; his days are as a shadow that passeth away, unless he has trophies."

Can anyone identify the part of the verse above that's not actually in the King James Version? We trophy in vain, is Vada's point. Trophies belie the simple fact that we live, and can live, only in the present tense. Bodies age, triumphs fade. There's no use trying to hang on. If you do, you'll look like the chrome-domed pentagenarian down at Skink's who, having dispatched the biscuits-in-redeye-gravy breakfast special for the two thousandth day in a row, shimmies into his decades-old letterman's jacket—blue wool body, vinyl sleeves gone from white to tallow, the *L* on his chest the size and subtlety of Superman's *S*. Ollie Odom (Vada doesn't speak much to his breakfast-mates, but he's come to know who they are) knows better than to give his fellow patrons the satisfaction of watching him try to snap the jacket at the waist—you can't pen a sow in a saucer, and may as well not try—but still they have to avert their eyes in kindness when he shambles down the tight aisle between tables. The thing is a straitjacket, and Ollie has to strain his shoulders backward and keep his hands a foot six inches behind his hips. He looks like a man being goose-stepped by an invisible jailor. Ollie long ago learned to take out his cash before he gets up, to avoid the Houdini-ish arabesques required to produce his wallet at the cashier's stand. Used to be Ollie Odom could take a punt to the house through broken field. Now he can't snag a mint or a toothpick without ripping a seam.

51

Death the Disambiguator

Likewise, your trophy house can't be lived in lest its value diminish. Trophy gravestone may dwarf the neighbors', but neighbor-dwarfing may have lost its savor; you're *underground,* pal. Trophy roadster will set you back fifty bucks a week in detailing at Caw-Caw, and you'll end up parking a hundred yards from every destination to minimize the danger of a ding.

Nor can trophy wife make you young again. Soon, to keep up the illusion, you'll need blue pills to . . . you know. That's what trophies are, if you think about it (and you'd better believe Vada thinks about it)— they're false engorgements, the magnification of one part in preference over others that have the same right to swell. Ollie Odom might as well shrug into a sandwich-board facsimile of the senior-year report card that cost him a scholarship to the Citadel back in 1972 and doomed him to sit for thirty-five years in a little lean-to fireworks stand on the bypass and watch for assholes pitching cigarettes as they honk by. Any moment can be his last. Any moment can be anyone's last.

Plastic surgeries, too: the sharpened nose, vacuumed neck-wattles, the bosom amplified to entice a stranger's gaze (and to remind you that once, gazes didn't need enticing). But when you make a trophy of yourself, where does the real you go? Vada once saw a cable show on which they claimed that if you look at a surgically altered person under ultraviolet light, years after, you can still see the slack skin or rippled fat or nose-hook that was carved off—these register as a ghost or halo, a cityscape's envelope of smog. All surgery avails you, seen in the proper light, is blurred edges rather than sharp ones. You look like an oldster in a tintype who yielded to an itch.

Death doesn't care about the edges you've roughed off. Death has no truck with illusions you've bought. Death, grunt that he is, humps a heavy pack—did you really think it wouldn't include a black light? Death, the grand disambiguator. And today—this minute—he trains his beam on Vada.

52

Taking a Vada from Vertex to Vortex

Celeste never tired of telling Vada, when he was revved up about something trivial, "None of this will matter in a hundred years." This was supposed to be *cheering*.

Sure, Vada, at the town's spring follies you had to wear a barbershop-quartet outfit including boater hat, spangly vest, and arm garters, had to ride your bike in a slow-motion ballet at the head of a train of younger kids, most on training wheels, the last few pedaling spiderlike on trikes. Yes, the only reason you had to do this was that your mom was in charge of the production number and forced you to participate. Yes, the music was, nonsensically, "A Bicycle Built for Two," though that seemed the only self-propelled vehicle *not* on stage. Yes, the choreography was adapted from an old Esther Williams mermaid movie, one of Celeste's favorites, even though the audience couldn't see you from overhead and you weren't underwater, or at least were underwater only in some inward way. And yes, the stage was far too small, especially when every mother in town started lobbying to add her two-year-old to the comet's tail. And in the finale when you rolled forward, your big moment, to be what you proudly called—you'll deny that pride, and it's true you hated the idea at first, but you warmed to your role, and on the day before the performance when your mother was gluing pretty yellow-and-green streamers onto your handlebars and you spoke this word, gave yourself this label, there was no mistaking your tone, and you were jazzed up about the arm garters, too, yellow on one arm and green on the other; now don't be a revisionist, Vada, the world is full of revisionists and they're dishonest—when you rolled forward to be what you proudly called the "vertex" ("Mom, you think other kids will be jealous that I get to be the . . .?"), it's true that your tire slipped off the stage's lip and you fell into what would have been the orchestra pit if the orchestra hadn't been merely a jam-box on a stool, both of which, stool and jam-box, crunched beneath you with a sound like, well, you can't help remembering, it resounded over the microphone so beautifully—a sound just like a potato chip underfoot . . . but the point is, History shall not pause over the event.

Celeste's motto never had the desired effect. It certainly kept no one at school from saying, "Yo, Knievel. Why didn't you wear that bowtie at Snake River?" Nor did it stop his classmates, for years after, from calling any face-forward plunge a "vada."

Also, where was the boundary? If it won't matter in a hundred years, Vada was left to wonder, why should it matter in a hundred days, or a hundred minutes?

There was an important distinction that Celeste refused to acknowledge, one Vada had good reason already to know (item #34 in what's seeming more and more a Catalog of Ignominies—rubber handlebar grip, still sprouting homemade pompons from the end). To wit: Defeats are made of sterner stuff than victories. They might not make the hundred-year plateau, but they last. There's a difference between the things other people retain about you and the things you'd *like* them to hang onto. The things they retain are humiliations. The things you'd like them to retain are trophies. And you can't force them to see it your way— poor Ollie Odom—by buying an *aide-mémoire* and wearing it wherever you go.

Remember that time I won, everybody? Remember the moment when I was great, and the world bent to my will, and rivals curled at my feet, broken? No one will remember that. But when at last you lie curled at your rival's feet, broken? That's a different story.

53

The Difference Between a *Fascis* and a Fucking Mess

Vada should mention that he's a one-time trophy professional. He first met Wayne Albergotti, in fact, when he worked for him at a shop downtown called Jax' Plax-Max. His career ended after three months, at just the moment when Vada allowed himself to believe he'd found, at last, a workable calling. One afternoon Vada was in the back, engraving "Sharpshooter" onto a trophy for the Civil War Reenactment Society. The rear door opened, and in swept Wayne. At the time he hadn't yet morphed into Il DUCE, but already he was developing his stagecraft. By the time Vada saw him, he had let loose the knob and the dented metal door was crashing into the wall. Wayne's head was glossily shaven— an embrace of totalitarianism that did, Vada admits, work better than the close-shorn male-pattern baldness he'd made do with before—and he had as backdrop a blinding rectangle of sunlight. Actually, he had nine-tenths of a blinding rectangle of sunlight, with the lower right corner impinged upon by a dumpster in the alley behind the shop, but these were the kinks in his mastery that Il DUCE would work out later.

Vada, no fool, gleaned from the entrance that something major was up. He took out the jeweler's monocle he'd taken to wearing, pulled his burin away from the trophy, flicked off the spotlight he'd clamped to the table-edge, and blinked. Wayne's shaven bean gleamed like a waxed apple. "Hi, Wayne."

"I've told you. Over here my name is Jax. Jax with an apostrophe."

"Hi, Jax. Jax with an apostrophe." Best to keep it light.

"A man wants all his honors and his punctuations"—Wayne scowled at Vada, who'd broached this little issue of grammar the previous week— "even if they're not technically correct. This is the principle on which the trophy industry is built." Wayne seemed to like the sound of that, and he got distracted for a moment, gazing at his eloquence projected on some inner screen. Might it make for a good inspirational banner to hang on the far wall above the new laser engraver, or out front in what Wayne— Jax'—called the Piazza de Piggly Wiggly? He had, in those days, a sense of humor about his Italophilia. But humor was for the *accidentally* bald, not for those who chose razor burn as their destiny. He'd turned a corner now. "I have a proposition for you, Prickett."

A second guy edged in through the open door—one of those nineteen-year-olds, common to the South, whose weak chin occupies the midpoint of a straight line between his Adam's apple and the nose under which he's cultivating a starter mustache. He was skinny enough to make you believe in pellagra all over again, and his *Giro d'Italia* T-shirt told Vada all he needed to know about what sort of "proposition" it would be. He was to be replaced by this hick apparatchik.

"How would you like to work outside?" continued Wayne. "Mussolini believed that outdoor work was ennobling work, made the *paysans* pull together. 'Fasces' means bundles of sticks, strength in unity, and if one stick in the bundle is pointing sideways, it's not a bundle, it's a fucking mess, and there's *molto differenze* between a *fascis* and a fucking mess, my friend. What I'm saying is that all this"—he pointed to Vada's work surface, the antique tools he'd bought off the internet, the font chart he'd puttied to the wall—"makes you a sideways stick. I don't want to fire you, but I sense that engraving's not your gig. I keep getting calls from pissed-off customers; people don't like to do their bragging in a script no one can read anymore. It defeats the purpose. Look at you back here, hand-engraving with some fucking caveman blade or something when we've got a wall full of machines over there that I paid good money for and that can do basically everything themselves, including spelling. Yeah, yeah, you're an *artisano;* I can dig that. You're the kind of *artisano* who can fit a thousand words onto a bottlecap. But size matters in this business. Do it up, big scale. Mussolini understood that. I understand it.

The kid here understands it. A detail man like you—I think Caw-Caw Car Cleaners is the place for you. You start this afternoon. Or not. Your choice. *Capisce?*"

54

Immortality via Duotone Resin

In his stint at Jax', Vada had ample time to contemplate. It was winter, and trophies are a warm-weather business, so the bell seldom jangled, the phone rarely rang. Most of the time he was the sole employee. What else was there to do, besides sweeping metal tailings, reorganizing and re-Windexing the sample cases, making sure he had a good glue bead going when the time came to attach fifteen Pelion Pelé League Indoor Soccer/Runner-Up 2004 nameplates to fifteen duotone resin plaques?

So he contemplated, and because his own life was a poor source of material, he turned his attention to trophies. He read about their history. He did internet searches. He checked books out of the same library he and Wyatt visited with Celeste almost twenty years before. If fate was going to make him not a large-animal vet but a trophy engraver, he'd seek what distinction there was to be found in the field. He'd do the best he could with the resources available—what more could anyone ask? Building kids' self-esteem by screwing plastic athletes into stone bases and inscribing a few terse words of remembrance—it was an honorable occupation, right? These things did tend to *last*, at least. The bases were sturdy, and it was hard to stack household shit on top of the cheap plastic part, so they tended to stay intact. Thirty years from now, Vada's handi-work would *still exist*. In 2035, some hipster might fork over two bucks at a garage sale for Vada's haiku masterpiece, Sandy Branch Bowling/

Kegger Kegel League High Game/11/04. If that's the only immortality available, you grab it. You learn medieval scripts; you go online and buy a burin, a loupe. A man needs his little consolations.

And then you get exiled to Caw-Caw. And keep your burin as a trophy—item #24 in your catalog, Darla. It's the thing in the plastic pouch that looks like a crude dental instrument. The monocle? Vada flung it at the dumpster in the alley.

55

The Central Axe

Some of what Vada knows: Many trophies bear a taint of cruelty. This is especially true of the old kind, the kind not a manmade object, injection-molded or miter-cut, but a natural thing torn from its right context and then displayed to celebrate the thief's might. Assyrian soldiers may have had some better use for their foreskins than to see them clipped to the breastplates of Roman soldiers, for example. The northern pike ten feet above Vada's head now, no matter how iridescent its scales are in the specially mounted tungsten spotlight, no matter how lifelike its fight ("Most taxidermists can't capture torque, Vada, but this guy's *good*. And gets paid like he's good"), probably preferred the water to Wyatt's wall.

Trophies serve two distinct purposes. The first, straightforward, is to celebrate and commemorate. The second, subtler but no less important, is to intimidate. You, too, may have your balls repurposed into medals at any time. And your fight? Not your worry anymore, fish—your gills have gaped their last. Fight has ceased to be a verb. Just leave it to the grammarian with the cotton wool and clear varnish.

What Wayne left for Vada to discover in his researches was that the fasces themselves were a trophy. They were clutches of sticks that represented the Roman magistrate's power, and were carried around by lackeys as a symbol of imperial jurisdiction. As Jax-with-an-apostrophe said, they were supposed to represent the strength in unity, but as usual the emphasis was on the power to enforce that unity. No one could miss the bloodred ribbon that bound it all together, or the implication that unity wasn't a choice but a duty. Knuckle under to the power of the sticks, or else.

Or maybe some people could miss it. Some folks, laggards at symbolism, need clubbing over the head, and a bundle of twigs bound with a ribbon is of little use in head-clubbing. So the Romans, in wartime, decided to *enhance* their symbol. They placed at the center of the bundle a much stouter stick, and on its end an axe-head.

Presumably this is the axe that's been used to chop the sticks into perfect uniformity and order. So strength through unity, yes, but a unity enforced at the point of a blade. And not exactly a unity anymore either, if you think of it, since somebody gets to be the axe while the other poor schlumps have to be the sticks who mass around it and look pathetic and spindly next to it and absorb whatever chops may come.

What Vada said a while back about how wins are less remembered than losses? He amends it. A few lucky souls have the knack of commanding symbols, can turn others' memories to their wills and ends. Such people are axes and not twigs, and their whole lives are trophies. Such people, in Vada's experience, are called Wyatt Yancey.

56

Lacuna Beach

Vada never intended to become what he is. What fly intends to drown in amber?

It's just that his parents died, and then he dropped out of school for a brief while that became a longish while that became a decade, opening up first the kind of résumé hole that would need explaining and then, eventually, almost a generation gap.

Was it worth it to go back to college after five years, or seven, or eight? If he returned he'd need to retake courses, and he'd have to either reapply for financial aid or mortgage the lake property, since he had no remaining savings. He'd be called upon to explain what he'd been doing all these years. He wouldn't know anything about pop music anymore. He'd never sent or received a text message, much less file-shared or emoticonned or blogged. And as newspapers never tired of reminding him, today's college kids were the first post-9/11 generation, wary and worldly, and he was . . . not. He'd be eaten alive.

Even if he did scrape through, he'd be, what, a thirty-two-year-old graduate vying with his youngers for spots in vet school? By now some of the large animals Vada had intended to work on might be extinct; global warming had come a long way in the last decade. That's the problem with a time gap. It starts small, expands quickly (those melting ice caps! those ozone holes!). Creek becomes slough, then bay, gulf, ocean, and before long you're clinging to the last dwindling spit of sand, Lacuna Beach.

Vada didn't want this. It just happened, bit by bit. Nearly four years ago, he'd filled out the paperwork for a Pell Grant and braved the registrar's website and was all set to re-enroll when Wayne hired him at Jax'. So Vada put off his return for one more semester, then one more and one more, and soon Wyatt came home, and that was a setback, too, needed adjusting to, and then last summer the registrar's website migrated to a new server, whatever that meant, and though all Vada had to do was click a link to follow it, his finger stayed poised above the key. It had been a lie all this time—eight years plus—hadn't it? He'd been *hoping* for some kind of saving migration, so he could say he'd tried to hang onto the flock but failed and therefore had to circle back and roost for the winter and hope he stayed warm enough to survive right where he was.

He had no choice, in that fugacious and thank-God-rare moment of self-recognition last August, but to see that his parents' house—hard even now to think of it as *his*—had become a kind of annex to Wyatt's trophy room. Vada's role was as a lifelong side-by-side comparison that would never turn out to his advantage.

These last months, while Wyatt's romance with Darla has blossomed, the situation has seemed less and less endurable. He sees them playing croquet in old-timey Newport whites as a gag, and their laughter is a lash. Their vintage Vespas tooling up the driveway; candy-colored kayaks spooning atop her SUV; their matching Mondrianlike bike jerseys, the glossy tights with optic-yellow slashes up the inner thighs.

To Wyatt, all the world is sporting goods. Jodhpurs, clay pigeons loosed by remote control, luminescent footballs, ping-pong paddles that, like rocket ships, contain titanium. Meanwhile Vada's only sport is survival, and he clings to an ever-shrinking beachhead in a life more lacuna than not.

57

One Practical Lady

A last anecdote about Celeste: The autumn before she died, she asked Vada to "squire" her to the neighborhood association's early December pig-picking. Duck season was in, so his father was working long days policing hunters, and she didn't want to go alone. "Just drive out after class. I'll show off my handsome boy, brag about your grades a bit, and you'll be back in Columbia by nine."

The neighborhood's summer barbecue has always been a festive affair. Affluence comes earlier and earlier, it seems, to the go-getters apt to go and get it, and thirty-somethings were moving out from town with their spouses and toddlers into subdivisions featuring two-story foyers and bricked-in mailboxes. So at the July *cochon de lait* there were lots of children about (sometimes trailed by nannies from Chiapas or Bangalore), older kids home from college, and friends and family down for a visit.

The late-fall barbecue was grayer, more sedate. December required a scrawnier pig, a narrower pit. The young couples stayed away to spare their children the weather; the college kids were at school. Which was sort of the purpose. Instead of a hundred people, some of whom you wouldn't even recognize, maybe twenty would show. This was a meeting for the old guard—northerners who'd retired early and bought cheap land here in the 1980s, the remnants of the "pioneer" families who'd settled the lake a decade or two before. Celeste, in her fifties, was on the youthful end of the spectrum; Vada was the youngest attendee by two decades.

Even as a child, Vada had liked the autumn barbecue better. It had about it something pointless, masochistic, therefore appealing. He preferred somber yang to the giddy yin that seemed to dominate American life, at least suburban life, more and more—how was it that most people's lives seemed easier, all the time easier? But eventually bills come due. Banks foreclose, the repo man comes creeping on little crow's feet. Nothing is free, as Vic always said, and let us rejoice in that.

Summer was borrowed time, faintly unreal. The slate skies and leaflessness of December were the payback, were what Vada thought of as Real Weather. The fall pig-picking was a happy reminder that life was supposed to be hard, if standing around in a slight chill in a wealthy lakeside neighborhood eating pork counted as hard. *Relatively* hard, which was, to be honest, the kind of hard he was suited to. It was less work, in such surroundings, to believe in bankruptcy, or failure, or death, and he wanted to believe in them—wanted other people to be made to believe in them, too.

Vada found comfort in these thoughts as he stood beside the chain-link of the tennis court, twenty feet from the conversational circle, and zinged into the woods the waterlogged lost balls of summer, just now exposed by the grass dying back. He was working up to squiring; he'd squire after he got his first drink down the hatch. It was always easier to like things in the abstract, he'd found, and the old-folky jibber-jabber at the fall barbecue was no exception to this rule. He inched farther away, used his sneaker to nose loose another ball buried in the thatch, leaned to pick it up. He was alternating throws with sips of a High Life (another sign that life was hard, or *relatively* hard).

The part he looked forward to would come later, after buzz had risen and night fallen. At the fall barbecue, people stood in the dark around a smoking hole and kicked wet leaves and kneaded the cold out of their knuckles, even if it wasn't chilly. They drank toddies. They told nightmare stories of the family Thanksgivings that had ended a week or two before. Every year the same people laughed when Rex McGuinn, pretending to shiver at the pit's edge, pulled out his fingerless driving gloves for warmth and made a joke about upper-middle-class hoboes, the end product of Democrat administrations.

"This is it for me," they all said toward the end of the night, "never again. *Why* do we have an outdoor party at this time of year? Whose bright idea was this?" And didn't mean a word of it.

Ten minutes after Vada and Celeste arrived, there was a loud report from the parking-lot side of the tennis courts—the sound of a cane thwacking a tetherball in passing. "That'll be Rouse," someone said.

Rouse Hartwell was a red-faced old cotton factor from the Lowcountry, jolly and jowly, and vaunted himself for his humor. He liked to twit the alleged Yankees on their alleged Yankee habits, so as he approached the wine drinkers grouped around the smoldering coffin-sized hole, he wagged his cane and complained, "Chardonnay? Just *look* at yourselves. Would General Wade Hampton drink fruity piss-water?" He produced a fifth of Dickel from his jacket pocket. "General Wade Hampton would not. On a day like this you need some warmth going down."

There was a silence. Rouse *had* to vaunt himself for his wit, as no one else seemed up to the task. People were just waiting the three seconds required by politeness before they could go back to hearing about Vera Hutto's mischievous grandson, who'd smashed a whole shelf of her glass-frog collection. Today's kindergartners just had no respect at all for breakable amphibians.

But Celeste jumped in. "You know," she said, "that won't save you. If you're dying of thirst, I mean, drinking urine won't save you, no matter what they say in the movies. I read an article on it. Urine's filled with metallic salts, so it'll only dehydrate you faster, unless you can figure a way to desalinate it. *Then* it might help."

Vada had been about to hum a ball into the woods, but he paused, weighed it in his hand and looked over. Celeste leaned forward, aglow in the dusk-light, which had a yellowish cast this time of year. She'd been itching to share her research, and Rouse had given her an opening. Busted frogs be damned—this was life and death.

"That's disgusting," said Eva Poteet, the pretty second wife who was, at forty, the second-youngest there. "I can't even *say* that word, much less *drink* it. I'd rather die."

"I bet you wouldn't, if push came to shove," said her husband, Nate, clearly glad to have a way to bust her chops that had no overt link to her out-in-the-open affair of the previous summer. "You drink that goddamn Fresca by the case, and piss can't be worse than that. You're talking about your life, now. You'd pee in your palms and *like* it, honey-pot. Desperation breeds strange . . ." He realized here that he'd trodden too close to "bedfellows," so he tacked. "They say it softens calluses, too, so maybe you could lay off the . . ." Oops. That way lurked disaster, too, in the word "moisturizer." Eva's beau was a salon manicurist, which made him in Nate's eyes a double scoundrel, guilty not only of tomcattery but also with theft by imposture. It wasn't right for a straight man to soften women's cuticles—it especially wasn't right if he wore a nametag that said "Madge!" that the women all tittered about. Nate hadn't worried about him until it was too late.

"Can't we change the subject?" asked Lucy Council. She could mean either subject, or both. There were people there who'd probably rather drink waste than see a reprise of the Christmas-party argument last year that had resulted in a threatened assault charge against Eva for mangling Nate's hand in the door of her Lexus.

"I've started calling Max Destructo, but my daughter seems to think I'm being funny," tried Vera Hutto. "I tend not to be funny on that subject. I've been collecting those frogs on fifty years, and she knows it."

"I could do it," said Celeste, quietly but firmly.

"Anybody want to switch over to red about now?" interjected Billy Council.

Celeste forged ahead. "You'd have to use your clothes as a filter to evaporate the salts, somehow. But you could make it work till you got either fresh water or help. The nub of it is, you do what you have to. You make the best of your situation, whatever it is." Celeste seemed to realize she'd gone too far, but the only exit strategy that came to mind—Vada couldn't do much, but he could read his mother—had the effect not of mitigating her speech but of emphasizing it. She quaffed the last of her wine, wobbled the glass by its stem like a censer, and headed to the cooler for a refill.

There was a silence of four or five seconds. Vada still held the tennis ball; he could feel a row of dog teethmarks in the felt. Lucy and Eva exchanged sour looks, and Maggie Welsh discreetly poured her wine onto the ground at her feet. Kendall Proehl prepared, as usual, to fill the breach with a few dozen mentions of his son Harry's being in a singing group at Yale. Every time he said "a cappella" it would be followed like clockwork by a mention of Harry's *girl*friend. Rouse Hartwell settled onto the camp stool he'd brought on account of the gout—which was, he'd be tempted to tell them, basically a sickness caused by your flesh drinking your urine. People should stop acting like urine-drinking was glamorous; his goddamned feet *screamed all the time.*

Beyond, under the tin picnic shelter, Celeste bobbed for a screw-top bottle in the ice of the cooler. She didn't look back, at them or at Vada. The last thing she'd said had been for his benefit. *She* was willing to filter her wastes and imbibe them. *He* balked at standing next to his mom at a party and letting her say the phrase "dean's list."

It was Nate Poteet who spoke first. There was neither praise nor censure in his voice. What sense does it make to praise an avalanche or censure a typhoon? They can't be judged by the standards of party palaver. All you can do is marvel at their power.

"That is one practical lady," Nate said.

Amen, thought Vada. And then, because he was after all his mother's son—*You do what you must*—he sidearmed the tennis ball into the trees and turned to join Celeste and suffer her bragging for a while. The nub of it is, you do what you have to.

58

Tapping the Bladder

While Celeste was alive, her practicality saved Vada from having to be practical. But after she and Vic died, his life became a trackless desert, in storybooks the worst kind, and "trackless" an adjective one didn't see fronting any other noun. It was an unmitigated desert with the trackless gall to wipe out his mother's footprints, footprints Vada needed. So he wandered. But when Darla came into his life, "trackless desert" ceased to be just a phrase. The sand scraped his eyeballs raw; he started seeing mirages in which Darla was dressed like Barbara Eden (sorry, Darla). And when the wedding plans were announced, just six weeks ago, Vada realized that the time had come for him to stop staggering blindly through the dunes.

Among Vada's beloved books in adolescence was a compendium of phrases and their origins, and one example sticks in his memory. British sailors voyaging home from Trafalgar, having drained every barrel of rum but one and jonesing for strong spirits, were said to have inserted long straws into the final, forbidden cask . . . in which Admiral Nelson, killed in the battle, had been temporarily interred.

Vada, too, has been moved, bit by bit, to action. To ACTION, damn it all! The seamen tapped the admiral. For Vada, it's come time to tap the bladder.

59

To Action!

Sometimes, Wyatt, the things we've stuffed and mounted and urethaned—sometimes, even after years of a torpor that may look like death, they rise up in mutiny.

Armageddon has a way of getting your blood flowing. After that night, Vada decided to seize the hand of the woman he loved. He *acted*. He went down to the gun show and bought two knives and a snubnose .38. Also a camo shirt, in a pattern called Swamp Amoeba that's favored by Asian mercenaries. He paid cash. He wore his father's clothes, burned them when he got home. Two weeks later, Vada streaked his cheeks with Vic's old Kiwi shoe polish, pulled on black sneakers, and crept through the woods to Wyatt's, hunter for once instead of hunted.

No, he didn't.

When you're not a man of action, when you are from way back an unman of inaction, you don't suddenly drape yourself in bandoliers and open fire on your enemies.

60

OK, So It's Pretty Sorry Action

No, Vada's idea of blitzkrieg is to get a push broom and sweep out the old storage barn, haul a couple vinyl chairs and chipboard dressers to the curb for pickup (even *furniture,* Mom and Dad—the groundswell of public outrage was enough that the county trash trucks will pick up *furniture*), and start assembling and labeling. If you can't beat 'em, lampoon 'em. Vada's barn exhibit is a burlesque of Wyatt's trophy hall, with its oiled woods and its ibexes and dik-diks and crystal loving cups and six-foot-by-three-foot novelty checks from his golfing days. The difference is that *Vada's* miscellany of knickknacks is intended, all of it, for an audience of one.

Vada knows it'll take explaining, his decision to fight fire with irony. Paper may beat rock, but fire will whip irony every time. Come to think of it, in the real world wouldn't paper over rock be a major upset? Face it: Paper never beat *anyone* straight up.

61

Late Mom

The first time Darla came into Vada's house . . . when she walked into the kitchen and cast her eyes around, Vada abruptly saw his life not as the trophy-free zone he'd thought it to be but as just a sadder, damper, dimmer trophy room than Wyatt's.

He'd kept his whole adolescence. Vada's shoes were lined up under the old church pew Celeste used for a mudroom bench. Countertop cans, green with bright fake gilding, still held bouquets of pencils with Celeste's hortatory messages, translated into movie-Indian to save space and money: "Best Way Have Friend—Be One" and "Make Virtue of Necessity." Celeste's cookbooks still rode their rack; even the sticky-notes marking pages were undisturbed.

Darla took it all in. She plopped into a seat at the table, with its centerpiece of plastic lollipops girdled by plastic ribbons, in a rack designed to look like a Christmas tree. "Your décor: I take it the style is 'Late Mom'?"

62

Lingua Vada

She was right. Everything one chooses to keep is a trophy—whether you store it in a $100,000 humidity-controlled sanctum or just in memory. Vada has nine trophy rooms, stacked high with junk supposed to preserve the myth that once he had potential, once he had hope, once he had parents. The difference between him and Wyatt, as usual, is that Wyatt is better than he is, at curating as at everything else. You might as well keep the things that are most flattering to you. That only makes sense.

Darla dumped the pencils onto the kitchen table and read them aloud, funningly. And though Vada was too busy to realize it as he slid Darla's coffee mug across the table, scooped the pencils back into their holder, and whisked away the lollipop centerpiece (out of sight, out of conversation), his plan was set into motion then. For once, he would Make Virtue of Necessity. If trophies were the *lingua wyatta* of love, he would have to devise, at last, a *lingua vada*.

The form it would take? Easy. Darla confided in him that night her distaste for Wyatt's trophies, all those "ghouls with glass eyes. And no matter how good the taxidermist is, the place smells like meat. What sort of girl wants to live in a meat house?" Vada sniffed as she spoke and, smelling only must and pine cleaner, thanked Fortuna for making him forget to thaw hamburger that afternoon.

The Trophy Room in the Barn? Darla would have laughed with him, would have found bracing its nothing-hidden honesty. She might have melted.

63

In Defense of the Pun

Puns are often dismissed as low humor, the lowest, and of course they're abused by pet groomers, headline writers, the owners of hair salons, and so forth. But puns are an improvisatory art, right? That's why Darla loves them. Like many reporters, she takes pride in her ability to think on her feet, to make something of the world's messy and unpromising givens. You take the cards you're dealt and build a hand of them. Armed with native wit, you leg it out to the heart of the matter. You stitch a monster from the available corpse-parts, and hope that creature won't track you to the earth's ends and then usurp your name for all history.

Facing fourth down and a mile, Vada knew what to do: drop back and pun.

64

A Buttload of Bottlecaps, a Big Basement

When Vada says he decided to seize the hand of the woman he loves, he means of course metaphorically seize the metaphorical hand. His mistake. Metaphors, too, are a kind of trophying, forcing one thing to stand in for another, something wishful for something real, and are therefore useless. The barn's contents will be read as a suicide note, the quirky last testament of a man whose end has kind of been *awaited* all these years. The neighbors will shake their heads and say, in the sage way of neighbors quoted in aftermaths, "I'm shocked, but I'm not really *surprised*."

Or the barn's contents may be written off as the insane act of one of those deep-sea-dweller-looking losers still living at home in their forties, the kind of guy whose mother, after he succumbs in his sleep, finds the scale model of the Twin Towers he's made from YooHoo bottlecaps in the cellar, and to make the tragedy *mean something* she calls the newspaper and declares him a hero and a martyr. He never *wanted* to drink a case of YooHoo a day and die of diabetes. What was unquenchable was not his thirst but his patriotism. He belched and glued all those years not out of idleness or to sate a sweet tooth but to provide a profile in courage, to fulfill his country's need and his art's. Semper fi and all. Whereas you know the guy had his own reasons, namely a sugar jones, a buttload of bottlecaps, and a big basement no one cared if he ever came out of.

Now, before Vada descends so far into metaphor that he'll never escape, let him admit that these nine years he's stayed put not out of reverence for his parents but to have a covering excuse for the failure he would surely have been anyway. *Oh, right, the promising young man undone by grief. Did you know that before his parents died he planned to be a large-animal veterinarian?* This life and this house are the snail shell of a narrative that he crawled into and never left.

A metaphor that, for all its demerits, at least accounts for the slime trail oozing out beneath him onto Wyatt's slate.

65

Two Films, Summarized

We'll Always Have Plaster of Paris

Lonely guy, home nurse by trade, yearns for the girlfriend of his childhood buddy, an investment banker with wallet of gold and heart of tin. Desperate, the nurse decides the only way to capture his beloved's heart is to injure her and lay her up for a few days. Then he can contrive some alone-time, and he'll win her with gauze dressing, bedside manner . . . possibly sponge baths, if he's lucky. He knows better than to outsource his mayhem, á la Tonya Harding, so he dons a tracksuit with hood and—while the boyfriend is away on a two-week business trip—jostles her on the sidewalk in front of her apartment. He means only to sprain her ankle, but her spike heel catches in a manhole cover and she breaks her hip. Nurse hurries around the corner, sheds jogging suit, composes himself by clamping his hands over his ears to dampen her screams, then calls an ambulance and "happens by" in time to trundle her into it. Just before she's released, the nurse tells his beloved that her insurance company has assigned *him*—coincidence of coincidences—to attend her. During her convalescence she falls in love, as he'd hoped. But it's an honest love got dishonestly, and guilt tortures him. Turns out *he's* the brute and the creep; the investment banker's heart is not tin but a finer metal—not gold, but something between tin and gold.

The nurse knows he doesn't deserve this wonderful woman. His friend doesn't either, but at least his friend hasn't caused necrosis in any of her major joints. Rather than confessing his crime and making her either hate him, have him arrested, or both, the nurse concocts a story about having volunteered months ago for a mercy mission to Mozambique that has finally come through. He'll move away, he believes, and preserve a pure memory of their love. There's a weepy leave-taking. He helps her chip open the cast, revealing an alabaster leg that seems to have suffered no atrophy. "We'll always have plaster of paris," he jokes. She cries. He cries. Fade to black.

Cut to: Years later, having figured out the truth, she tracks him down to his houseboat near Seattle, whacks him in the hip with a bat, and as he lies on the blond wood of his deck and stares up in Nancy-Kerriganesque perplexity at his assailant, we see, beneath his bared-teeth grimace, a sort of smile. They're even at last—and as she drops the bat beside him and dials the ambulance, he notices there's no ring on her finger.

The movie ends with them rocking side by side in old age on the same houseboat deck. She comments on a coming barometric change. He says, "I know, honey." The camera backs off to see each of them slide a palm to an anciently injured hip and smile at the damage done. Those same hands then link across the armrests. Cue music.

Lodestone

Woman avoiding a traffic snarl cuts through a neighborhood across town, sees her husband's ice-cream truck parked streetside, stops in, rolls up the metal shutter to catch him in the act with a high school girl. The flagrante delicto involves the very popsicle we saw the wife coveting a moment before on the signboard. Worse, the teen has cake cones adhering to her nipples, and the woman's husband is serenading the child with "Vogue."

Wife threatens to press statutory rape charges, runs the horny rat out of town with only the clothes on his back. Then she decides to hold an event that's part yard sale, part exorcism. She hauls his possessions onto the lawn. *Everything* is on offer, no matter how intimate or embarrassing: his shower shoes; Members Only jacket; jumbo tube of jock-itch cream, squeezed from the middle; music (he seems to have escaped with his Madonna collection, but the camera lingers on homemade mix tapes with titles like "Horizontal Bop" and "Happy Birthday, Little Chicken," then closes in on a bootleg tape labeled "The Four Original Members of the Supergroup Asia, Together Again! Benton Harbor, 1997"); soap bar with hairs glued to it; twin Fudgsicles he ate one of, sealed with masking tape, set in the freezer, and forgot about. Also the apron he shed that fateful morning, the napkin dispenser he used to blot their secretions and the popsicle's . . . plus two cake cones, slightly used. Hubby's truck is parked in the driveway, its calliope tinkling, his melting stock free for the taking.

Word quickly gets around town until it's like an orgy, hundreds of people tramping through the yard on a bright June day, plundering the booty of the booty-caller while treats drip down their wrists. It's mostly couples who show, and they're weirdly avid, pawing and gawking, laughing too long and too loud, trying to reassure themselves that, sure, our relationship may be touchy from time to time, but you have to admit I would never wear Knight Rider flip-flops, in the shower or anywhere else.

The movie's main characters are one of these couples—young and newlywed and confident, but a little worried underneath, as what sane person wouldn't be (could *my* medicine cabinet survive this scrutiny, or my stack of albums? The Barry Manilow was a *gift* from my *sister*), so they too laugh aloud and scurry from table to table so as not to miss anything and, the culmination, pick up the husband's apron with kitchen tongs their host has thoughtfully provided. Like the others, they slowly rotate it with the tongs, which scintillate in the sunlight, and they gaze at the apron stains and speculate about which are innocent ice cream spatters and which are more sinister.

At last the husband buys his wife a souvenir, a magnet in the shape of a cartoon halibut. Everyone's doing this: a way of bringing home the feeling that, whatever frailties our relationship may have, it's sturdier than *this*.

Six years later, things having gone the way things go, the wife clears out one day, and leaves her husband a kiss-off note . . . which she pins to the refrigerator with the magnet. *This*, Vada recalls, *is where the film fell apart*. The guy keeps trying to convince himself that she's coming back because of a bunch of blarney that has to do with the lodestone, in olden days, having the power to draw wayward wives back to their husbands.

And then, in that arty student-film way, there is suddenly an imaginary friend (the ice-cream husband, magically reunited with his apron) whom the dumpee can see in mirrors, and Dumpee explains to him the lore of magnets—the guy teaches community-college metallurgy, or something—and the guy with spooge on his apron (did the filmmakers think we'd forget?) thoughtfully wipes his hands on it and nods and says nothing because he is a nonspeaking ghost. *And the whole thing turned boring. Don't they teach in film school that inwardness is a drag?*

Vada remembers thinking, *It's a fish. It has no special powers.* So when, inevitably, the wife returns—she's come to retrieve an insurance policy left in a drawer, and it *just so happens* that her (ex) husband's car is in the shop, which fools her into walking right in, and he's canceled class because he's so miserable and is sitting in the kitchen, droning at the ghostly ice-cream cocksman whom he sees in the toaster's chrome, and he's fingering the trophy fish, of course, so that when she opens the door she finds herself face to face with him . . .

66

Strange Attractors

And Vada, being the sort of fool who learns life-lessons from movies, took from the first film, it seems, the idea that puns can eventually make *anything* come out right, no matter how fucked-up, and gleaned from the second—a movie he denounced as stupid even at the time—that objects are magic and can be used to lure home the woman one loves.

What a load-stone.

67

United in Love and the Rheumatiz

Listen: this is important. The movie nurse *wanted* his Maimed Beloved to ferret out his hiding place, or he'd never have left her with the wordplay that gave the film its title. He must have honed that parting witticism for weeks, tried it out before mirrors, with different tones and tilts of the head.

How far might one go, having struck upon a line like that, to deliver it? Pretty far. Vada's theory: the leave-taking line *preceded* the nurse's decision to take leave. Till then the guy had been playing out the string of his deceit, and he had no incentive to give up the pleasures of the Maimed Beloved's company until either she recovered or he was exposed. Face it: our lives are mostly holding patterns, delaying actions—we act only when forced to. So why sprout a conscience? What made him opt for "noble" retreat, right at the point of getting what he wanted?

Happens all the time. We find ourselves in a familiar narrative, and then we behave in the way the story requires. The most successful people are those with a gift for writing themselves into heroic roles rather than being extras who stagger from set to set looking for something better to play than Skate Punk #3, Vertex, Orphan, Corpse on Floor.

That's the genius in the nurse's exit line. On the day the cast comes off, it's almost painless to leave her, because he *knows* she'll come back. The storyline requires it. Throw in the hand-squeeze, the wistful smile, and she'll hear the same pizzicato tempest of violins that the filmgoer does. Make sure, too, that you leave some small sign, to be discovered later, that *you* were the brute who injured her. To do all this is to enter a script whose final scene you both know, the script of the weepie that can only end with the two of you on that boat deck in old age, patting your cranky joints, united in love and the rheumatiz. That cliché is a space you can occupy together, a tale you can mutually tell. Which is what love is, right?

Reader, we are donkeys who pin on our own tales. And if we are *skilled* donkeys, those appendages do more than cover our asses.

68

The Underwater Undead

You'll need to know more about Wyatt.

They grew up together, nearly the only children in what was in the 1970s still a sparsely populated place. The lake's shoreline was dotted with trailer parks or tin-and-cinderblock fishing camps, and a few A-frames had begun to sprout, weekend places for doctors from Aiken or Orangeburg who seemed caught in a fantasy half Dixie pinewoods, half Swiss: "Rat von Trapps," Darla calls the few chalets still standing now. Back then there were many spots on the water where the only landmarks were shoal markers mounted on drowned sandbags. It was impossible to navigate by looking to shore, because every vista was the same: a dense tourniquet of trees applied to the open wound of the red clay banks.

During construction of the lake in the late 1920s, a dozen small communities had to be abandoned or relocated. Their remnants lay underwater now. This led, of course, to playground speculation about zombies with gills. Graham Gossett claimed to have been to the bottom in the deepest part of the lake, 360 feet, where he and his father saw tiger sharks cruising among stones in an old boneyard. It had been daytime, he said, so there were no dog-paddling corpses about just then. But the graves were disturbed; the zombies were definitely real.

"How do they know it's daytime, that deep?" asked someone. It might have been Vada. "Isn't it dark?"

"Zombies are smarter than you think."

"Do you and your dad have, like, a sub?" asked someone else. Or maybe that was Vada, too. "With spotlights?"

"Bathysphere," said Graham. He smirked. Sixth-grade science is a dangerous thing. If you could come up with a specific term, nobody could contradict you.

Vada knew better than to flat-out deny the existence of underwater undead, but he did point out that the elder Gossett had only a panel van with a rusted-out rear quarter panel and BUSTED PIPE PLUMBING on the side. Besides, there were no lake marinas with deep enough water to launch a bathysphere. And didn't he mean *bathyscaphe*? Bathyspheres weren't self-propelled; they were lowered from ships on cables.

For this offense against romance, the guys gang-tackled him at recess, took his shoes and shirt, and tossed him into the dumpster behind the home ec room. As Vada sprawled half-naked (not for the first time) among gallons of spoiled egg salad and badly basted skirt hems, he tried to console himself with the knowledge—he for one had *read* the lesson in their South Carolina history text—that before the lake was flooded, the cemeteries had been deconsecrated, the remains and tombstones moved.

But knowledge was puny compensation. He lay amid the eggy fetor, awaiting the bell and wondering about the more everyday stuff in the muck of the lake-bottom: broken plows, stripped Model T's. Barnwood outhouses with birds' nests still wedged in the eaves. Gourds now housing crabs instead of purple martins. Blackberry brambles through whose ruins eels slithered. The skeletons of moles that poked up through the soil one night to discover that someone had replaced the air with water.

Just before fifth period Wyatt, having cajoled the others into returning Vada's stuff, arrived at the dumpster. He didn't peek in, didn't speak. Vada saw his friend's hand and the clothes—the shirt stuffed in one shoe like a soiled flag—flash into his vision, and he warded off a sneaker that nudged his face like a friendly fish. "You need to stand up for yourself," said invisible Wyatt. "Seriously." Vada didn't respond, but he sat up, wiped off as well as he could with fabric scraps, and pulled the shirt over his head. Wyatt had rolled it tightly before stuffing it in the shoe, to protect it. As if sensing that Vada was noticing this little solicitude, Wyatt spoke up. Gruffly. "Hurry," he said as he walked away. "Bell soon."

69

A Shining Subdivision upon a Hill

Wyatt's father, Reid, was bequeathed a major stake in the electric company, and in the late 1950s, soon after he turned thirty, he got a sweetheart deal on ten thousand acres spread along the lake's southern shore. He built a handsome but modest split-level atop a knoll with a three-sided view of the water and settled into a squire's life of hunting, fishing, and adventures on the tractor that became his hobby, boon companion, and—or near it—religion. He worshipped at the Church of Massey Ferguson by way of endless regrading, drain-tiling, brush-hauling, sodding. His tithe took the form of custom attachments he commissioned from metal fabricators all over the Midlands—tillers, scoops, trenchers, aerators—and the shed space to accommodate them.

Now and again Reid sold timber or granted hunting leases for ready cash, and he was an untutored but, it turned out, gifted horse trader. Bartering with the government over right-of-way along the new four-lane at the southern verge of his property, he managed to parlay minor concessions on his part, slivers of scrub that eminent domain would have allowed them to seize anyway, into a network of public streets through his holdings . . . including a paved road that at the time amounted to a four-mile-long extension of his driveway. Then the suckers granted him a lucrative long-term contract to keep that road's shoulders clear and its berm mown. They paid him to maintain his property precisely as he would have maintained it anyway.

When Reid finally married, at forty-two, he and Penny decided to develop some land contiguous to the homestead. A king surrounding himself with principalities, the better to be awed and envied? Prone though he is to the sour view, Vada can't see it that way. Reid wasn't the lording-over type. Perhaps the decision was about constructing a ready-made neighborhood for the child they'd soon have, just as poorer folks slap up cartoon wallpaper and hang a mobile or two for a nursery. Reid probably conceived of the Shores as a way of sharing his bounty with others—and if there came a nice profit, it was simply further evidence of God's providence. This was the American way. A rising tide lifted all boats by their bootstraps toward their manifest destiny: a shining Subdivision upon a Hill. When you're a Yancey, the world seems just and sunny.

Penny named the development Keyhole Shores, after the shape of their headland. The Yanceys lived at the top, on a bulge that tapered to a wasp-waist, then widened: a circle mounted on a slender triangle, a ball balanced on a seal's snout. Surely the name reflected, too, the pride of the keyholder. Reid and Penny held a passe-partout that would turn any tumbler, trip any latch. They were king and queen, castellan and chatelaine.

Reid cordoned off thirty acres of lakefront for himself and Penny and divided the lower triangle into acre-and-a-half plots. The road he'd conned the county into building years before already bisected the peninsula, and he persuaded the powers-that-be (in part by selling the assessor a lot at discount) to create two new half-loops called Yancey's Oval that would provide access to the new homesites. He immediately sold a dozen lakefront lots, nearly all to weekenders. Many were bought as investments and wouldn't be built on for years. But there was an exception.

Vic Prickett had been Reid's friend for nearly a decade, since shortly after Reid moved to the lake. Back then Vic was the game warden assigned to the southern shore, more than twenty miles east to west, and on one of his first afternoon patrols he happened to chug into the cove as Reid was preparing to dump a tractor scoop of tilapia fingerlings he'd smuggled up from Florida. He'd bought them to eat the aquatic weeds that kept fouling his outboard (aquatic weeds he might have introduced to the lake himself the year before, when he'd stocked the area around Shoal 93 with fish).

Vic's soon-to-be friend watched—engine still roaring, the scoop poised to drop its writhing quicksilver—as the warden sped toward him, sounding an incomprehensible alarm, then hurled himself in full uniform into the water twenty feet from shore, a tight-weave seine net in his hands. He tripped on the net's lead plummets and got a faceful of mud, came up spluttering: "In the name of the law, pttttffff, hold your fish! Hold your fish! Pfffft. I repeat, keep the contraband *up.*" Vic pulled a little veil of froghair off his face, the better to assert his authority. Then, alerted by Reid's pointed finger, Vic swam in chase of his boat, which was idling toward an outcrop of boulders down the way. Reid cut the tractor engine, jogged along the shoreline, and caught the boat before it ran aground. A few seconds later, Vic swam alongside and stomped onto dry land, his shoes gasping and snorting like old men saved from drowning . . . and what had begun as a potential arrest ended with the two of them sitting side by side until sunset on the emptied scoop, drinking scotch ("Another cup of contraband, officer?") and swapping stories. While his khakis dried atop the Massey's ticking engine, Vic wore a hideous and unbuttonable pair of Reid's slacks. The little fish fluttered and died in a conical heap alongside them. "Sorry about that," Vic kept saying. "But they'll be good fertilizer, anyway."

"Never paid sixty-two dollars for fertilizer before," said Reid.

It turned out that Mother Prickett and Mother Yancey had grown up ten miles apart, in country hamlets flooded out of existence for the lake. The clapboard churches and blackberry brambles of their childhoods were gone, and their swimming holes were now pockmarks in the vast bowl of the lake bottom.

Often during Vada's boyhood Vic quoted Reid's poetic speech that day about their meemaws "never suspecting that one day their grandsons would fish the skies." Yap, yap—lyricism was for chumps. Besides, this wasn't what Vada had asked. He'd wanted to know about corpses revived via voodoo, the swimming abilities thereof. At school he'd had the facts, but they had not sufficed. Fact just marked you as a kid who thought you were smarter than everybody else; fact didn't stand a chance against the sort of truth that could heave you into a dumpster. But it was Vada's only weapon, so he was hunting up new, more potent facts, to be backed by his father's authority as a native of the lake and a sort-of scientist.

Vada had a personal stake in busting up the myth of the Subaqueous Undead—any lakebed zombies might well be his kin. And even Bathyscaphe Graham didn't deserve to meet up with Vada's father's folks, whom the few extant photos revealed to be scowling Baptists with weak chins and square shoes. Hatchet faces, bent beaks—try that on for heritage. He tried in vain not to think of his grandfather as a scrawny turkey buzzard who'd developed, after death, both gills and a taste for human flesh. It had been two weeks since he'd been able to make himself swim.

Aboveground relatives were trouble enough, and for the most part they didn't have peeling faces or a craving to eat folks.

70

Piscinity: A Strained Metaphor
(Gotta Charge Extra for Artistry)

During Vada's childhood, Vic and Reid often repaired to the Pricketts' back deck after dinner, striking matches on the rail to light the fat cigars they favored, and as soon as the tips glowed orange, both men would compress their lips rapidly five or six times to make the stogeys draw: "glooping," Vada called it. Once their cigars caught, smiles overspread Vic's and Reid's faces, and they'd lean into the blue plume and disappear into a companionship on which no one dared intrude. The men didn't complain if wives or sons came to join them, but whenever Vada drew back the sliding door from the kitchen the conversation lulled.

Guilt would always ruin fishing for Vada. By hauling a creature out of its element, one diminished it. Under water, he thought, fish might be unconstrained by bodies. They were pure abstractions, thrash and hunger. Only when yanked into air did they become the pop-eyed, sad-mouthed, listless things Reid dropped into his bucket and later, with a few deft incisions, filleted and gutted. Nothing that yielded its bones so easily could have had them long.

It was best to leave the gloopers to their murk, so on most cigar nights Vada would take a quick sniff of the tobacco, then shut the door and make common cause with his mom over the dishes. As he and Celeste scrubbed and dried, puffs of sud drifted up like containers for the dialogue they had no need to speak. Meanwhile, his father's boisterous laugh rattled the glass.

How did women come to marry such men? In the photo albums Vada consulted like runes after his parents' death, Reid's and Vic's clothes from their bachelor days were baggy and bloodstained, their nails ringed with grime. They displayed braces of quail, stringers of bream. Beer cans were heaped at their feet like tribute to drunken lords. It was hard to imagine either of them courting anything that couldn't be caught with a cricket or felled by a bullet . . . yet they were married in quick succession.

Vada couldn't conceive of his father and Reid discussing matters of the heart. They had tackle vests and ammo cases, not emotions, and their only cologne was the acrid niff of gunpowder. Affection had to make itself known—if for some reason it felt the need—in talk of gear differentials, field dressing, and varieties of fish or fowl. Could it be, though, that Vada underestimated them? When that sliding door thunked shut did they change, become back-porch Wordsworths who talked of plundering fish from the vaults of their ancestors' heavens, blah blah blah? He has no guesses. Who knows what fish do once engine noise has bloomed overhead and the boat's shadow has dragged itself away and night sifts down through the water?

71

A Truth Universally Acknowledged

Oh, reader—sorry. Vada left out a scene change there. Now it's six minutes ago, and Vada is thumbing shut the spout of the fish-scale fertilizer he sprinkles onto Celeste's rose bed three times a year and plucking off his garden gloves one finger at a time. July's no time to fertilize, but he's dawdling near the road so that if he hears the motorcycle downshift for the stop sign at the head of Wyatt's driveway, he can wave Darla away.

Again Vada wonders what the hell Wyatt is doing here. The liar had told his fiancée he'd be downstate at a chukar hunt, one of those all-day events for which a kid gamekeeper, fresh from his wildlife major at Clemson, drives to Charlotte, picks up birds ordered online, drives the cages to the Lowcountry, and releases the cooing prey into the scrub a few hours before the plutocrats arrive with their silver flasks and die-tooled shotguns. That gives the gamekeeper just time enough to gas up the ATVs and chill the champagne with which they'll celebrate the successful hunt.

Vada was to meet Darla "at noonish." Six minutes ago, that would have been *any second now*. Which—Vada apologizes for not mentioning it earlier—is why he got so agitated when he saw Wyatt bounce up the driveway in his cart to fetch the mail. Ever since, he's been watching and listening for Wyatt to leave. Please. *Please*. Because "meeting" is too weak a word for what he intended with Darla. All morning Vada tried on "rendezvous," toyed with "assignation." But "meeting" was her term, appropriate to her purpose if not to his, and he would always defer to her. Meeting it would be, at least at first. She wanted to show off her wedding gift for Wyatt, an Italian motorcycle with matching leather suits and his-and-her helmets canted backward like ants' heads, and after Vada contributed a few oohs and ahhs and perhaps a quick buff, carwash professional–style, to spruce up the chrome, she wanted him— the business that would need transacting—to garage the bike until next weekend's festivities.

Which he'd do, *in the barn.* Reader, this is his plan, such as it is. Such as it was.

72

The Thunder of Disclosure

Vada didn't forget his precious chronology. Did he leave off, before, with nine minutes to go? The refrigerator door open, wasteful cool bathing his face? Oops. It's been open now for fifty pages or more.

He'll recap quickly.

First he shut the fridge. A blunder there—distracted, he'd meant to open the freezer instead. All morning he'd been thinking of his reward for mowing, the albino salami of cookie dough that he'd devour while standing in the open door, listening to the ice cubes crack and feeling the motor's shuddering exhalations. Eight minutes fifty-some seconds ago, Vada gnawed two inches off the dough, folded over the wrapper for a next time that would never be, sealed it in a freezer bag. Then he went to the window above the sink and opened it, the better to hear the sound of an approaching engine. He ran the tap over his wrist until the water got cold, then turned his mouth under the faucet and drank. He washed his hands and face, dried them with one of his mother's dish towels. It had a hippo on it. The hippo, threadbare at the snout, had seen better days, the kind of better days symbolized by a threadier snout. Feeling sheepish about his unhealthy lunch, Vada reopened the fridge and took a bite of the onion sandwich he made last night, then promptly regretted it, as he couldn't take the time and risk of running down the hall to the windowless bathroom to brush his teeth, and thus had sentenced himself to reeking of sulfur when he made his play at the . . . meeting. He spat the bite, still-crunchy, *barely used*, into the trash, but the damage was done. Then he headed back outside, hurrying to minimize the time he'd be underneath and then on the wrong side of the house and thus unable to intercept Darla. From his father's basement he grabbed the fertilizer and the gloves as props. They would be to him like Lauren Bacall's cigarettes in old movies. Eight minutes ago, basement door, at a trot. Seven found him in the rose bed.

Six minutes. As Vada stood listening in vain for the motorcycle and trying to make the glove-doffing last and last (Bacall had been even more skilled than he thought), he realized he'd been so locked in on *that* noise that he'd been ignoring a growing raucor behind him. Now the sound became intelligible. Here was Wyatt just twenty feet off, in his cart, pointing through the pines at a delivery truck parked five hundred yards away at his door and shouting. "Vada! Come on! Hurry! We've got a grizzly to move."

Vada's first thought was, *A delivery truck? How did that get past me?* As the sentinel worked cold dough around his mouth or tried to suck shreds of Vidalia from his teeth, his empty mind must have wandered.

Wyatt said, "Pull the glove off already, Gypsy Rose. Let's *hustle*."

What could Vada do, hearing his friend's imploring tone, but comply? As he hopped onto the seat beside Wyatt, he made sure to drop one glove alongside the gravel driveway—but to signal *what*, exactly? This was no fairy tale, and even if it were, and if Darla knew how to interpret the Garden Glove of Warning, the Grimms would invent some sort of polka-dot-glove-eating crow to fuck him over per usual.

They got to the truck five minutes ago, just as its impatient driver was spinning the latch and yanking the door's nooselike fabric handle and unleashing that upward thunder Vada has always liked. The thunder of disclosure.

But wait.

73

No Man's Napkin

In retrospect, Vic's friendship with Reid seems based in a fatal inequality, mostly financial. Reid sold his friend this plum acreage at below market value and asked Vic to agree to a covenant stating that neither he nor his successors, be they heirs or buyers, would subdivide the land. In a sense Vic was paid to provide a buffer, to interpose himself between Reid and the world. The lessor, the lesser.

But Vic never seemed diminished by Reid's largesse, which he seemed not to take notice of, and for his part Reid never demanded or expected any quo for his quid. Vada imputed this to kindness, but his mother was inclined to a darker view. In his early teens, Vada asked one morning why Mr. Yancey let Vic hunt and cut firewood on his land. Celeste flipped down her paper and peered at him over dime-store half-glasses, as if gobsmacked that her dull son could ask a sharp question. "A man doesn't begrudge his napkin the crumbs it catches," said Celeste. She paused before flipping the paper back up. Her face bore the intensity of the coin-operated arcade soothsayer who, when you grabbed her plastic hand, coughed out a phrase of turbid advice. Did he see?

Vada nodded, wanting to live up to her hopes, but the drift was uncatchable.

Now he sees. Celeste always hated driving the orange Ford—referred to evermore as Penny the Pinto—that Penny Yancey passed down when she got her Eldorado. Nor did Celeste like displaying, at Vic's insistence, the pricey gewgaws the Yanceys showered her with on Christmas and birthdays or to reward her for feeding the cat when they were in Gstaad or Gpalmbeach: cloisonné dolphins, waterfowl prints with captions in Gothic script, lamps made from glazed and braided twigs. And it drove her crazy to come home from errands in town to a ringing phone; Penny had spotted her namesake turning into the drive, and, well, the patroness's curiosities must be satisfied.

Vic's obliviousness infuriated Celeste. How could he not see that being lightly starched, ruffled, and frilled into a table garnish, then shaken out, lap-spread, and dabbed at stray sauce or spilled wine . . . how could he not recognize that this was demeaning? The Vic she'd married was No Man's Napkin.

Vic wouldn't hear her criticism. He set his teeth, closed his eyes, tightened his grip on the steering wheel—a faint tapping at the door of anger's anteroom, the knock of a man who hoped to find no one at home, but nevertheless the closest Vic ever came to pique with his wife. In its way it was intimidating, this near-anger in a man so mild, like spotting a whitecap in the bathtub. "Reid is our friend," Vic would say—elocute—at last. "Friends help friends."

74

Mr. Jefferson's Colossal Cowpie

For all those years, the fathers were inseparable. Often at dusk they sat in their tractor seats on the bluff alongside Reid's house and drank thermos coffee from dented cups like cowboys on the range—senior cowpoke high on his behemoth Massey, stirrup boy below on his economy nag. On wet Saturdays in the fall they'd gather under Reid's tractor lean-to and touch up duck decoys, meanwhile passing a bottle of scotch and hooting like schoolboys as rain pelted the tin overhead.

They did most of their waterfowl hunting barely a quarter-mile behind the Yancey house, surrepting themselves before first light along an isthmus that emerged from the lake every autumn, when the electric company drew down the water level. Reid had started with three dozen identical mallards, cheapos resembling painted footballs, with aluminum keels, bead eyes, and tucked wings. But wet Saturdays piled up through the years, and just as the toy-soldier hobbyist graduates from one smudged gobbet of general astride a footless stallion to a basement Shiloh so meticulously re-created that the trees are flayed of bark by gunfire and dying men clasp severed limbs to their chests and the blood puddles have sodden peach blossoms afloat in them (you'll have to bend close to see, but that's *not* dandruff), Reid and Vic eventually had to splash about in predawn dark for twenty minutes to deploy a raft of a hundred ducks. There were pintails, buffleheads, teals, in a variety of poses: preening, swimming, squabbling. There were even a few ("asses" for short, as in "Make sure you grab the asses, Vic") that consisted only of tufted white hindparts tipped up to approximate a diving duck. The men made these by attaching cotton pads and real tailfeathers onto a sheet of tricot mesh and then gluing the mesh to a round rubber buoy.

It's easy, Vada thinks, for the unwary hobbyist to turn fanatic. His father and Reid didn't *choose* hunting. What they chose was each other. The hunt was an afterthought. Shooting was beside the point. Even if days passed without either of them lifting his gun, the men sat vigil every morning of the season. Accompanied by Reid's dog Rosa, who panted in the weeds behind them, they roosted on camp stools inside the double blind Reid had built. He'd designed an innovative hinged door in its side. He was Thomas Jefferson, and that blind was his Monticello.

From Wyatt's window, four hundred yards distant and thirty feet above, the blind had looked like a tank turret, a colossal cowpie, or—that's it—a *shoulder-high volcano*, and their fathers were lava gods waiting patiently to erupt. If you watched for movement, you could see the gunmetal thermos of coffee pass back and forth in the gathering light. If you listened, you could almost hear them whispering. Equals.

"I don't get what you're looking at," said Wyatt from bed, where he was reading *Captain America*. "They never even *shoot*. They're the boringest hunters in the world."

"I don't get why you like that musclehead," said Vada over his shoulder. "He doesn't even have *powers*."

"Captain America hunts *Nazis*," said Wyatt. "He doesn't sit on his butt in his own cove." Vada sighed. Later today, as Hitler, wearing a trenchcoat whose hem would drag and a grease-pencil mustache, he'd be harried all over creation by Captain Wyatt America, in flag T-shirt and red galoshes and carrying a trash-can lid he'd sail at your head if you stopped and tried to stand your ground.

Now, after two hours of suspended animation, their fathers crashed into the water to yank up the decoys, which were anchored to bricks by a ski rope. It would take twenty minutes to wrap and stow them in the slat-sided wagon Reid had attached to his golf cart and covered with a tarp. Vada put down the binoculars. "That's it," he said.

"Finally." Wyatt pushed himself onto one elbow and yelled down the hall. "Mom! Breakfast time!"

75

Spreading Thin the Raspberry Corps

Vada is realizing that he missed a lesson or two along the way. It's been that kind of a life.

Take Farny, Senior Vacuumist at Caw-Caw, a goofball monomaniac who dresses in a gray Confederate cap ("That ain't no cap, boy—it's a kepi!"), digs his own chicory for camp coffee, and weekly waxes his flowing mustaches. He refers to himself as the Colonel. Four mornings a week he attacks the Union garrison/breakfast buffet commanded by ruddy-cheeked General Big Boy and located two doors down from the carwash. He refers to this as "swarming Coronary Hill," and says to his gum-snapping aide de camp, "Lois, the Colonel will have a Denver with extra ham, hash browns, and toast points, double brushed." Then he re-creates the Battle of Seven Pines on the tabletop, using salt shakers, hot sauce, jelly packets, the strawberry-shortcake promo card. If you stir your coffee with the Chickahominy River or spread General Sumner's corps on your English muffin, he is not amused.

But surely Farny didn't *set out* to be a caricature. What he wanted to be was a *colonel* (thanks, Il DUCE, for the old fascist try, "Colonel of the Sucking Apparatus," but even Farny saw that was too steep a price to pay for an acronym). And what was it he got for his wanting? He's a middle-aged man with eccentric facial hair who lives a hundred and fifty years in the past and is so fat that after the toast points he can't walk the fifty yards from Big Boy to work. Instead he has to drive the spavined Buick Electra the carwash wags call Traveler.

Reader: Desires warp us, and collections accrete. It's their nature; it's ours. Nobody plans to back himself into a corner that requires chicory digging or mustache wax. And nobody plans to become a failure collector, either. It just happens.

76

Smart Capitalism

What does all this have to do with Vada and Wyatt?

Beyond the neck where Reid and Vic hunted, the isthmus widened to a two-acre island of red clay and pines almost three hundred yards from the summer shoreline. The fathers occasionally pounded golf balls at the island, an aerial bombardment not seen in these parts since Doolittle's Raiders did low-altitude training runs forty-some years before. Vada and Wyatt waded the shoal for the shots that fell short or went astray.

Wyatt was paid a quarter and Vada a dime for each ball salvaged, and it didn't take long for the boys to realize that they'd make more if Vada ceded most of his haul to Wyatt and took a kickback. This was "smart capitalism," Wyatt insisted, and the deal did pay for tons of Marathon bars and *Daredevil* comics Vada would have missed out on . . . but it took a toll to see his father's disappointment when the boys walked back across with their burdens—Wyatt striding, his stiff-bottomed leather satchel held over his shoulder and stuffed nearly to capacity, the balls clumping as thunderously as cavalry crossing a bridge, and Vada trudging along with downcast eyes, silently boloing his smaller drawstring bag, quarter full, around an index finger.

77

Führer Bee

As with sons so with fathers, and on up the generations. Wyatt's maternal granddad was one of Doolittle's pilots, had screamed over the lake in a B-25 and dropped payloads of concrete onto makeshift targets, often scraped-together woodpiles but on one notable occasion, Reid told the boys, a giant tarpaulin on which Hitler's mug had been painted by the Ladies' Auxiliary. "They had themselves a Führer Bee," he said. "They signed their initials in lipstick along the edges of the tarp. Who knows? King Kraut's mug might have been spread out on *this island right here*. It was one of the target ranges, you know." Reid told Wyatt and Vada to keep an eye out for tatters of that sheet when they went diving for shag balls. Only the borders would have survived, he claimed, because Wyatt's grandfather had been the pilot chosen, and he'd popped old Adolf with a payload of grade-A local cee-ment: "Blew that smug little caterpillar under his nose to kingdom come. Whammo, right in the kisser."

Meanwhile Vada's grandfather, handicapped by weak eyes, had been in charge of dispensing fuel for Doolittle and his flyboys. His precision aim had been spent on dropping a nozzle into a tank.

Ontogeny recapitulates phylogeny, Vada learned in his pre-vet classes (only to discover that he'd been taught this as an example of the idiotic errors of a past put safely behind us), "The development of the individual is a progression through the forms of adult ancestors." In his case, that meant moving through feebleness and deference and nozzle-holding on the way toward . . . more of the same, the next subservience down the line. Oh, to come down on someone, just once, like a ton of concrete.

78

Under the Microscope

Property taxes and electricity are expensive, if you're eking by in a succession of minimum-wage-or-barely-better jobs. For eight years Vada lived off the insurance settlement. But that money finally ran out, and this last year, to hang onto the property, he has been forced to move some merchandise. Jewelry. Furniture. His father's tractor and fishing boat. He has kept the things, lawnmowers and chainsaws and the like, that help keep up appearances, and he has resisted selling items like his mother's cookbooks and inspirational pencils that would mean little profit but great anguish.

The result is an increasingly sparse and echoey house. In the last few months Vada's done all he can to avoid entertaining and to repel intruders at the door, not out of shame so much as from fear of the real-estate sharks who swarm Keyhole Estates. These days it's not possible at any price to get twelve acres attached to lakefront, which makes him what the real-estate folks like to call a "unique opportunity" (OK, a "very unique opportunity," but Vada is a kind editor, as he hopes you will be).

And when there's blood in the water, everyone's suddenly your chum. Pa-dum-pum. Vada dreads fielding offers every time he ventures to breakfast or barber or just to curbside, where he often runs into his cross-street neighbor Cynda Neely, one of three realtors on West Yancey's Oval. Cynda's the one he fears most, in part because every time he goes to town he sees her vulpine grin, teeth sharp as fence pickets, from a billboard along the highway. He's imagined the scene. He, wheeling his garbage up the slope; Cynda, idling in her Mini Cooper and commiserating/angling, one part sympathy to nine acquisitiveness. He'd sound crazy if he asked her to pipe down out of respect for—here a wag of the head toward the hunter-green cart that's always looked to him, and all the more so now, like a giant jack-in-the-box—you know, The Dead.

The one time he did let someone in, on Armageddon Night, only confirmed the wisdom of his policy. Since that night Wyatt, presumably alerted by Darla, has several times offered to buy back, at hefty price, an acre or two of pinewoods. Every time he asks Vada for help these days—lifting a trailer onto a hitch, dragging a stuffed elk out of the way for dusting—they go through a pas de deux in which Wyatt insists on giving him fifty bucks for his trouble, Vada refuses, Wyatt jabs at his hand with the bill, Vada flicks it away. Then Vada finds it in his mailbox in an envelope and caves.

The cash cow most difficult to slaughter was the expensive microscope Vic and Celeste gave him on their last Christmas. Even after he liquidated most everything else, he kept that instrument, with its stereo zoom, its reagent-resistant finish, its coaxial fine and coarse focusing knobs for each hand. It's humiliating now to think how much he begged for that thing. He figured it was the object that would *make* him become a large-animal vet. Once you had something as fine as that, you'd begin to love the work, or not *begin*, he means to say, but you'd love the work even more than you already did love the work (he loved the work), and the work you'd have available to love would be no longer the dreary bookwork of prereqs, which would undermine *anyone's* determination, but instead would be the real work of examining microbes ("Mr. Prickett, do you see the marker that identifies this as camel-borne *Brucella melitensis* rather than its unexotic cattle cousin?"). And once you'd invested that much money, or caused your loved ones to, you were in for the long haul: no turning back once you're in the hole for nearly two grand worth of magnifying power.

A decade ago, without meaning to, he'd committed the brochure to memory. The effortlessness of this feat reminded him of the death-struggle the catechism had presented a few years earlier. He had to take care, when begging for the present, not to echo the marketers' wording or to tout so fluently that they'd know he was spouting a script. After his parents' death, the microscope had represented a promise to himself that he would in due time return to school. Eventually it devolved into a relic, vested with the power to taunt and shame. But he couldn't part with the three color filters (and here church-rote came mistily back, "the three divine persons, Father, Son, and Holy Spirit") or the extra lens that came in a velvet sack like a gemstone or fancy liqueur. It was—still is—a gorgeous machine. Until two weeks ago it had pride of place on the tower of milk crates that, together with his bed and his jam-box and the massive old console TV Reid had entailed to Vada's parents years before, made up the only furniture in his bedroom.

Two hundred bucks, by the way. That's what he got. Two lousy bills.

79

Revenge Is a Double-Edged Sword Best Served Cold

Wyatt was a great champion of the wet willie, and Vada his favorite victim.

This is what it comes down to, their relationship: the willier, the willied. Ah, the desolation of the sap with wetted ears, the done-to. What recourse is there as you stand in the hallway amid laughter, alien slobber leaking down your lobes, ear canals itching from nail scratches? To claw at your head is undignified and gross, and passing the humiliation on isn't an option, for reasons more practical than moral; everybody's going to be watching for you. So you go to the bathroom, there to ream out your ears with brown paper towels and think harsh thoughts. Your inwardness is your revenge, only it's the dumbest possible revenge, and not importable into the world, because then it ceases to be inwardness and becomes susceptible to the world's rules, which stipulate that you are a loser and get the shaft or why would you have had to resort to inwardness anyway? Captains of industry, hostile takeoverers, buccaneers, action heroes, and Mafiosi have no need of inwardness, and everybody likes them or at least envies them, which are the same thing or which we pretend are the same thing because it takes time and finesse to sort out the difference, and precisely what we like, or envy, about such people is that they don't trouble themselves with parsing bullshit distinctions like the difference between like and envy. Time is money. Finesse is for pansies. Mighty is the finger that, licked, plugs some schmuck's ear for giggles.

It's a matter of firepower. "Fuck the pope," Stalin is said to have barked when an aide suggested that stringing Catholics from lampposts might be an idea with bad consequences. "How many divisions does he have?" Vada got this in his carwash orientation from Il DUCE, who got it from Hunter Thompson, so who knows if it's true—but the difference between true and false is just another technicality that doers shouldn't trouble themselves with.

80

Nanook of the Penumbra

At Dartmouth, Wyatt earned honors in economics and reaped the media curiosity that came from being the northernmost golf All-American in decades. For a profile called NANOOK OF THE IVIES, *Sports Illustrated* posed him on a sled, mushing huskies with a seven-iron.

Then he spent seven years traveling, playing various international tours. This is the period Vada views now as the Age of Dwindling Penumbra. From safely afar, he was able to like his friend again. When Wyatt won the Bangkok Open . . . well, bully for him. Vada knew nothing of Bangkok except pop-culture tidbits: Yul Brynner in pouchy silks; the canal chase in *Man with the Golden Gun;* the 1980s Murray Head song in which a chessmaster declines a come-on by saying, "I get my kicks above the waistline, Sunshine." At this distance, goodwill was possible. To begrudge Wyatt success halfway around the world would be, well, a kick below the waistline. Vada's not sure that came out right.

Wyatt could have afforded not to make a cent. But he did well, even pledged 20 percent of his Asian earnings to the amelioration of poverty on the continent—a stand that won him lucrative endorsements and allowed him to start a charity called Bettering Par. In a Catching-Up-With puff piece, Wyatt's pals at *SI* pronounced him "fourteenth on the Asian Tour money list, but first in the Order of Merit." Nanook of the Far East. Vada enjoyed the interregnum. In those years he saw little of his friend except in magazines. Usually this was easy, what with Wyatt ten thousand miles away. But during Wyatt's winter layoffs, there were times when Vada, hearing the familiar upbeat knock, hid in an inner hallway as if waiting out a tornado.

He did, though, grow closer to Reid. A year after Celeste and Vic's death, Penny and her private yoga instructor absquatulated (or ab-downward-dog-ulated) to Arizona, and Reid and Vada became the Left Behind, scarred veterans with grim miens and poor dietary habits. They didn't *see* a whole lot of each other, but they grew friendly. There were the awkward but pleasant five-minute encounters in the woods, less conversations broken up by silences than silences plugged by broken sentences. These almost always ended, their peak of eloquence, with a misgripped handshake, a shoulder pat, a "Hang in there." They were skittish creatures, more comfortable at long range, shouting unhearable words of greeting over engine noise as a tractor or fishing boat trolled by. Sometimes they'd only wave, but that wave, repeated three or four times during the day, with a gusto and affect neither had much call for otherwise might be the only social contact either had, and they treasured it.

But last September, ten months ago, Reid dropped dead of a heart attack, and south and west came Nanook, slouching toward new orders of merit. Vada should have seen it coming—there were only two compass points left to conquer. Wyatt's thirtieth birthday was coming up, and with his father's affairs to arrange and estate to handle, and with his standing on the Asian money list having sunk to thirtieth, then fifty-third, then eighty-ninth, he figured it was time to settle down.

Umbra cast away his Pen, and down rang the Arctic night. Vada always knew whose bushel his light would be hidden under. He just didn't know it would get so dark so fast.

81

Yahweh's Subtrahend, Mommy's Monster

It was a headline Vada assumed he'd see someday: YANCEY IS HERO.

When they were boys, the words had seemed printed everywhere (stitched on his mom's crochet samplers, written on vapor in the sky), so it wasn't a shock to find the phrase, finally, in newsprint. But he wasn't prepared to see it here and now, on a warm, rainy November Thursday, in the same cart shed they strafed together as kids—not like *this*. Couldn't Wyatt have been, at least, the *dead* kind of hero? Vada would be glad to honor his memory, RIP and godspeed; he just didn't want to have to see him on *Oprah*.

The cart shed's bay door overlooked the pond that guarded the eighteenth green, but the building's backside abutted the driving range, where punk kids—like Vada himself years ago—pounded hooks into the corrugated sides, to amuse themselves with racket and to keep the lowly jumping. A few years back the club had planted spindly crape myrtles around the perimeter as a screen, but the barrage of range balls shredded and stunted them. Though the ends of a few branches sported pompons of fuchsia blooms, they looked like something dreamt up by Dr. Seuss and then napalmed.

Every time the exterior wall twanged and shivered and Vada jumped again, he berated himself—for being such a perfect little creep back then or for finding himself still counted, at almost thirty, among the Lowly Who Jump. Or both.

It was of course one of Il DUCE's schemes that landed Vada back here at the club, solo, hand-washing cars that cost five times his annual wage—and doing so in the same shed he and Wyatt used to target with three-iron fusillades. "Rapid fire," Wyatt would shout, and he'd set out ten balls and blast them as he walked down the line, like a trick-shot artist: three-quarters takeback, head down, confirming his accuracy only by the metronomic tattoo of surlyn on metal. Then they'd duck into the row of parking-lot redtips or hunker behind a trash bin until Seth the carts hippie, dizzy from the din and post-spliff stress disorder, ambled up—and seemed shocked to find the range deserted. It wasn't nice to do this to a paranoiac like Seth, who was forever being menaced by what he called "jack-booty'd thugs." Back then the shed had held a cache of powdered donettes and bear claws. Seth insisted that convenience stores open late were all DEA fronts, so he bought his pastries at the day-old shop. Wyatt and Vada howled at the thought of Seth being tracked by black helicopters on his way home from a munchie run. Now Vada sees him as a brother HA. They're everywhere: the Hosed Association.

At some point the club had built an air-conditioned shed and converted the old to storage. Now it housed drums of greenskeeping chemicals, ancient aerators, spiders, dirt daubers, in the corner a bin of long-lost clubs, and a trash can of gray range balls. Old-style battery chargers for carts were still coiled around the rafters, cords dangling, like something from a medical thriller. And Vada, warehoused here too, with his buckets and rags and vacuum, scrubbing and rinsing sports cars and tract-house-sized SUVs.

This was one of Wayne's marketing innovations, the Buff While You Duff Special. Vada had thought of explaining that "you" actually handle only the duffing, not the buffing, but what would be the point? People are whores for rhyme, and accuracy be damned. It's that kind of world. Whatever. Vada suffered on. He bleached whitewalls and dug cicada corpses out of grilles and, whenever he could, fired up a joint. Hail, Seth the carts hippie. Nothing soothes the chronic like the chronic.

What had brought him back to this moldy shed and the range-ball artillery—it was like being inside a helmet—was a ploy by Wayne to bypass the membership waiting list. Il DUCE had struck a deal with the new pro: Vada provided a Deluxe Hand-Wash, just like at Caw-Caw, but with a 20 percent surcharge that got kicked back to the shop. Wayne chose Vada for the job, he said, because of his "familiarity with the venue." Part of the service's popularity derived, Vada knew, from sympathy. Allay the conscience, give the down-and-out son some trade. It was a chance for Wayne—Vada too—to cash in on Ma and Pa Prickett's tragic deaths. And the job *was* easy, maybe ten cars a day if Vada opted for a Monday-to-Thursday schedule and avoided the weekend, which of course he did. This left plenty of time to nap, so long as the assistant pro kept an eye on the junior bombardiers.

"You make your own luck," the DUCE said smugly whenever life dropped another gift in his lap. Vada wanted to believe there's a difference between the main chance and *la bonne chance,* but a man in his position couldn't afford moral superiority, so he learned to play along. He dug change out of crevices, buffed it to a shine, and placed it on the console—twenty cents' worth of conspicuous honesty often paid off fiftyfold in tips. Make people feel better about human nature. Let them forget that they themselves are adulterers or crooks or all-round assholes, and their hearts swell and their wallets itch and they'll fork over a tenner to the sudsy bloodshot guy whose parents' remains, that fateful day, had to be protected from soon-to-be fryers by the boots of deputies who held handkerchiefs over their noses. Vada still imagines the scene from time to time: the upended cages, the birds screaking, the feathers drifting and settling, gravity suspended, time slowed. It seems never to have sped back up again.

Vada did plunder the cars for reading material, though—his one concession to curiosity. On rainy afternoons there was little to do, so he sat on a mildewed chaise retired from the club's pool and either snoozed or perused his swag: church bulletins, GOP campaign literature, alumni newsletters, to-do lists, junk mail, newspapers, and magazines ranging from *Cigar Aficionado* to *Golf World* to something called *Collars & Cuffs,* which turned out not to be about haberdashery.

He also spent time reminiscing. How could he help it? The shed faced the pond at eighteen, site of his childhood's lowest moment. It wasn't a childhood that lacked for perigees. Amazing that he could identify a superlative, even, but he could. Wyatt Yancey was at its heart.

It wasn't that Vada was *bad* at golf. By the time he was fifteen he'd whittled his handicap to four, but his game didn't travel well. It was just that he knew how to bend himself to his place, *this* place. He'd memorized every swale and rill, every bowl of hardpan, every bail-out position and collection area, and he lacked the recklessness that tempted others into assaulting tucked pins or trimming doglegs. On the greens, to calm his twitchy right wrist, he turned around and putted left-handed.

It had become clear early on that success in golf, or in anything, would depend on stifling his nature, on choking the *himself* out of himself. Before Vada finished high school, nerves graduated him first to a crosshand grip, then to a belly putter, and then—by which time every lag putt had come to look like linksland seppuku—to a case of the yips so severe that no trick or gadget could keep it at bay. Still, he was skilled enough to be perennial bridesmaid in the junior club championship, the Mutt Gerard. This might have felt like an accomplishment, had it not meant that he was forced, year after year, to witness Wyatt's sovereignty at close range, in the final pairing.

Wyatt got to carry a red-white-and-blue All-American bag with "W. Yancey" stitched on the pocket in gold. It came equipped with the collapsible tripod that would later become standard but that back then seemed magic—the *Homo erectus* of golf bags, first to haul itself upright and lord it over the meek and earthbound. Lying beside it on the dewy Bermuda, Vada's boneless brown sack looked like it was pleading for mercy.

Which depressing train of associations—entertained in this of all places, on this of all days (that *newspaper:* Vada's half-sprung chaise groans when he gets up to confirm that the headline says what it appears to—yep, YANCEY IS *STILL* HERO)—led back, unavoidably, to The Worst Day of Childhood.

It was the 1993 Mutt Gerard, final round; Vada and Wyatt were sixteen. On the penultimate hole, a par-three, Wyatt's tee shot hung up on a bunker rake, and when he was able to extricate the rake and the ball stayed put, it looked like the gods were smiling as usual. But after he addressed the second shot, the ball not only rolled (a penalty) but also— guided by Vada's hateful wish, his only success at the telekinesis he'd been cultivating for years—trickled into the sand. The resulting triple bogey put Vada in an unfamiliar spot: tied for the lead, one hole to play.

Eighteen was a five-hundred-thirty-yard par-five, a lay-up hole for Vada, who hit two safe irons and left himself in the center cut at wedge distance. Wyatt, looking rattled—visor askew, the usual banter dammed to make way for the free flow of sweat—hit a sweeping hook off the tee that left him with no choice but to bunt a short iron back into play. His second, through an avenue of pines, was well done, but it took a skanky kick through the fairway and skidded into a tangle around the hundred-fifty-yard stake. The mowing crew had spun around the marker rather than yanking it up, so the stake was the center of a kikuyu tangle just three feet in diameter.

"Where'd it go?" Wyatt called. Anxiously, for once.

"I've got it," Vada replied, and strode toward the ball in a show of sportsmanship. Wait till he saw *this*. Welcome, Fortune's Child, to mankind's natural state: damp, mute, aggrieved. *Fucked*.

What happened next isn't, even after all these years, clear. As Wyatt trekked through the trees dividing ten from eighteen, Vada walked along the roughline looking for the ball . . . or not *looking for it*, exactly, since he could see it clearly, sitting high as a wedding band on a bolster of purple plush. Not even Wyatt's bad breaks turned out badly. The Lord giveth, the Lord taketh away, and once again, for the zillionth time, Vada would end up Yahweh's subtrahend (thanks for the word, Mrs. Carson).

Vada was sick of standing, year after year, in front of the plywood scoreboard—capped with a cute cedar-shake roof so the ink wouldn't run—on which every number but Wyatt's was marked in the black ink that meant over par. Just the day before, at the stoplight just outside school, a stringy old dude in a porkpie hat had handed a pocket New Testament through Vada's window, and as he made a show of thumbing through and then flipped it into the backseat, Vada just had time to register that the pages of the Gospels looked familiar. Why? Like Wyatt, Jesus spoke in red. His words were winter cardinals, flares of crimson in a black-and-white world. And now the lesson came home: what that roof reminded him of. The Bavarian clock on Grandma's wall. Its chimes and weights, the two little doors that flew open. Thought you'd beat him? Cuckoo, cuckoo, cuckoo.

When Vada reached the ball, he leaned and pulled the stake loose. A *courtesy*. In doing so, he lightly (by accident?) tamped Wyatt's ball . . .

and was spotted doing so by the scorer, a middle-aged lady in a yellow hardhat of a visor—Celeste, whose squawk suggested that she wasn't buying the accident theory. Yet there *must* be an innocent explanation: Had he tried to pull the stake from too far away and lost his balance when it grabbed the weed-tops, just as the rough tries to strangle an iron shot? Surely he didn't *raise and then stomp* his foot, didn't lift his chin then to whistle in a show of casualness and discover Mom's cart idling ten feet away, the shriek gathering in her throat? Memory's tricky. How did Celeste (pressed into duty and paying fitful attention, fiddling with a shopping list she'd composed on the scorecard clipped to the steering wheel and also ticking off shots one by one, every fifth a diagonal slash across the previous four) . . . how did Celeste see it and gasp and, once and for all, peg her son for a cheat?

Her scream had made him tread the ball deep into the turf, and Wyatt got a free drop. His eight-iron nearly ripped the pin out of the hole, resulting in a birdie that was unnecessary because Vada, unable to see or breathe, dumped five balls into the pond. He kept one eye fixed on his mother. There were tears on her cheeks, and he watched her mark, with a horrifying, evenhanded lack of flourish, like St. Peter tallying sins, those eight vertical lines and the two slits across: *three in, four out; five in, six, out; seven in . . .*

When Vada finally holed out for deca-bogey fifteen, Wyatt extended his hand and said, "You'll get 'em next time, Bubba." Vada stomped to the edge of the green and swung his putter like a carnival mallet, snapping it in half against a sprinkler head. The vibrations ran up his arms and electrified his teeth. He flung the pieces into the lake, one with each hand, Zeus loosing thunderbolts. Then he picked up his golf bag and hurled it in, too, watched it bubble briefly and sink. He was trying to decide whether this made him feel any better (maybe a hint?) when he turned to see Wyatt—selfless, annoying Wyatt—flick off his shoes and dive in.

Afterward, his mother said nothing either to tournament officials or to Vic. This only made Vada's agony worse. He'd subjected Celeste to a humiliation so deep that it made *her* shrink from justice. He'd dragged her into the sludge with him. Mommy's little monster.

And then there was the punishment of being forced at the presentation to stand by Wyatt, the dripping knight, for a photo. In it, Vada appeared to be wringing his modest trophy like a turkey neck, and Wyatt was a cross between Johnny Miller and Aquaman.

It would have been bad enough had Celeste's love for him glowed a bit more wanly from that moment on, but what dimmed in her was more than that. She was a quieter, sadder person, a flickering lantern. And then she got snuffed.

Vada tries never to think about that day, but Wayne crimped that plan by stationing him here in the old cart shed, where he could (where he must) look across the brown pond pocked with rain pellets and see—a spot of white against the backdrop of zoysia, pine bark, and the swamp beyond—that hundred-fifty-yard marker, the slender picket he unplanted fifteen years ago, the stake he drove through his mother's heart.

82

Toshiro from Encino, Malfeasant Flumist, Toting WMD, KO'd by WY, VIP

Back to the cart shed, last November. The rain has keyed up to a squall now, and Vada pulls his chaise back into the bay, out of the roof spray. For a third time he cracks open this morning's newspaper, which an hour ago he found folded on the dash of the pro's yellow Boxster. He nurses the hope that the words will have changed, but destiny never tires of playing her favorites. It's still there, lead headline in sports: YANCEY IS HERO. Below that, LOCAL LINKSMAN NIXES AIR TERROR PLOT.

Wyatt, homeward bound from Asia at the end of his final season, has "tackled a deranged killer" and "wrested away a serrated blade." It happened over Texas, on the last leg of his intercontinental trip. The article mentions the knife's serration twice, quotes a Texas Ranger who notes the "unusual crooked blade, for inflicting maximum damage." But it turns out the "deranged killer," Toshiro from Encino, is a water-park employee under whose watch a child, a black-haired pixie named Ellie Rogers, drowned on a log-flume ride. He was headed to Atlanta to stay with a sister while recovering from his sorrow, and the weapon, one discovers near article's end, was a grapefruit knife he intended to use on himself in the lavatory—a freebie that came with the sack of citrus he was bringing his hosts as a bread-and-butter gift. (The unusual crook at its end? *Damn* the grapefruit for its roundness!)

Toshiro probably smuggled the knife aboard by accident, and interpreted its getting past security as an omen, a nudge from the Reaper. He tried to use the in-flight magazine to distract himself until the crisis abated, but it was near the month's end, and all the puzzles had been filled in. Another deathward nudge, that, and two despairing, puzzleless hours to pass before Atlanta. Which left suicide and Skymall as his only options . . . that is to say, which left suicide as his only option. No doubt having reasoned that killing himself in first class would inconvenience fewer people, or would inconvenience people more deserving of it, Toshiro made his way forward. But in the lavatory, the heartsick flumist chickened out. He pressed his forehead to the mirror, hoping the vibrations would jump-start him to courage. Five minutes passed. Now other passengers waited outside, shifting from foot to foot, and one must have knocked and said something like "Hey, we've got complimentary martinis to offload," thirty seconds later "Come onnnn, guy," finally "We're drowning out here." That last phrase—the voice of dead, bedraggled little Ellie!—so unnerved Toshiro that he yanked back the bolt and hurried out before quite getting the knife reconcealed. Eagle-eyed Wyatt, in the front row, noticed the blade and tackled the poor schlemiel (or schlemiel-san), then sat on his chest until the plane could land at DFW.

The local rewrite guy, embroidering on the wire report, said Wyatt had received an ovation during the descent, and then he puffed it up further: The passengers had sung "God Bless America." To dispel any lingering doubt about the heroism, Rewrite Guy had the "unidentified Texas Ranger" scoff at Toshiro's explanation: "I've seen a Harry Caray knife. That was no Harry Caray knife." No doubt Toshiro—now conclusively identified as dangerous and alien, a non-Cub fan, a non-Bud man—planned to saw open the reinforced cockpit door and halve, section, and sugar the pilots.

Vada feels for Toshiro—like him, underemployed in one of the wetting industries, prone to excesses of grief, and unfortunate enough to stray into the orbit of Wyatt Yancey, Hero. They probably *did* serenade him—or, worse, Wyatt asked his fellow passengers to join him in a chorus to show the evildoers a thing or two in song.

Vada would like to protest the use of "hero" to describe a man who chases a dimpled sphere through meadows for a living, and does so wearing yellow slacks that bear the name of a *citrus-juice company* (the papers have no use for irony). He's prone to dwell on the elements that are obvious fictions. But why bother? No point begrudging a good story; people like good stories. Sure, poor Toshiro's mistake gets punched up to villainy by way of a racist shortcut, and sure, only those who sit in first class have the chance to be heroes, but what else is new?

Besides, how can Vada deny the power of a narrative he himself has been writing for years? It's easy to see Wyatt, after he pinions Toshiro's upper arms with his knees, surrendering the knife (handle-end first, for safety) to a flight attendant and then for the duration of the flight protecting his prisoner from the liquored-up mob of business class. He uses phrases like "fellow citizens" and "proper authorities" to appease them, spreads a lady's sweater over Toshiro's head to spare him their killing glances. He asks the dewy-eyed attendant to ply them with another round of cocktails. His wish is her command.

Easy, too—easier yet—for Vada to put himself in Toshiro's place. He has a mouthful of rivets and buzzing carpet, and his countrymen are baying at him in rage and fear, schoolyard racisms he hasn't heard for years (hey, people: Encino is *in* America). Yet he deserves it, because little Ellie is still dead and will stay dead. Deserves it even more for noticing—wistfulness is an unforgivable sin in a suicide—that the tan cardigan shrouding his head bears the scent of his ex-girlfriend's pillow, which he often laid over his face as he waited for the alarm to go off and summon him to . . . to drown children by daydreaming about things like his girlfriend's aromatic pillow instead of keeping watch. We pay for our failures of attention, and then we pay for our failures of nerve, and now he finds himself pinned by something he'll never get out from under.

83

Vada, Come On, It's Time

On the afternoon in question, with that old vista before him—sheets of rain swept the pond like wiper blades, and the flag at eighteen was snapping, a loose sail—Vada's nostrils clogged, and the hemispheres of his brain itched, and there was that pain behind his eyes that meant the tears had begun.

Wyatt would soak up a hero's hospitality in Dallas for a day, but he was headed here, headed *home,* where he'd resume his fatal proximity. It was over. Whom was Vada kidding? He'd never go back to school. He was already running out of household things to move for cash. The word *friend* had been so devalued that to use it, he had to define it down to a tractor-borne neighbor, now dead, that he used to wave to.

Wind lashed the aluminum, and fat raindrops battered the shed. It was as if Vada was being pelted with range balls fired by boys from every angle. Or a spooky shivaree, everyone he'd ever known standing overhead and pounding a pot to celebrate . . . what?

He not busy living is busy dying. And what did Vada do for a dying? Washed cars. Lied to himself about future plans. Sold off his parents' junk. Acted like some sort of paralytic, like a man pinned to a floor at thirty thousand feet and going nowhere fast. The rain gave way to tiny balls of hail—a million clocks ticking simultaneously. *Come out, give up.*

You're surrounded. This was no epiphany; the world had had every exit covered for as long as he could remember.

He thought back to The Worst Day. When Wyatt hoisted the golf bag onto the bank, water sloshing from its pockets, and climbed up next to it, Vada ignored him, sat hunched on the cattail border and glared at the caps of his shoes. Wyatt had the sense not to press him. He rolled away, and Vada might have stayed there forever, might still be there now, mossed over, grown into a gargoyle-shaped hummock along the bank, had Wyatt not returned fifteen minutes later to summon him for the trophy presentation.

Vada saw his shadow first, blotting the sun behind. Then he heard the sound of joints popping as his friend squatted alongside, felt the faint heat of a knee near his ribs. Had Wyatt clapped a hand on his shoulder and said something blandly soothing, Vada would have dragged him down the verge and pummeled him to death while the ducks quacked encouragement. But Wyatt bypassed the shoulder, spared the clichés. Instead, Vada felt a hand grip his head and nape the way Ms. Gillum had cupped Wyatt's five years before. Wyatt's hand lingered a moment, and then he slid his fingertips to the soft spot below Vada's occipital bone and fluttered them a little, as if playing a chord—a gesture so weirdly tender that it ceased, almost, to be weird. Wyatt stood and issued what amounted to an order, though one spoken gently: "Vada, come on, it's time."

What does the loser do at last, once his exertions are over and his rage spent, once he's done his worst? He has no choice. Reader, come on. It's time.

84

The Hero Accountants of the Apocalypse Crunch Their Aftermaths (Biff, Pow, Nnnfff)

Vada's friend Tisha blew town in late February. Abruptly. That's the way it is with people who *act*, rather than letting impulse be the end of the line. They do things, and then they're done.

Yes, grammarians, "they're" is ambiguous, may indicate that either the things or the doers are done. The point is that *doers* don't care which. Stuck, they make a choice. Not a "fateful" choice. Doers scorn the adjectival. Faced with the end, they behave like hero accountants of the apocalypse. After- is merely another species of math. They act, and their actions have consequences, and then they clap on their eyeshades and crunch the numbers: biff, pow, nnnfff. "Back in your column, infidel integer, or suffer the algebra of justice." Usually they can massage the figures, wriggle free from history's audit. And if not . . . hey, it's there in black and white: "Your number's up. Deal with it."

For doers, the far limit is chapter 11. Chapter 84? Come on. Were Tisha poleaxed to Wyatt's slate floor with organs failing, she wouldn't have lingered long over the math; she'd be dead by now. You'd like her book better. So would Vada.

But only a wee spell to go now—Darla, the last few minutes. And Tisha's the way to Darla. Tisha was the way to Darla.

85

Under's Easier (A Tale from the Age of Shivery)

They became friends at Caw-Caw, where Tisha, soured on academe (her version) or fired for staging an open-mike comedy act that consisted of idiotic lines from student papers (the grapevine's), came to work late last fall. The weather had turned too cold for Buff While You Duff to be profitable, so Vada was back to his old haunts, his old hose.

"Well, Professor," Wayne smirked as he led her into the main bay, "I'mo put you under the toot-lage of Vada here. He prolly can't diagram a sentence like you, but he sure can handle a hose." To illustrate the final phrase, Wayne did his lewd two-hand lariat-pantomime. For a certain kind of despot, masturbation jokes never lose their luster.

As soon as Wayneolini swaggered off to kneecap a rival or whip some train out of its habitual tardiness or ask some other newbie the difference between old W-olini and a jock strap (dictator, dick-toter, haw haw haw), Tisha turned to Vada and rolled her eyes and said, "Fucking Duce-bag."

She was attractive even before she said it. Though barely five feet tall, she seemed to occupy a larger space. Or not larger—sharper. She was like a slide viewed under an electron microscope. She bore a higher resolution than the rest of the world.

Tisha's dominant feature was her nose: long, broader at a spot up the bridge as if broken once—a characteristic that always, for some reason, inclined Vada toward a woman. Was it the hint of past suffering, or of the tendency to stick one's snout into things that Vada would call derring-do? Or maybe he just found the little swell of cartilage sexy. He'd bet the scar tissue would turn colors when she smiled. Tisha's nose was lovely, vaguely dorsal—and, as it cleaved the air, left behind a wake of corkscrew curls parted down the middle.

Tisha was the kind of person whose conversation partners should be lowered in a cage. To talk to you she needed to poke, sniff, palpate. She looked Vada up and down, leaned so close that her curls spent their static charge on his chin. Then she tapped his chest through the coverall, pincer-gripped his upper arm, smiled (sure enough, the little nose-knob went white), and said, "Not that your tutelage isn't perfectly able, but I prefer *over*, not *under*. And my skills should get me by. I've watered Nonnie's flowers, tortured for the CIA—all the usual hose stuff."

Vada was dizzied by her scent, and he wondered how she'd risen high enough to discharge her hair-voltage—Vada's height hasn't entered his story much, but in the glory days of verticality he was six foot one. Patchouli! A woman on tiptoe, or even jumping a little!! But he didn't want to let the exclamation points get the better of him; a third would be fatal.

And there was a clear message in her touch. Even he could recognize it as a way of staving off real flirting by way of the fake. At a glance Tisha had sized him up as the sort of mope who, confronted by a woman with a color-shifting scar and hippie scent and Medusal hair, would shut down. He planted hands in pockets and stammered shoeward. "Er, eh . . ." He was working up to mumbling. Tisha's feet, he noticed, were smaller than his hands; she'd had to triple-fold the bottom hem of her coverall.

"Hey!" she said. "I'm up here. Even my tits are up here. Some lech you are." When Vada lifted his eyes (having closed them so as to prevent any chance of his gaze brushing the aforementioned), Tisha was standing with her head tilted sideways, wearing a thin-lipped but friendly smile. "You *are* a hard case," she said.

Yes. She'd put a name to it. He *was* a hard case, only not in the unreformable-criminal way. Or maybe in the unreformable-criminal way, but for crimes of excessive interiority and fear. Did other people, even in thought, use the phrase "derring-do"? They did not. That's how far Vada was from either daring or do. They were like folktales from another century. He'd entered, early on, an Age of Shivery.

He felt a chill, but was grateful to know that it wasn't infatuation, a nicety he would have missed—*that* quickly he would have been down the funhouse chute and sore in love—had Tisha not pointed it out. Thirty seconds into their acquaintance, she'd put him in her thrall. No surprise there. Yet somehow she'd made clear that it wouldn't be, for once, the kind that made him moon and babble. That hair-zap had carried not the tickle of desire but the serious voltage of a stun gun. This would be a better, a different, thrall. They'd be friends.

"Actually," said Vada, and was shocked at his ease, "under's easier for me."

"Friends, then." And that was that.

86

The Meat Journalist's Chauffeur

In late November and December, the first six weeks of their friendship, they watched a lot of TV at his place. Partly this had to do with Wyatt. Vada was lying low. He didn't want to see the news-channel vans or answer reporters' questions about what it was like to live next door to such a paragon. He couldn't stand to hear the hero's story embellished just that one iota more with every telling.

But it's Tisha he was talking about, it's Tisha Vada wants to be thinking about. If a woman's car is parked in your driveway at all hours, people make assumptions, and those assumptions can turn out useful if you're hoping to discourage—repel—visits from an old friend newly home.

For her part, Tisha loved having a sidekick. Also physical therapist, sounding board, errand boy, straight man. The TV phase could have gone on forever, as far as Vada was concerned. He didn't mind the massages. Tisha's feet were minuscule and pretty; so many bones, and every one sharp, in need of kneading. It was nice to adjust his shopping, too, to the needs of another: to buy the cucumber-melon lotion Tisha favored, her citrus-infused Swedish rum, to cater to her hunger for novelty with ventures into exotic snacks: barbecue-flavored corn nuts, all manner of things embedded in olives or encrusted in wasabi, even chocolate-dipped crickets. It was pleasant, too, to imagine the neighbors' mistaken perceptions.

Her car in the drive, day after day—it made him seem, for the first time, sort of formidable. An adult. A player. Wyatt kept his distance.

And the TV? For Vada the couch wasn't lark but lifestyle. Outré snacks and flavored rum and *My Mother the Car* were plenty to get by on; they had to be. But Tisha had that rare adventurousness that's unslakable by snack foods, no matter how weird. It was fate, he supposes, that she'd draft him to be her henchman—like those poor goons in leopard-print tunics who attend Catwoman and have to maintain a macho air despite felt ears on their caps and the fact that every line they speak has the word *cat* in it. Tisha sat still for weeks of *Mannix, Mission: Impossible,* even *Barnaby Jones.* But Jerry Van Dyke being carped at by his mother, who's been reincarnated as a '20s jalopy? That was too far. She didn't care how many goddamn channels he had; they were going *out.*

Once the gates opened, she could barely go a week without a new hobby. First they dragged out a field guide and catalogued the birds in the cove: bald eagle, blue heron, coot, wood duck, bufflehead—also something they identified as a plover before they learned that plovers disdain the sub-Arctic. After Vada told her about the World War II bomber runs, they putted around the lake in Reid Yancey's skiff, hauling a metal detector Tisha had bought at a pawnshop, to sweep uninhabited islands for ordnance. Then Tisha stepped it up, started dressing her biddable boy in thrift-store costumes and false identities. Spirit gum appeared in his medicine cabinet, and pancake makeup. She put him in an old-style cravat and dragged him to watch paddle tennis in Aiken. She posed as a meat journalist—the kind of meat journalist who wears Jackie O glasses and employs a driver—and wangled their way into a Vienna sausage factory in hog country. Journalists, any one of whom could turn out to be an Upton Sinclair, are usually barred from the floor, but Tisha's internet research and her flattery of the plant manager won them entry into every nose-stinging corner.

They accepted a beachfront-timeshare vacation, and after a free night's lodging she got them kicked off the tour that was its price by means of some slapstick involving colostomy bags. In his yard they planted collards and heirloom squash, for the sake of old times neither of them had ever had. They smoked a lot of dope. Did he mention that already? Sorry, he must have spaced.

"Girlhood is played out," Tisha said one day. "I'm tired of the whole girl paradigm. So I'm trying something else for a change. You're my running buddy, Vada. What do running buddies do, besides get high and shoot the shit and fire guns at road signs? Want to have a belching contest?"

"Men don't really have those."

"How would you know?"

"Point taken."

"Just for once, Vada, I'd like to see the point not taken. If I dump the girl paradigm, you don't get to hang onto it."

She was always hatching schemes, like her idea for a series of detective novels set in a doughnut shop, the shamus-hero a baker by trade. "Bakers are up in the violent part of the night," she said, "in bad neighborhoods, and the job's lonely and hot. You're like to get brown lung and cynicism, which a detective needs. Marx called bakers 'white miners,' which would still be a good line if you didn't have to stop and explain that he's talking about flour and not making a racial remark. Plus so much flour now is whole wheat. That's what brought down Marxism: the failure to anticipate. Of course, if he'd called them 'floury miners' that would have posed its own problems. Damn homophones. No one ever said fomenting revolution was easy."

"No," said Vada, when it became apparent that a word was required of him.

"I think I'll call the first book *A Cruller Twist of Fate*."

"That's awesome," said Vada. "I get it."

"No you don't," said Tisha. "Not if you think it's awesome."

87

Baker's Man

At first Vada enjoyed their adventures. They were a team, no matter how small his contribution. He marveled at how Tisha could flirt, gab, or bluster her way through anything. But wasn't there cruelty in these games, too? Vada knows this marks him as an incorrigible pussy, but hey, he's an incorrigible pussy. What about the sausage foreman who'd gone to the trouble of having aprons embroidered with the VIPs' fake names? He'd wait in vain for the article about his hock-trimming innovations to appear in *Hogs Today*—seemed already to suspect that he'd stay unsung when he escorted meat journalist Letitia Marble and her chauffeur to a . . . Ford Festiva with its tailpipe tied on with a scrap of water-ski rope? Vada even felt sorry for Giles the timeshare-seller, who'd after all tried to be compassionate, had comped them a double roll of paper towels for the road. Some people wore the kind of colostomy bags that weren't filled with tea leaves and fruit pulp—why tempt the gods who might, if you think it's so funny, flip a switch and unbenign those polyps that make you bleed and strain from time to time?

Vada was glad when, after the new year, they were driven back to the TV room on the heels of a prank that involved trapping a raccoon and taking it to a groomer for a flea dip. This misadventure ended with cops being called, Vada fleeing the scene on foot, and a solemn young paramedic shining a penlight in Tisha's eyes and asking over and again whether she believed this to be, in fact, an animal of the species dog. The guy kept saying it just that way, and every time he paused and said "in fact," Tisha roared, she told Vada later. Her laughter and bloodshot eyes and the wreckage of three boxes of Dunkin' Stix in her car seemed to make the cop's antennae quiver, and he'd have found her stash except that, well, a policeman's diligence extends only so far: When hissing and baring its teeth had no effect, the raccoon, in its cage on her backseat for the drive, had shat (perhaps this was divine revenge for the colostomy-bag incident—the Lord, like a raccoon bowel, moving in mysterious ways).

So they were on the shit list for free vacations now, and sick of disinterring not '40s bombs but '60s beer cans from campfire ruins on islands . . . and whatever that deceptively ploverlike thing was, it wasn't in the damn book. They'd reached the limits of public tolerance, of their meager finances, perhaps even of Tisha's imagination.

Cable it would have to be. Vada was glad—no collateral damage that way, no disguises. But wasting her life in front of the tube wasn't for Tisha. She cut back her visits from three or four a week to two, then one. And when, despite all the deodorizing firepower available at Caw-Caw, the raccoon reek proved irremovable, she traded in the Festiva for a 1980 Impala and started spending her time souping it up.

Shadetree mechanic's aide wasn't a role Vada could play—not that she asked. His flight from the groomer's had been the beginning of the end, he knew. When she picked him up an hour later, loping home along the route where years before he'd collected pull tabs, Tisha was philosophical. "What did I expect? That. I *hoped* for more. But what sense does it make to be mad at you for being who you are?"

Vada said, "Thanks?"

Two weeks later, at work, Vada tapped Tisha on the shoulder and asked whether her gumshoe baker might, in the novels, have an apprentice: "You know, like, to save on soliloquies. Maybe beat dough, too." He was joshing, he swears. It was supposed to be a *parody* of pathetic.

Tisha made a little moue, like Letitia Marble sampling bad sausage. "My baker never met the dough she couldn't beat herself. She can handle her own pastry tube, too. No Hose Associate needed. Don't do this, Vada."

"Maybe just a running buddy, or a neighbor she hangs with?"

Now she lost her temper. "You don't see me actually writing books, do you? No, you see me spritzing dashboards and tucking cellophane bags of candy into cupholders. A few months ago I got fired from a job I actually cared about; now I have to take my lumps for a while. And I am. My fingers stink day and night of orange-blossom spray, and I get ordered around by the only moron on Earth you can call a fascist and mean it literally. So yeah, I have steam to blow off. Yeah, I pull some pranks for shits and giggles. Soon I'll get disgusted enough with myself and/or the world to break the cycle. That's the point. But you—the reason you take it so seriously, like what we're doing isn't just fucking around? You've turned pro. This is your life. When you say you're fucking around, you're *not fucking around.*

"I thought you were hiding the edgy, angry you behind this ironic mask, but it's the irony that's fake. You're like a Jehovah's Witness who goes door to door proclaiming the one great truth, and the one great truth is how helpless you are. Which nobody wants to hear, least of all if it's *true.* Twenty-nine years old, and you've packed it in. Vada, aren't you sick of your life? Isn't there something, or someone, that you'd be willing to change it for?"

But I could crimp a mean cruller, thought Vada. *Can't you just think about it?*

Did keeping these thoughts to himself count as nadir's new nadir, or was it progress? Was Tisha right? Did self-loathing have a bottom, and if you found it you could propel yourself back toward the surface?

"I'm sorry," Vada said.

Tisha grimaced. "That's just it. For once, you need to be unsorry. Please."

88

Dorito Ergo Sum

So on a February Friday, after weeks of seeing her only in passing, Vada was taken aback when Tisha sought him out and volunteered to come over on Sunday.

"For TV?"

"Sure," she said, and that long nose swung downward like a dowsing rod. "TV." When she turned away, Vada saw that she was wearing her hair in a loose bun held by a yellow pencil. He wished he had some way of filling her with the irresistible impulse to write something down. But it was, he knew, too late to say "I'm unsorry."

In the listings, Vada was pleased to find a *Dark Shadows* marathon. A good omen. The Saturday of Thanksgiving weekend they'd watched one together, he and Tisha, a makeshift American family: Vada stretched on the floor (he'd just sold the couch), she in his father's lounger (soon to go) behind him, snacks on the ottoman (a part of the empire he would never part with). No football, no turkey. Traditions were for the lazy, the convention-bound.

When his parents were alive, that Saturday would have been the day the three of them drove to the tree farm and alternated swings with an old red axe, Celeste having rejected Vic's chainsaw as insufficiently Currier & Ives for this purpose. When Vada's turn came, his mom always backed up a few steps and could be seen in his peripheral vision with fingers crossed, like a superstitious schoolgirl. Scared, yes, but tradition meant letting your son have his whacks; the backing-away was to keep him from becoming an accidental Lizzie Borden. Vada had loved the way aromatic shards collected around the trunk, and Mom always brought a plaid thermos of cider.

Those days were gone—but maybe here was a *new* holiday tradition, every bit as good. *Dark Shadows* had axes, too, and one didn't rub finger blisters by sitting on a couch. Plus no Perry Como Christmas tape on the drive home. *This* was his new idea of community: sitting before the tube with another eremite, a fellow traveler of the idea that traveling is useless and leads only to foreign ruin rather than the perfectly good ruin that awaits you at home. Vada liked world-weary wit as much as the next person, but he liked it best when he didn't have to bother with earning it by going out into the world and getting scuffed up. The world can weary a person just by being out there, right?

As they'd marveled at Barnabas Collins's mighty cool and committed suicide by nacho chip, they talked less and less, fell into a fairy-tale stupor. Before long the only sound was the TV. Fifteen minutes of silence, half an hour, longer. It was comfortable, comforting. The quiet piled up like slivers of pulpwood. They were chopping away at something. Eventually it would fall, and they could tie it to the top of the car and drag it home and rally round it for a while. Finally, during a commercial in the marathon's fourth hour, it happened—the crack of timber.

Or crackle of chip. The voice came from above and behind him. "Dorito ergo sum," said Tisha.

At the time this seemed to Vada the rare perfect moment in a life. Her tone conveyed, Sure, we're losers, but not so much that we can't get off a pretty good one about our loserdom, a pretty good one with a tinge of defiance and also a minor-key bitterness that the world has let potential like ours go to waste. But contentment, too: it's *fun* to watch Barnabas chew scenery and say things like "Listen! Time, howling, withering with its relentless blast!" Dialogue like that makes time's relentless blast seem a little less withering and howling. Irony's not the bad guy everyone makes it out to be. It can damp a sting.

This seemed the closest Vada might ever get to domestic bliss, and he'd been determined not to ruin it. He didn't ooh and ahh, didn't repeat her line and tell her how good it was and ransack the kitchen for a pencil so he could write it down to tell at work come Monday. Instead he summoned a Barnabas-like self-possession, and without pulling his eyes from the screen, he'd done his part, delivered his performance of Solidarity's Haggard Laugh. He reached up and tweezered a last few ontological crumbs from the bowl. Sure, his stomach hurt from chip-glut, and a sandwich of leftover turkey would've hit the spot now, warm cider too (whatever happened to that plaid thermos?), but the show must go on.

"Mmm-*mmm*," he said.

89

That Little Tricorn Glow

The February visit, of course, was good-bye. He knew it as soon as he ushered Tisha into the TV room. To be honest, he'd known it already on Friday. Or even a week before, when Tisha showed at Caw-Caw with her new car painted black and bloody fangs spanning the hood. Vada had to hear the name from a Goth nitwit named Casper, a waxer with a diaper pin through his nose. "She calls it Vlad the Impala, dude. You copy?"

Days of silence. The Number Two bun. Her cleverness expended elsewhere. Vada copied, all right.

Now, seeing the recliner gone and the Persian rug rolled up in the corner, Tisha winced. She tugged one of the corkscrews at her temple and perched, stiffly, on the ottoman. The room smelled stale, and the orange of the Doritos in their bowl (a sentimental touch) looked obscene. Vada noticed that the curtain was snagged on a table leg and admitting a triangle of winter sun, like a page crimped to keep a reader's place. Tisha's eyes locked on that little tricorn glow. This room, its ceiling grease-splotched like the lid of a pizza box, the floor strewn with pillows sporting Celeste's favorite Franklinisms ("Plough deep while sluggards sleep"), was his place. That triangle of sun was hers.

Vada picked up the remote, aimed it. Tisha snared his eyes, spoke before he could pull them loose. "Please," she said. "You know why I'm here."

90

Aubergine Trebuchet

She spoke for several minutes straight. Vada can only try to piece together what she said. He was preoccupied, gazing at his remote and wondering what percentage of its buttons he'd ever used or ever would. Even the things you think you know best, the things you should know best after all these years, you don't. Meanwhile, Tisha talked.

"I'm out of here. Out-of-Dodge out of here. I'm moving to Charlotte to teach SAT prep. Also to pursue autocross. Charlotte's the big leagues. There's this promoter up there who's Junior Johnson's nephew, and he says Auto-X is the Nascar of Generation Y. Anyway, I wanted to come over so I could say in person: You should get out, too. Look at this place—it's a crypt, and cryptier by the minute. It won't make your parents any deader if you leave, and it might make you LESS dead. Are you even listening?"

Vada awoke from his fugue state to find her gone. He heard the door slam, rushed to catch her. Had she . . . maybe she'd been saying he should come along to Charlotte with her? Did they have co-pilots in autocross?

When he got to the carport, though, she wasn't peeling rubber. She didn't have to show off her auto-x skills by swerving around Vada to escape. She was standing at the driver's door of Vlad the Impala, looking at a mangled purple oblong thing twenty feet behind the car. "What the hell?" she asked.

Answer came in the form of Wyatt's golf cart bumping through the trees. "Are you all right!?" shouted the incomparably beautiful passenger.

"Isn't that the new weather minx?" asked Tisha expositorily. "From TV?"

"Thank God you're OK!" said the new weather minx. What compassion she had!

"Sorry about that," said Wyatt when he climbed out. "It was such a pretty day for winter, so I surprised Darla here with a catapult . . ."

"Trebuchet," corrected Darla. "The story makes no sense unless you say 'trebuchet.'"

"It won't make *sense* either way," Wyatt said. Petulantly, as both Vada and Darla noticed. Their eyes locked, their minds melded, their souls commingled. Was Wyatt looking a little doughy? Their four locked eyes and two commingled souls were unanimous—he was. "But sure, OK, a trebuchet. Darla here was telling me about a report she did in broadcast school about pumpkin-chucking, and I thought it'd be fun to try. We ran out of pumpkins in about ten minutes, so Darla raided the crisper, and eggplant seemed like our best bet."

"Aubergine!" corrected Darla. "It's not an eggplant catapult. It's an aubergine trebuchet."

Vada loved her. How could he not?

"Right," said Wyatt. "But eggplants are too light, or I must have loaded it wrong, and *somebody* didn't forecast gusty winds this afternoon, and . . . anyway, we're glad nobody was hurt. Pardon me, ma'am—we haven't been introduced." He cut a reproachful glance at Vada. "I'm Wyatt Yancey. This is Darla Dietz."

"Bitchin' wheels, ma'am," said Darla. She was wearing a German barmaid getup—a white shift with lace at the neck, but superimposed over it a tight black cuirassy thing, a corset bristling with strings. Warring impulses of purity and sultriness, with the right side winning. "And I'm glad I didn't cause them any harm. My mama always said that if you're going to fire vegetables from a medieval weapon, you should choose the vegetables based on aerodynamics, not rhyming. Hey—are we interrupting something? Wyatt, I think we're interrupting something. Anyway, sorry. Hope we'll see you two soon. Maybe we could all have dinner together, to make it up?"

"So much for eggplant parmesan," said Wyatt. "But we could order pizza."

"Hush," said Darla. She turned back to Vada and Tisha. "Really. Just give us a call. We don't know any other couples out here."

They smiled, hopped back in, and drove off, leaving Vada and Tisha in silence. Vada watched the cart rattle across his lawn and up the slope, then slip into the pines.

"I know you won't listen," said Tisha, "but remember I said this. That woman. You are doomed. Leave this place NOW."

Vada snapped his head around just in time to see Tisha's head disappear and hear the door cronk shut—1980s Detroit took a backseat to *no one* when it came to satisfying sounds of closure. And she was gone.

91

Busman's Holiday

Right you are. Vada lied. How did you figure it out?

Yes, Tisha came over, told him she was leaving, warned him to leave too, rushed out while he fiddled with the remote. Yes, he chased her, too late—she *was* peeling out when he got there. The car was agile, all right, and its agility under perfect command. Those broad taillights stayed dark as she squirreled out of the drive. No hint of brake.

The rest he made up.

What gave it away? Did the catapult make it seem too meet-cute? Was it the St. Pauli Girl getup? Maybe you knew that Vada's eyesight isn't good enough to let him see, at a hundred yards, that Darla's beauty was *incomparable*. Was it the crack about Wyatt looking doughy?

Or most likely it's because you, sagacious reader, recalled that he's already catalogued his exhibition's Objet #1, and you knew that it *wasn't* a pulped eggplant scraped from the driveway that afternoon by a Vada who was, thanks to Tisha, in full and helpless knowledge of his fate.

Vada can testify to the corrupting power of narrative. He half-believes his own lie, even now can hear the scrape of his father's flat shovel as he collected the nonexistent eggplant in a nonexistent freezer bag. And, false memory within false memory, he can see himself afterward—the aubergine stowed in the freezer behind his cookie-dough billyclub—hosing the spot it had occupied in the driveway, his thumb expertly regulating the spray.

Lies within lies. Busman's holiday.

92

Five Snapshots

Love Makes a Hash of Our Metaphors

Early March. Vada goes to borrow tinfoil from Wyatt. Trying to heed Tisha's advice to change his life (and also to economize, the property tax assessment having jumped again), he's decided to forgo cable for a month. He's returning to the old days of rabbit ears with foil pennants, a semaphore Vic was once master of.

He knocks. About thirty seconds from now, Vada will redevelop an interest in perfect reception of local channels, and before an hour has passed, he'll have canceled his cancellation. The tinfoil will never be used, or will be used only in the usual Vada way. There's a dingy, compacted square of silver in his wallet right now, souvenir of a landmark night, soon to baffle the paramedics—and then his old pal Ghoulie the Cricketer, who might tell everyone he had a stiff in his drawer the other day who carried a charm to ward off green men and their brain-controlling rays, at least to ward them off from a wallet-sized block of one butt cheek that must have seemed especially vulnerable to the brain-controlling rays of green men. When you're dead young and by freakish means, people have to reassure themselves that you're not like them. Your eccentricities get promoted up the line to barking madnesses. You pass into fiction.

Wyatt answers the door, ushers Vada into the kitchen, and introduces him to the beauty sitting on the butcher's block, swinging her legs.

Heathery skirt. Hollows beside her kneecaps. Tiny translucent socks like the disposable ones at shoe stores. She looks like an innocent about to submit to some horrific medical exam. She doesn't know what she's in for. "Darla, Vada. Vada, Darla."

"I've heard so much about you," says Darla. "Pleasure."

Vada lashes himself to the mast of the errand at hand. "Tinfoil," he says. "Got any? Borrow? Oh, yes, pleasure meet you too."

"Is game?" laughs Darla. "Talk like telegram? Jane play too."

The phone bleats. "Gotta take this," says Wyatt. "I've got a line on a javelina hunt in west Texas. *Bow* hunt," he says to Darla as he darts into the next room. "So it's fair."

Darla turns to Vada and says, "*Fair.* Seen any rich javelinas flying east to double-lung a golfer from twenty-five yards?"

Vada puts his head back down. "None. Right. Yes."

"Oh, sorry. Forgot game. What foil for? Leftovers? Voices in head?"

Back in Vada's lie, Tisha had been right. It was the TV prognostica-trix, the one with tied-back hair and scrimshaw collarbones who said "thunderboomers" and "frog-stranglers." When she promised "your forecast for the weekend," "you" sounded singular.

Vada pulled it together enough to ask how she liked her new job, and Darla, in Columbia for only a few weeks then, began rip-ping her producer. This was a woman with no use for coyness. Her eyes stayed levelly on his—at least that's what it felt like, his eyes having fled south as usual. It was exhilarating. There was nothing but meanness in her, but it was superficial; there was no *meanness* in her, none of the bitter furtiveness he recognized in himself. She seemed Vada's photographic negative: light where he was dark, dark where he was light. Her raillery wasn't meek and aggrieved but fero-cious and playful. And she was funny. Often it's said that someone's wit is rapierlike, and hers had that quality—but after she'd let you know how curt the blade might be, she would touch it to your shoul-der, blunt end first, tenderly, like an accolade. Talking to her was like being knighted. It was like being knighted by a schoolgirl about to undergo a gyno exam on a butcher block. Love makes a hash of our metaphors.

By the time Wyatt returned and fished out a flashing silver baton—"Here, Vada. Take the roll. I seem to have lost the box, but it'll tear just fine"—Vada was done for.

The snapshot, though, takes place before Wyatt interrupts. Only two people are in it. Her legs are swinging in rhythm, like an abattoir's rotating knives, and she's carving, carving: "It's my luck that the noon producer is sleeping with the world's dimmest intern. She's from *Highlights* magazine by way of Up with People. Not brains enough to grease a saucepan. Every time she speaks, Bruce breaks out in winces and hives, but she's twenty-two and pretty, in a bowhead moron way, and he's her 'mentor' . . ."

The socks flash, the teeth too. In the photo, foreshortening makes him look like he's at her feet, Sir Lanceseldom in Love, basking in the mordancy she keeps hidden beneath the dangly earrings and pastel blazers.

A Man Called Intrepid

Two weeks later. Vada's reading the paper at the bagel shop downtown when a shadow looms over the sports page. "You're brave to risk sesame," says Darla. "You could go all day with a seed on your face. Or choke. Good to see you taking risks." Then she's gone, rattling her bag as a wave good-bye, but not before she lets her fingers—at least two, possibly three—brush his shoulder.

But wait, back up a minute. Take the shot . . . *now,* at the moment of first contact. Count fingers with him. That's three for sure.

He was brave, ten minutes later, to stand up without support.

Learn the Litterbox

April now. Darla has asked Vada to bring in mail and feed the kitten while they're in Provence, and he's come over for a morning tutorial. Darla has run through feeding procedures, shown him where supplies are, given emergency numbers. Now she points toward the stairs. "Got to learn the litterbox," she says.

Vada's feeling great, alone here with her in the sunny kitchen, glow of cobalt bottles lined along the windowsill, view of clenched calf when she used a stepstool to reach a cabinet. "I already know," he says.

"Let me just show you where it is."

"I'm trained already. Squat in a corner, scratch it in. Or scrape up a pile of grass and mark it like a puma. I was a vet student, you know. I can pee like *lots* of animals."

Darla smiles. "Aren't *you* giddy today? New girlfriend to tell me about?" Vada says nothing.

"Come on," says Darla after a second. "The box is in the trophy room. Wanted a live animal in there to scare Wyatt straight. Maybe Telltale— that's his name, Telltale, and Wyatt pretends not to get it—maybe Telltale will resurrect some peers and get them to eat us in our sleep. Serve us right. Him, anyway. I hope they'll decide I don't deserve eating." She beckons him down the hall.

Vigilant photographer, SNAP NOW! She's looking over her shoulder. The raised hand, index finger uppermost. Neck tendons flexed above the collar of a ratty Dartmouth sweatshirt, split at every seam. Parachute shorts. Tennis shoes, no socks.

"I know he's in there somewhere," she says as he follows her down the hall. "Hiding. As a former vet student, you'll recognize him right off. He'll be the only one that's blinking. I hope."

Telltale!

May 1. Darla on air, against the green screen, tracing a map that's not really there. Vada feels, every time, a proprietary flush. But this day, when they zoom in on her face, Vada spies a wisp of tabby fur riding the lapel of her red suit. *I know that cat,* he almost says aloud. *I know that lapel. I know that woman.* It's like being privy to a magician's secrets. If he were there, he'd palm the fiber, brush the lapel, cup her chin.

This, thinks Vada, is intimacy. *Finally.*

Sitting on Something Too Deep for You

Mid-May. Nearing dusk, Vada's deck. Wyatt is away, and Darla—"Tired of flying solo, so let's fly solo together"—has invited herself over for a drink. They lounge side by side on chaises made of rubber belts. Darla's chairback is let out all the way to horizontal, and she seems serene as an odalisque. She rests on an elbow, and her other hand holds one of the beers she's brought. She encircles the bottle's mouth with thumb and forefinger and stretches her other fingers—like someone making the A-OK sign, or the way rude boys used to make the vagina when they were pantomiming sex. Vada, meanwhile (or therefore), has his chaise-back almost vertical. His legs—stretched straight in front—remind him of what it was like, as a boy, to sit on something too deep for you. He's already been up twice: to fetch her a second bottle, to bring out snacks (*classy* ones—florets of raw cauliflower, shaven-down carrots the size of finger joints).

For twenty minutes Darla has been enumerating another day's worth of the world's follies, TV-newsroom subcategory, as they look over the lake. The vista is calm but for a few dopplery ski-boats in the distance and two flop-hatted oldsters fishing in the cove—or not so much fishing as biding there so that every ten minutes they can awaken from a coma of bobbing corks and hurl country insults audible across the water ("Great Caesar's ghost!" "Mother Hubbard, lad!") at Donny, the sun-bronzed teen menace who keeps buzzing them with his JetSki. Vada has the idea that all three of them are having fun. The fishermen need Donny, snake in their garden, fly in their ointment—handy emblem of the disrespectful generation coming of age—and Donny, well, Donny needs coots to wet. They shake their fists, actually shake their fists in unison, bow and stern. Donny, meanwhile, swerves hard, accelerates, and drops onto their heads his rooster-tail of splash—oh, those young men and their high-arcing streams. Donny bounces over his own wake, heads for one last circuit of the cove before dark. The old guys settle in for another few minutes of lure-watching and curse-marshalling.

And the battle of brash boy and fogeys illustrates what Darla's saying now, what she's been teaching him ever since he met her: *Confrontations are not all bad.* The old guys may have been pissed on figuratively, but they don't mind. A little dampening never hurt anybody, especially in this heat. And maybe they comfort themselves with the thought that Donny, too, will eventually face the wince and trickle of age . . . but there's no ill will in it. Let the young pee freely while they may.

Meanwhile Vada watches Darla's lips purse for a swig. Enjoy this while it lasts, he urges himself; dark will come soon. When did she take her shoes off? Click of bottle on wood, then the monologue recommences. She's carving up her boss, the Chief Meteorologist. "Every night he gives a shout-out to the wife: 'Mrs. Lamont's gonna need a light sweater for yoga tonight. Namaste, honey.' Meanwhile he's boning the intern-of-the-month, and they caught him two years ago in a whore-house raid in Cayce; he was cowering in a closet, wearing Pampers. A *specialty* client. Today after my noon broadcast, Bill comes to offer tips. He pats me, and his hand slips off my shoulder and onto my butt. So I say, 'Bill, Wyatt and I are thinking of having kids soon, and I'm won-dering: cloth or plastic? What do *you* think?'"

How is it possible to be this guiltlessly, cheerfully cruel? And to have it not ruin your beauty but deepen it? Darla is teaching him that fric-tion can be a kind of affection. Not until these last months, first with Tisha and then with Darla, did it ever occur to Vada that his over-the-top amity might not be what he's always imagined. Is he not a nice guy whom the fates failed . . . but a cold fish?

Vada has sometimes suspected this when he listens to high-lonesome ballads in his car and weeps and has to choke back a sort of ecstasy. *Look,* he tells himself, *there it is—profound human emotion. Look what you're miss-ing, people!* But he can't help noticing that he spends all that emotion on himself alone and next morning presents to the world the same smooth mask as always. Where are the sobs of last night, when he sat idling in the carport, watching exhaust dissipate in the rearview, while "Down in the Dumped" played at top volume? "I'm down in the dumped / My stomach needs pumped / I'm full up with poisonous youuuuuuu."

Now, for nearly the first time, it's contact he craves, rather than soli-tary weeping over missed contact. That's Darla, on a chaise not eighteen inches away. Her lips are still bee-stung from having rubbed off the "warpaint" she wears at work. He can see her chin quiver when she sips. Vada jerks his head sideways and kisses her . . . or as she bobs down to grab her bottle, he bumps the top of her head with his lips.

Snap! Hurry. It's only an instant. In photography, timing is everything.

The next second, he's lapsed back into his chair and staring water-ward. Fool. Rat. Donny's nowhere to be seen. These oldsters don't merit a last pass after all; somewhere there are girls to spray. He hears Darla sip slowly, calmly, hears the sound of an empty hitting the deck.

"That was sweet, Vada," she says. "But please don't do that again."

He understands. He takes it back. But by then the snapshot is safely in the book.

93

A Dental Irony

Vada has no idea what Wyatt's business deals are, besides lucrative. The image in his mind's eye is of his friend in top hat and monocle, like the Monopoly guy, jetting about to pick up canvas sacks with dollar signs stenciled on them, then heading into the field, having shed monocle for binocle and top hat for camo vest, to stalk the prairie chicken or the mastodon. But he's grateful, because ever since Apocalypse Night, Wyatt's toings-and-froings have given Darla and Vada time together— to run errands, walk the woods, work the crossword, swim across the cove to Weed's Landing for foot-long sleeves of Tom's hot peanuts. They've grown close.

Wyatt has encouraged the friendship between fiancée and "oldest pal." It's a patronage Vada half exults in (motive plus opportunity are supposed, eventually, to add up to *crime,* and the spree was set to begin today) and half resents (because it implies he's not a fit rival). Wyatt sees him as the eunuch neighbor from every sitcom, a goofball named Lunky, Bama, Pooh. And is right, as usual. You see where this should be leading, reader—only you know it's not leading there, but instead *here,* to Vada trapped and leaking beneath a quondam bear.

But back to the days of hope and glory. Since Darla moved in with her betrothed, Vada has dropped in for coffee most mornings when Wyatt's away. They often take it in the humongous trophy room Wyatt added when he came home, a hall done up in club leather and dark wood and used to display the fruits of the hunt. At first, Darla told Vada, she'd been puzzled but amused: Boys will be boys, she reasoned, and rich boys will be boys on a grand scale. Her only protest was to slosh, saucerless, in a sanctum where liquids were forbidden.

But more and more the room distressed her. All those eyes, for one thing—even the crocodile's seemed doelike. Worse than the animal cruelty, though—and she'd learned not to use those two words together, lest she endure a lecture about the steward's huntership of the earth, blah blah—was her gradual realization of just how far Wyatt's lunacy extended. He'd already told her he couldn't go to New York with her to see the Christmas lights because Yule and Duck share a season, and he'd be out by dawn every morning. The hall table was piled with gunsmith magazines and two-hundred-dollar penlights and calendars from the half-dozen dove clubs he'd joined. Worst of all, after dinner he'd walk her through the trophy room while providing commentary: "Look at those tendons, love. Only an artist can do musculature like that." Once, when she asked whether he'd love her always, he kept his eye on his taxidermy magazine and said, "If that spot on the okapi is bacterial hair slip, it's done for."

Darla's *hombre obsesionado* had hired a Salvadoran cleaning woman to come every Tuesday, and he provided a list of instructions translated into pidgin Spanish. The gist of "Groom with an old toothbrush and a blow dryer set to gentle" came through, except that the idea's being so *chiflado* made Señora Estorino assume it had been mangled and ask Darla's help in translation. There was this baffler: "Use only a humid rag, and clean with the corn of the skin." And then, in big red letters at the bottom, NUNCO VACUUMO. For the wall-mounts, Wyatt equipped her with a special eight-foot feather-duster attachment not unlike the angled pole Vada uses to change the specials on Caw-Caw's marquee. Every week the señora Q-tips all eyes with Windex, and she has a palette of ten polishes to brush onto fur as needed. She examines all mounts for evidence of insects, and any breaches or stretchings she repairs with putty and surgical thread. She replaces the low-heat spotlight bulbs, monitors the air-filtration and climate-control systems.

Yes, Wyatt can afford this, and it's his house after all, and it's not like Darla's *jealous* of what she once, on a bad day, called "Wyatt's *other* mounts." She's not the bossy type, she tells Vada, and never intended to move in and start issuing ultimatums. But Darla heard a crash one evening and rushed to find her beloved on the slate floor, beside a toppled stepladder from which he'd been straining to reach the boar's tusks. In his hands, tooth-whitening strips. For once, God showed himself on the side of good, and demonstrated a command of dental irony: In his fall, Jack sustained a broken crown.

Darla's laid down the law. Wyatt's days of footloose head-gathering are over. If the doors stay closed, she'll consent to Wyatt keeping his current menagerie, but he can add nothing new. She'll not be crowded out of her own house—and if he doesn't want it to be her house, then better for all concerned if she learns now instead of later—by deceased things with blank eyes and no-wax shines . . . and he's not allowed to give them better dental care than he gives himself.

Encouraged, Vada pressed on with his plans for a trophy room of his own, into which Jill might come tumbling after.

94

What True Love Looks Like

First task was to clear and clean the aluminum barn Vic had put in to provide extra storage, and then to refill it. It started as a joke, yet this he took further than most of his stillborn whims, spending a hundred hours over the last two months crashing around the basement, rifling chests and closets, choosing card stock, and finally even (take that, Vic) more or less successfully installing track lighting. Eventually, Darla's seeing the trove started to seem inescapable. Here was mission-creep in action. If you build it, she will come. OK, if you build it and then drag her over here, she will come. Someone has to *enforce* the decrees of fate, but that doesn't make them your decrees rather than fate's.

Yes, he foresaw the outcome. He'd find himself estranged for good from Darla and Wyatt and home and history, a laughingstock, forced to move far away. This was his way of learning from Tisha. He'd get himself fired from love, drummed out of the human race. Then he'd torch the barn and split, and try not to think of himself as wimpy Tony Franciosa in *Long Hot Summer*.

So, today, with Wyatt supposedly away, he arranged to show Darla the shrine he's built, show her at last what True Love looks like. If she melted into his arms and whispered "Hold me," he'd be the happiest man alive. More to the point, if—*when*—she covered her nose and half-turned to spare his feelings before honking out her guffaws, he would at least be forced to *do* something.

95

Pièce de Vichy

Six minutes to go. Five and three-quarters (oof), five and a half (yeowch). As the golf tumbrel bounces over rough ground toward Wyatt's driveway, Vada grits his teeth, hangs on to the roof support, and puzzles.

No he doesn't. *A grizzly to move?* Wyatt is as figurative as tree bark. He means what he says. *That's* why he's home in stealth. He plans to smuggle one last trophy through those oaken double doors before marriage slams them shut and paints them white. Darla has "negotiated a compromise." Wyatt will be allowed to hunt, but only for animals he's willing to eat. To offset that indulgence, he has to sell the two game freezers in his garage and pitch out the exotic meats he's saved to preserve his illusion that he's a sportsman rather than a carcass collector. A sportsman, Darla says, is a carcass collector who can afford big freezers, plus a few bucks a month for the juice to keep them going. Wyatt doesn't *like* wild game. He's a steak and chicken guy, but God has seen fit to make beef unfleet and poultry flightless, and furthermore to stack them in cages or cram them in pens on corporate farms, which crimps the thrill of the chase.

So long as the meat stays in the freezer, Darla says, Wyatt doesn't have to confront his moral culpability. He assures himself that in some alternate world, some subjunctive mood, if the circumstances were right, he might eat his kills.

"Moral culpability?" asks Vada. "Did you *say* that?"

"Like one day he might salt and cure his reindeer into jerky. Or make Brunswick stew out of flying squirrel."

"But 'moral culpability'? Really?" It's a phrase that would make Wyatt draw up to his full height in fury. For every syllable you can bring, he'll shed an inch of slouch.

"When the first freezer got full, he tried to pawn some off on the food bank. They wouldn't take it. The poor don't like picking shot out of quail any more than he does, or yak steak either. I heard Wyatt cite that to a buddy as proof the needy aren't needy anymore, they've gone soft from too much government cheese. Too much government cheese? When your fiancé says that, it's time to bring the lumber. If a marriage is going to work, you have to be willing to hit where it hurts. And where does he hurt? You know it: right in the *moral culpability.*"

Five minutes twenty-five seconds. As they bounce and jostle at top speed, Wyatt is talking. The grizzly, he says, is a gift for Darla, is his collection's pièce de résistance. Does Vada know that she looooves bears, and on their second date he won her on a midway, by way of his skill in mole-whacking, a life-size bruin, and so, just after his proposal last month, when he was already on the West Coast, it had seemed providential when a friend invited him to the backcountry. Wyatt decided to bag her a grizzly.

Wyatt has seemed Magoolike before, blind and charmed, but never *delusional*. It should be fun to see his friend, for once, doing the squirm of self-justification. But Vada doesn't have the time to revel in that. Instead he's nagged by the role he's about to play. Wyatt's pièce de résistance feels like Vada's *pièce de Vichy*. He knows where they're going, and to do what. He knows Darla's feelings. Will he be a gutless collaborator, or is he going here and now to stand up and be counted? Man or mannikin? Grizzly or teddy?

But if he dawdles, Vada thinks, Darla will give up looking for him at his house, come over here instead, and catch them in the act. The bulk of the blame will fall, as it must, on Wyatt. She'll know Vada helped only under duress. Maybe he won't even *have* to show her the barn and its mistreasures.

They're still forty feet away when the impatient delivery driver yanks the ripcord and, as Vada reported some time back, up thunders the truck's rear panel.

Five minutes.

96

Black Panther, Brown Bear, White Devil

The truck is white. It carries no insignia, no stickers or vavavoom mudflaps, no 1-800 number for reporting erratic driving. It's the kind of thing a wedding tent might emerge from, a sea of crepe, a frothy flour confection big as a chifforobe. But the hulk under blankets in the back, trussed like King Kong in the age of bungee, is no cake.

Wyatt remonstrates once more with the driver, a wiry black man who resembles a famous singer: Marvin Gaye? Teddy Pendergrass? It's a heated discussion, and Vada would like to introduce a note of levity (smooth R&B, a shared language!), but he doesn't want to offend this man. Vada's the kind of white Southerner afraid of African Americans because he imagines that if he were black, *he'd* be pissed and unpredictable. And this guy's wearing one of those colorful African skullcaps, the kind that screams "militant." Vada usually abases himself in front of such men by apologizing, apropos of nothing, for some Jim Crow atrocity. No African American seems to want to hear, as he seals salmon steaks in butcher paper or shimmies on his back to wrench loose a sinkpipe, how awful Vada thinks the murder of Emmett Till was or how much he hopes Bull Connor suffered from mouth cancer, "from the snuff, you know" . . . or to hear how he *almost* confronted Wyatt's father once about the Labrador retriever he named Rosa Barks, but didn't, not out of a failure of moral courage or anything but because the name might, after all, have been meant in tribute. Rosa was an excellent bird dog, a credit to her race.

"Clipboard's clear," Pendergaye or Marvingrass is saying. "It says I don't go in, and union rules say I go by the clipboard. I was told you'd have a crew. Might take four people to haul it inside. Weight's no problem, but the bulk . . . You gonna try it with just *him*?" He points at Vada without looking. Vada's too puny to merit looking.

Wyatt is agitated—not like himself. "I'll gladly *rent* the dolly. A hundred bucks if you'll help get the bear inside. Cash money. What's your price? But please hurry."

The driver taps the clipboard again, coldly. His mind's made up. Vada recognizes this from Caw-Caw. Wayneolini likes, when he knows his mind is unchangeable, to let the pleading go on and on. It's sport, a chance to watch someone beat his forehead bloody in pursuit of a desideratum it's in Wayne's power to deny. Why doesn't Wyatt see this? Does he have so little experience with *no*? He does.

Every second is one tick closer to their discovery by Darla, so Vada's content to stand aside and watch.

"Got another delivery to make," says Pendergaye. "Contract says I get it out the truck, so I'll get it out the truck. What you do with Yogi after that's up to you. It's like I-raq. You shoot it full of holes, you own it. You own it, good luck."

Wyatt switches tactics. "Have a heart. Please. My fiancée . . ."

"Got no heart," interrupts Marvingrass with a barely suppressed smile. "Got a clipboard instead. Black man can't *afford* a heart."

"Are you giving me a hard time because I'm . . . a honky? Is that what this is about? All I want is the dolly I paid for."

The driver seems never to have seen air quotes accompany the word "honky." He grins. His teeth, Vada can't help noticing, are lovely. Is it racist to notice this? To think about a black man's teeth? To compliment them? He wants to compliment them.

Brother Pendergaye speaks calmly. "I got nothing to do with your dolly, friend. Your dolly's your own business. Historically, you know, it hasn't been healthy for us-like to share a dolly with you-like." Missing Wyatt by only a foot, he yanks down the metal ramp, secures its tabs.

Wyatt probably shouldn't have conducted this man up the driveway (Vada allows himself to imagine) with an impatient-looking cavalry wave, amid a horn-flourish that must have had some unexpungible echo of "Wish I was in the land of cotton." He might, too, have done better in wardrobe: In Vada's vision of race war, it's the dudes with monogrammed golf carts who are introduced to the torch first, and he's pretty sure brazier number one will go to the fatcat wearing a burgundy track suit and speaking a racquet-club jive complete with air quotes.

Now Pendergaye flexes the edges of his thick clipboard with powerful hands until the clasp gapes like a mouth in pain and momentarily lets the pages loose. He smiles again. He's won. "Sign here," he says, and Wyatt complies. Even he sees it.

The hypnotic cap and its owner walk up the ramp. Wyatt stands there looking irked, every few seconds swivels to check down the driveway for Darla, of whom there's still no sign. The only sound from the south is the languid drone of July.

Vada has less than three minutes of life left. From inside the truck he hears the music of ripped tape, buckles gone slack, dolly wheels on metal deck, and at once Wyatt's looks of surl and worry are supplanted by joy. "God," he says. "It's beautiful. Absolutely beautiful."

For those of you worried about timing, don't—fate never blows its cues. It's arranged for Pendergaye the Black Panther to skate the edge between professional and miracle-worker. It takes just sixty seconds for him to free his cargo, get it down and clear, stow the dolly and ramp, and re-secure the door. In another twenty he's turned the truck and is speeding back down the drive. Which leaves Vada to begin the last ninety-odd seconds of his time on earth on Wyatt's flagstone path, in a cloud of dust, beneath the sheltering arms of a male grizzly on hind legs, seven feet tall. Up close like this, you can still *smell* it, some pelt musk that can't be covered over by chemicals and glue.

"It's magnificent," says Wyatt. And he's not wrong, or is wrong only in his chosen tense. It *was* magnificent—being alive, Vada knows, is a prerequisite of magnificence.

The beast's nails look like rake harrows, and its yellow teeth guard a jaw open wide enough to admit a human head. This is not, he thinks, your average bear.

97

Gravity's Slack

Impossible to imagine *this* specimen on a bicycle, at the end of a leash, wheezing its way around a fire hydrant that looks like Uncle Sam as pygmy robot. There's nothing comical about the way it strains its seams, and its paws' pads are big as catcher's mitts.

Vada upon the flagstones. D minus sixty seconds. He's wasted the last twenty donning a chamois shirt and driving gloves, then being directed by Wyatt on how to kneel and take his burden. Now, blind, he has a mouthful of grizzly hump, right behind the shoulders, and he's wobbling backward as Wyatt, gripping the flat feet, steers him toward the house.

How can something that is at heart florist's foam or polyurethane be *this fucking heavy*? Vada bore the pall for Reid Yancey, or one-sixth of the pall, and the casket seemed oddly light, as if it was the body and not the soul that weighed only a few grams. The main job had been to keep up the *appearance* of great weight, to take up gravity's slack; it wouldn't do to swing the box on one finger, like a purse. The stuffed bear, though, is causing his spine to make noises like a rock-polisher.

But maybe the problem is a simple inequality. Wyatt, under no strain, keeps up the bright, unbreathy chatter. Mostly he's lauding the taxidermist. He had the work done locally. The hide was degreased, pickled, and tanned in Alaska, then shipped to this *genius* in West Columbia—has Vada noticed the quality of the handmade jaw set, the mottling of the bear's lower lips and gums? Guy used a palette toned with brick-red and tincture of blueberry, so it's not too pink. You're looking for shock but also accuracy. Muting is the name of the game, Vada, this isn't a baboon's ass. At higher latitudes, colors tend to be calmer—low light, you know. And check it out: Did Vada ever see a more lifelike dampness of nose?

Vada has noticed none of this, of course, since he's staggering backward under a wall of fur and smelling wild balsam and tundra, maybe, beneath the preservative funk.

"Careful. Threshold coming. Pick your feet up and bend your knees—got to clear the overhang." How many ways does Wyatt think Vada's spine can hinge at once? Meanwhile Wyatt's steps shove Vada steadily back, and he feels like he's teetering on the edge of a precipice at the point of an adversary's . . . bear. It's always that way with Wyatt, and it's nice to have the feeling be physical for a change. He *is* on the edge of a drop—they're turning to Vada's right in preparation for the second double doorway. Then five shallow slate steps into the trophy room.

"Whole rig cost almost ten grand, counting shipping."

Halfway there. Thirty more seconds, Vada thinks. But he's wrong—his lifespan has dwindled to twenty-five. Vada calls for a rest, but no sound emerges through the fur gag. He leans back, repeats himself: "Hold up a sec." When Wyatt sets down the feet, Vada steps aside, rests his elbows on his thighs, and touches his forehead, at knee height now, to the bases of both thumbs. Wyatt keeps talking: "I appreciate this, V. You're a pal." Five seconds pass. "Darla'll be here soon, and she's on the warpath about hunting. We need to get it behind closed doors. Ready? The steps shouldn't be too tricky."

When Vada once again screws his brow to the sticking place, or whatever (he's dead tired, and soon to be tired dead), he feels the fur tickle his eyelids. He locks both elbows to his ribcage and lifts. He has just ten seconds to live.

98

The Antonym of Shipwreck

Where's Darla? Her meeting with the wedding planner, Roz Robison, must have taken longer than expected.

One of the best moments of Vada's life came five weeks ago, soon after Apocalypse Night. Darla pulled up to the top of his driveway, where Vada, still in his coverall, stood behind his idling car fetching another day's catalogs from the box. Without a word, Darla handed Roz's card through the open window, and when, after a few seconds of not-quick-on-the-uptake, a smile overspread Vada's face, she threw her head back against her headrest and laughed out loud. What a joy it is to know what a woman is thinking, or what she recently thought—like waking to the sound of water through a bathroom door and reaching over to feel warmth, still, in the sheets. She was here. She was *here*.

The card was fancy, with letters raised like tiny islands on an ocean of the creamiest cream. But the reason she'd hired Roz wasn't the tasteful card with its Palatino archipelago, not exactly. It was the pun. The business's name: Robison Trousseau, a joke irresistible even to Roz, whose living depends on her ability to convince couples that marriage is not sinking and maroonage but the *antonym* of shipwreck.

Today is Saturday, the wedding a week off. And Vada? Vada is Friday, a day past expiration and fast going sour.

99

Wedding Cake

This morning's crisis had to do with the cake—that's why Darla called to postpone their meeting from eleven to noon. Another complication of planning a big wedding on short notice: the baker turned out not to have the proper icing on hand for the lavender cascade, which meant either a lavender cascade that would shift toward blue, or a cascade of another flower altogether.

Seven afternoons from now, just yards away, under a bunting-clad gazebo overlooking the lake, to the huzzahs of three hundred guests, Darla will carve into the first canto of her Dantesque nine-layer cake. Vada won't be there—wouldn't have been. He lied, told them the DUCE wouldn't give him the day off. When Darla looked hurt, he laid it on thick, said that in the detailing business a July Saturday means all hands on deck [small wince from Darla], besides which that's the day Wayne gets to display the pace car for next spring's 500 in Darlington, and nobody likes a well-waxed ride like the Nascar fan docs, so they'll be out in droves [bitten lip, lowered eyes, Wyatt's hand finds her shoulder] and Wayne will stand around in the Caw-Caw racesuit he's ordered for the occasion, illustrating down-forces, he's the foremost expert I know on down-forces, ha ha, so sorry to miss the festivities and if I could make it you know I would I'm so happy for you two lovebirds . . .

Later Darla rallied. She promised to save Vada a wedge. She said, too, that she'll freeze a slice, and on their first anniversary she and Wyatt will thaw and share it. With a single fork, passed lip to lip.

"I thought the first one called for paper," Vada replied with what breeziness he could muster. Had she said "lip to lip"? *Darla?*

"It's wedding cake," said Darla. "It'll *taste* like paper. That's the point—you're brought closer by hardship. Marriage is about weathering storms, and the ceremony gets you off to a start. The trial of relatives. The agony of soaped windows and rice in your hair. The wretchedness of cake that cost you the GNP of Guam."

It's touching, her faith in ritual: cascades and buntings, rings and garters, the borrowed and the blue. The Zip-Loc seal of marriage: yellow tab into blue groove equals green for all eternity. To her, "Robison Trousseau" is a joke, not an omen. But comedy is never *light*, Darla. Vada's in a perfect position just now to say so. And by next July the cake will be forgotten, buried under butterbeans and Lean Cuisine. Vada imagines that in eight years, or four, or probably even sooner, Darla will be clearing out freezer-burned game—venison, dove, whatever else her estranged husband has stockpiled to taunt her for taking his basement stand-alones—and she'll happen upon the warped icing and have a good cry. Wedding cake as keepsake: bagged and stowed, then remembered only when either freezer compressor or marriage goes bad.

And if Darla and Wyatt *do* eat the saved slice next year, it'll mean things have gone wrong. People don't follow through on such things unless there's trouble. They set the cake between them on the tablecloth to thaw, sip red wine in low light and speak, trying to recapture lost magic—but the purplish wine-shadows on the linen seem sinister rather than romantic, and they run out of things to say before the cake softens to edibility. And what to do with the freezer bag? There's no place in the symbolism for a plastic sack, so Darla will fold it into her lap, where it will sit like a cold hand. In a few minutes, giving up, they'll nibble in turn at a frost-rimed edge, suppress their gag reflex, then pile the whole mess into the garbage and laugh and pretend it doesn't mean anything.

Where is Darla?

100

Giddy

The ten-second mark found Vada on the second step down.

For the mount's protection, Wyatt had said, shrugging, as he handed Vada the gloves and jacket. He should have required a stocking mask, too: Vada's only points of skin-to-bear contact now are his forehead, nose, ears. But burying his face in the wiry fur has benefits. For one, it muffles Wyatt's instructions. Vada can hear only the sound of his own heart, which seems by a sonic trick to have been displaced into the grizzly. Nor can he see. And the smell, a cross between lab and timberland that he'd like to call timberlab—the tanning chemicals might be making him high—blots out most everything. Both sweat and consciousness flow freely now. *Why is nothing ever described as wieldy? Because, dope, if it's wieldy you don't think about the wielding. Oh, to have Pendergaye's dolly now. Wasn't Dolly the name of that sheep that's like an android or something? Not android—clone.* He thinks for a moment of his hands, flexed just above his head. The knuckles, like all knuckles in driving gloves, must look obscene and mechanical, the android knuckles of Dolly the human dolly. Whew.

Vada should be appalled, righteous. They are dragging this behemoth—robbed of its real fierceness and then tortured up, until forever or mildew, into a dead and clownish parody of it—so that it might be secured with engine-block superglue to a fake rock in a hall of falsities.

The only true thing here is abomination. He should be thinking of saving Darla from this fate, lest she wind up in the hall of trophies, too, behind a Styrofoam anchor desk, hands knitted atop a page and teeth pearly as the boar tusks above her.

But Vada's fierceness is as false as the grizzly's, falser for having *never* been real. What is wrong with him? The task seems *fun*. His arms ache pleasantly, and the drone of Wyatt's excitement, so long as Vada can't make out the words, has nostalgic value, is the soundtrack of his life, and the underside of the bear's chin caresses the top of his head—how long since he was touched there by a living, or once-living, creature? God help him, he's *giddy*.

Nine seconds. Eight.

One more step, Vada thinks, then rest and regrip. Of course Darla won't show. Perhaps she'll learn about the grizzly later, if Wyatt's conscience makes him confess. Fat chance. You'd think this operation would give *WAY* time to reflect and repent, but reflect and repent aren't his style. Vic, in game-warden mode, used to say that the bigger the prey, the more twisted the soul of the hunter. Which meant that Wyatt's soul must feel about like Vada's neck just now. This *beast*. In Europe there are cars this size.

A shudder is Vada's first sign of something amiss, and when the grizzly rocks away from his face a couple inches, he hears Darla's indignant voice: " . . . the fuck is that? Wyatt, if that bear's dead then you are, too."

Five seconds. Four.

Vada hardly has time to think *There's my girl* before the bear pendulums back toward him, and he can hear retreating footsteps—or can't hear hers, as Darla flees down the avenue of carpet runners Wyatt laid out in advance of the truck's arrival, but can hear Wyatt's seven-league clumps, and then Vada tries to catch the bear that gravity and God and his former friend have flung at him, but all at once he's fur-blind again, and fur-deaf, and a-three, and a-two, and the last thing to go, just then, appears to be his equilibrium, and uh-oh.

One.

101

No Juiciness

Which leaves just one thing to tell: the life-altering night he and Darla spent together, in the aftermath of Apocalypse. And what did they *do* on that occasion that earned it the label "life-altering"? Vada's sorry if his holding out has made you think there's juiciness there. No juiciness. What they did was . . . truth be told, they baked cookies. Also played a little Scrabble. Ate hot dogs. Talked.

102

Vada Was an Angel

At nine that June night, just after dark, Vada heard a knock at his carport door and was surprised to find Darla there, still in her on-air ensemble.

"I suppose you saw the newscast."

Vada nodded.

"I hate to ask this," she said. "I was supposed to meet Wyatt downtown, but he's extended his West Coast trip, and . . . look, my phone is ringing off the hook." She held up the offending instrument, which—an obedient visual aid—started up its snake-charmer tune. She punched a button, and it went dark. "Would it be OK to crash here tonight? I know it's an imposition, but I just don't want to be alone. Right now you're the best friend I've got."

Vada succeeded in closing his mouth, taking a step back, and motioning her in.

"Thanks," said Darla. "You're an angel."

Vada was an angel.

103

The Five Sacraments of the Apocalypse

Gobblers in Throws

Darla sat on a stool in the kitchen, he poured her a glass of wine, and she began to talk. How did Wyatt expect to have a happy marriage if he's constantly off gallivanting—worse than gallivanting, *hunting*, which is where he must be headed because though his message was cagey, she knew he hadn't scared up a big financial deal in, like, the Klondike. What kind of business did they do up there, besides hunting?

Vada said "Ice cream bars" at exactly the moment Darla said, "And don't say ice cream bars." Then he blanched—she'd said *marriage* just now, he could swear it—and noticed at last the ring she'd been tapping against the stemware for the last five minutes. Oh, wait, he got it—when she'd said angel, she meant "sexless being." She'd been establishing rules. It was a compliment wrapped in saltpeter, to let him know what "I just don't want to be alone" meant.

"He proposed just before he left for San Francisco," Darla said.

Tonight, downtown, she continued, they were supposed to start planning. The wedding was to be biggish but soon, which posed problems. Earlier in the day Darla had identified a few planners who might accommodate them, but now Wyatt was gone, and she'd just seen a kid nearly stroke out in a rat suit on live TV, and then there was a riot, and her career was in the . . . "Hey, I'm hungry. What do you have in the pantry?"

Vada made pigs in blankets. He cut wieners in half and wrapped them in crescent rolls. Even now, in adulthood, his favorite part of the process—a process he loved far more than he loved eating hot dogs—was the tympani strike of the tube of dough on the counter's edge to open it. That *thwiiip,* and with it the feeling he'd had as a child that he was someone in a fairy tale rapping open a secret passage, thus saving a damsel in distress from scoundrels she'd thought had penned her in.

Darla polished off four, slathered in ketchup that she licked from her fingers. "Delicious," she said when she finished. "But I don't think it's right to call them pigs in blankets when you use turkey franks. You're insulting the grand gobble-gobble, which was once—I'm pretty sure I heard this from *you*—nearly our national bird."

Vada held up a frank. "This particular bird seems to have suffered worse insults," he said, hearing a distant echo of Vic, "but fine by me. Gobblers in Blankets. And actually, they peek out of both ends, which makes these pretty shabby blankets. I'd go with Gobblers in Throws."

"Aren't you going to congratulate me?" Darla asked.

"I thought that was bad luck," Vada said through a mouthful.

"It's not."

"Congratulations, then." The word seemed to have eleven syllables. He scarfed whole a gobbler in throw, to save himself from further comment.

"If Wyatt doesn't make you best man, maybe you could be my maid of honor."

Already, Vada was sure that if the day came—when the day came—he'd be long gone. She waited for him to swallow. "Or the caterer," he said. He swiped a speck of mustard from his nose.

Darla snapped shut the ketchup spout and popped a garlic-stuffed olive, which was serving as their vegetable. "No offense," she said, "but maybe we should stick to maid of honor."

Scrabble

After dinner, Darla made the one call she was allowing herself, to the hospital to check on Pablo the Bible-Believing Possum. He was fine, a touch of heat exhaustion, would be back soon to offer Christian witness through tomfoolery. Say what one might about the Shealys, they *had* sprung for a health plan. Then she went to scrub off her makeup. "OK if I raid your closet?" she asked.

"Second left down the hall. There are sweatshirts in the top dresser drawer."

Darla lingered in the doorway. She looked into the spartan living room, its furnishings now dwindled to the ottoman, the TV atop its crates, a nest of pillows, and an orphaned end table no longer at anything's end, a table there mainly to hold up Celeste's surviving chicken lamp. "You know," she said, "my fiancé has gone AWOL in the Yukon, and I may quit my job, and oh by the way I saw the world end a couple of hours ago, and it didn't end prettily . . . but right now I don't care. That's thanks to you, Vada. You're a good friend. Now set up the Scrabble board, OK? I'm assuming you still have the Scrabble board?"

"I do. But if you think that speech will make me throw the game, you're wrong."

"You won't have to."

Ten minutes later she returned in a ratty college sweatshirt of his mother's, a shirt older than Vada, along with a pair of Vic's tartan pajama bottoms he hadn't seen in years. She'd rolled up nine inches of leg. Her face was pink and scrubbed, and she'd tied her hair back with a bandanna. As Darla plopped lotus-style on a pillow beside the Scrabble board on his living room floor, she said, "Prepare, *mon ami*, to die."

She turned out to be one of those people with an arsenal of two-letter words, and she thrashed him in the endgame by deploying them in ruthless combinations while Vada spent his time and tiles to form oddities: "zither," "lummox." The turning point came when she added "ric" to "bishop" to claim a triple word score. Shark. "About time I got some benefit from the church today," she said as Vada toted up her score.

The wine drained away. The laughter mounted. By the end of the even-more-lopsided rematch, Vada knew that he would not be maid of honor, that he would not attend the wedding, and that he would do anything he could think of to keep Darla from attending it, too.

At eleven, Darla said, "I should suck it up and check the news, see how this is playing. If it's playing. Maybe they'll pretend it never happened."

No such luck. Bruce was milking the drama for every ratings point. Tonight there would be no bombings or plane crashes or famines, not in the Columbia market. Instead he devoted the newscast to what the graphic called BALLPARK CHAOS.

Things had degenerated even further after Darla left. Joe—heroic under fire—had kept filming. The tape showed a band of disaffected-looking kids, so thickly inked that they looked *blurry,* and wearing stocking caps (*Alleged atheists,* the anchor said gravely) clambering en masse over the exterior fence and engaging the yellow-shirted tribe behind the wall in right field.

"Why would you wear a watch cap on a hundred-degree day?" asked Darla.

"Good training for the Hot Place."

"Ski caps, but no shirts?" asked Darla again. She seemed to be probing at something, but Vada was distracted: On his screen, a riot had broken out. Kids were swinging folding chairs, and the watch caps bobbed among the yellow shirts like something from the mosh pits of hell. Within thirty seconds the vials of wrath poised above the outfield walls were being tipped, spilling their colored water, and the fray spread to the warning tracks.

The warning tracks! Millennialism as Christianity's warning track. All at once Vada understood Darla's questions. The watch caps, too, were costumes. How had he missed it? The *chairs*—those well-prepared Christians had made a study of wrestling, and they knew that a good riot's first need is folding chairs, so they'd stashed stacks of them behind the fences. No doubt the chairbacks were stenciled with the name of a church. A close-up would also reveal the alleged atheists to be clear-eyed and devout. Straight-edgers—sure, they wore skull tattoos, but with legends underneath saying "poison free." The Gothic monstrosity across the bare back of the guy toting the SATAN RULZ banner would read *"Libre de las Drogas."*

So why didn't Joe zoom in? Darla gasped when she realized. The angle was all wrong. Of course—Joe had hustled off when she did, while the getting was good, while the getting was gettable. It was the *Shealys.* You had to give them their due. These guys could sell stocking caps to the inmates of hell. For the next few days, this footage would be everywhere: Fox, YouTube, even CNN. In years to come, it would be a propaganda classic seen in church basements the world over. "Holy shit," said Darla.

"Why would Satan rule with a Z?" asked Vada, to show he'd caught on. "I'm not sure these kids quite get the spirit of anarchy. I don't think the rules the satanists want to overturn concern spelling."

"But why show it, knowing it's fake? This is like *War of the Worlds* meets *Triumph of the Will*. Bruce is smarter than that." Her anger derived in part from her sense that journalists were to be ungullible. But part, Vada understood, might have to do with being demoted from her starring role, deplore it though she might.

Despite himself, Vada was impressed. It was good theater, DeMilleish in scope, with Rapture in the balance. He rarely liked Christians more than in this moment. Like him, they resorted to foreign tongues when English would have made their sentiments seem uncool. Like him, they understood their lives to be trivial parentheses in a history unimaginably large and involute, surpassing understanding. How to get your mind around the fact that your world may be God's low minors, meaningless games contested in a backwater, and what seems to you the Culmination of All History may be just the first in an early-season ten-apocalypse homestand? The answer to the question of your triviality was that you *refused* to get your mind around it. People want to believe *the world ends when I do*. In the ways that mean squat to you, it *does*.

The kids were having at it tooth and claw. Shedding real blood, from the looks of it. Another difficulty in telling false finales from real: if you convince yourself that for your life to mean anything, yours must be the end-times, and if you have the means to strike the spark . . . hey, mightn't God be trusting *you* to Get This Party Started? So swing that chair, man. Alpha's left the building, and you may not get another shot at Omega.

The newscast cut away before the finale, which turned out to be that the voice of God Himself—or His proxy, a famed evangelist who *happened* to be in the press box—rumbled out over the PA, commanding that the fighting cease in the name of the Lord. That familiar rumbling bass elicited gasps from the crowd, and the fighting did cease pronto, and the former combatants stood shoulder to shoulder in the outfield (except for the injured, who made use of those chairs) and sang "Onward,

Christian Soldiers" with the assembled fans, and there was a tumultuous ovation, and then an altar call, and . . .

After fifteen minutes of "team coverage," the anchor announced, without ceremony, that the riot had turned out to be a publicity stunt. Then came the turn. "The events at Jesus of Nazareth Field tonight have sparked worldwide attention. Film crews are on the way from places including New York, Korea, and *Entertainment Tonight*." So *this* was their angle. If crews were on the way, and satellite trucks, then who could deny it was news? This was the Midlands' chance at the spotlight. A fresh-faced cub named Sylver, reporting from the now-quiet ballpark, said the local economic impact might eventually reach the tens of millions. She held up a T-shirt that said "Gilyard A-Mock-alypse, 2007." On the reverse, "Jesus Come Back!" As of 11:00 P.M., she said, twenty thousand orders had already been received at gilyardrisen.com.

"Now," said the anchor, "a tribute to the heroism of one of our own who was on the scene tonight." There loomed a full-screen still of the Darla pietá, and she was lauded for saving the life of young "Pablo the Possum, who has, at his request, not been otherwise identified."

Before the praisesong could go on, Darla clicked off the set and dropped back to the floor, stretched the sweatshirt over her knees. She kept her eyes on the now-blank screen. "I'll get the chair," she said in a dead tone.

"The chair? Huh? No one's dead. The kid will be fine."

"I mean the *anchor* chair."

And she was right. After the honeymoon, she'll take the helm on weekends.

Story Hour

11:30 now, and Darla has her phone out. This doesn't make her a hypocrite, she says, because she's counting, not calling. "Twenty-six incoming, eleven messages." She frowns. "Only four from Wyatt." The phone gives a depth-finderish beep, and Darla smiles. "OK, five—he's gaining on it, anyway. I do love a full mailbox."

Then Darla tells Vada a story—the story of her life. The part that sticks in his mind is the saddest part, the part that makes them kindred, friendred, soulmatedred. When Darla finished college, she too was at a loss about what to do, and she too was yoked to home. Her mother was dying of a liver disease treatable only by transplant—and though Darla's mom was a good candidate (or had been until the toxins built up and started poisoning other organs), there'd been no hope of finding a donor for an adult so small. Mrs. Dietz had always been tiny, barely five feet and a hundred pounds—and it turned out that when they called yours a "fragile" or "ethereal" beauty, they meant it: You had a head start on wasting away and going to ether.

Vada had never thought of what Darla called "the liver marketplace." Children got dibs on children's livers, it seemed, and the world was in short supply of teetotaling jockeys who came to violent ends. Darla, trying as much to stoke her mother's hope as her own, had installed the phone of her teen years—a bright red Princess—at bedside, but it rang seldom, and never with good news.

It seemed Darla's duty to stick around and see this through. If she'd had a high-powered job lined up, her mom would have insisted that she leave. But what kind of daughter abandoned her dying mother to hostess at ChiChi's or to intern at the WB affiliate in Scranton?

Her father was no help. Fifteen years older than Darla's mom, he'd retired the year before from teaching business at a small college. They'd always wanted to travel the world together before they were too old, and he'd quit as soon as he had the funds. Now, plans wrecked, he'd decided that if his beloved had to go, he should follow her as closely as possible. That didn't incline him to dote on his wife—if he was going to be her rock, he seemed determined to be the kind of rock you filled your pockets with before striding into the millpond. He grew grim and bitter, devoted himself to suicide by bad food and wan light. Day and night he holed up in his study with a bottle of Scotch to punch his calculator keys or play war games online. He'd come down only for supper at his wife's bedside, and afterward, when she was asleep, he'd complain to Darla about the "burn rate" of their savings, and thus of his daughter's inheritance. "But I'm going as fast as I can," he said. "Damn the actuaries, full speed aground." He laughed one of those laughs that staggered toward being a sob. "Sorry, I'm like some goddamn movie," he said. "And not a good one." He stole a look at Mrs. Dietz, dying there like an extra. Self-dosing button in her hand. Close-up on the red phone, unringing.

Darla stood behind her father's chair and cradled his head and tried to soothe him, but she didn't know what to say, and soothing wasn't what he wanted. He wanted his wife back, wanted years back. He was like the carwash's Colonel would have been had he married. Darla's dad wanted to go to the battlegrounds of ancient Greece and Sparta and drink ouzo with Mrs. Dietz under a café umbrella while he deployed olive-oil cruets or whatever exotic condiments they had there (now he'd never know) to explain the trap Leonidas set for Xerxes at Thermopylae. He wanted someone he'd never met, someone petite, with two healthy lobes of liver, to die—better yet, to have died six months before, when the damage was reversible. After a while he didn't even raise his arms to touch his daughter's. She stood behind him and clutched his head to her chest like a rebound she'd snatched, but no one wanted to fight with her for it.

That summer Darla's only refuge was the post office. She'd rented a box. It seemed important to have an address of her own, if only a four-inch square—a reminder of the independent life she'd put on hold. The box also gave her an excuse to leave the house every afternoon during the two hours when the hospice nurse was on duty. Which absence was the primary benefit, as both the box and the life it was proxy for were mostly empty. Slim pickings: grad-school brochures she sent off for as a fantasy, catalogs for kitsch and muffins, charity come-ons that included free ugly address labels, an occasional postcard from a friend traveling abroad. Most days there was nothing, just the consolation of that greasy key between her fingers, a key all the more valuable for its daintiness compared to the ruder, brassier keys on her ring, plus the tiny glass pane with its number, 242, painted decades ago in gold with a red border and holding up well.

One afternoon in August, only weeks before the end—Darla's father in his room, weighing the relative merits of Scipio and General Meade, and her mother wasting away in a sour cloud, pleading for more morphine—she slipped out for her mail check. Darla could see through the cubby's window that the box was bare, but she inserted the key anyway just so she could marvel again at the lock, that brass fist. Just *look* at it: Presently empty or not, any life that called for hardware as heavy as that *must* be meaningful. Then—there was self-awareness in this, Darla told Vada, not neediness but a parody of it—she stood, turned, and leaned against the wall of boxes. Golden knobs poked her cheek and temple. It was a long chute—she'd got her money's worth, depthwise—and her arm disappeared all the way to the shoulder before her fingertips wriggled into the back room, a spider tasting the air. It was as she'd thought, as she'd seen. No hiding scrap. Nothing. She clasped the cool metal lip of the box beneath hers (*Howdy, neighbor*), withdrew her arm, clicked shut the box, pocketed the key.

On the way out she was accosted by the froth-bearded crazy guy who seemed always at the PO, filling out change-of-address forms in the names of rock guitarists and reaming the stamp-machine slot for coins. He clutched her forearm, waited until her eyes swung up. "No one loves you," he said—no animus, no urgency, simply reporting a fact. Maybe he meant it as a lament, but lament was a tone he lacked.

Vada knew the rest before she told it. Frothbeard released her and shuffled off to visit the Most Wanted, leaving you, the least wanted. The door tinkled shut. Time passed, as it does. Mother passed, Father passed—as they do. The memory never did.

But the memory *did* pass, in a way. Eventually, in a new place, loved again, Darla could tell the tale. Audiences were appreciative. It was a howler. You? *You* unloved? The memory of friends' laughter ate away at the memory of the day itself. Eventually, with time and tellings enough, the laughter might supplant the original memory altogether, and she'd be left with something once dangerous but now with polished teeth and lacquered claws, a succor, a trophy. This was called mental health. It was what people did.

It was almost 1:00 A.M. now, and Darla had stretched her feet past the Scrabble board so that they nestled near Vada's thigh. She nudged him with a toe. "Hey," she said. "Don't be glum. You know I love you, Vada. Wyatt does, too. We'll be here for you. We've decided to stay. We're not going anywhere."

One, Vada remembers, is misery. Two's company.

What's three, again? Three is a number to subtract one from.

Cookies for Christ

"I'm not sleepy yet," said Darla. "Stay up with me a while. It's like an old-time girls' slumber party. You've never been to one, and here's your chance. Tell me something embarrassing about *you*."

If Vada was ever visited by inspiration, it was now. He hoisted himself off the floor, waved for Darla to follow him to the kitchen. First he plundered his mother's shelves for an old recipe file, then he rooted for ingredients. He vowed not to trouble himself with expiration dates. From the cabinet, sugar and vinegar. From the freezer, a bulging bag of pecans. Two eggs from the fridge. Salt. Wax paper.

"What are you making?" asked Darla from her seat at the island.

Vada brought out a meat mallet. "Would you run to the guestroom, all the way down on the right, and bring the Bible on the bureau? I'll also need the beanbag chair from my bedroom, straight across the hall. And don't ask—I've kept the chair because it's where I hide my bong, or something."

"Baking, maybe? But what's with the vinegar, and where's the flour?"

"Patience."

By the time she got back with Bible in one hand and uncooperative orange beanbag in the other, the oven was preheating and he'd separated the eggs. "In honor of the occasion," Vada said, "we're making what my Cub Scout den mother used to call Easter Drops. My mom made them, too, but with chocolate chips. She called them Forgotten Cookies. Now get over here and help."

He had Darla wrap the pecan halves in wax paper and pound them with the meat mallet. "This symbolizes how our Savior was savagely beaten by the Romans," he read from the recipe.

"With a meat mallet?" asked Darla. "Through wax paper?"

"It's the principle of the thing," said Vada.

"Ex-*act*-ly."

Then he had her sniff the vinegar, and he read from the recipe that when Jesus was thirsty on the cross, the Romans gave him soured wine. They tipped in a single drop. After this, the symbology turned lame for a bit. The salt was for tears; eggs symbolized life, also the fragile vessel that is a human body (see meat mallet, above). Sugar was the sweetness of everlasting life. Vada pulled out a glass bowl. "What's that symbolize?" asked Darla.

"The mixing bowl is always only a mixing bowl," answered Vada, "but I rinsed it out as Jesus rinsed dust from the feet of wayfarers."

"Do you think we could put in the chocolate chips?"

"But they don't stand for anything."

"A semi-sweet morsel need never justify its ways to men," said Darla. "Say it represents the believer's ambivalence—the joy of salvation, sorrow at the sufferings that produced it."

"Sold," said Vada, "if we have them." He fished a bag from the pantry. "Be warned, these are old enough that the ratio of suffering to salvation may be a little high."

"Let's risk it."

Vada may not be able to convey the tone. Though he was long lapsed, or semi-lapsed, from his childhood belief and Darla had abandoned hers in fury at her mother's illness, there was something *devout* in this. It was not a joke but a rite—the best two dented skeptics could do. It was a kind of worship. Wasn't that what ritual was for? You went through the motions, didn't you, so that when you couldn't quite believe in your heart, you might be brought back to it by believing in your hands, your hips, the tip of your tongue? Or maybe that's just an excuse, and the spiritual gets its usual back-alley beatdown from the grimy physical. Have it your way.

Yes, there was pleasure in the nearness to Darla. Their heads and hips nearly touched as they read the recommended verses between steps. Several times their hands mingled under hot water so that they wouldn't goop up the tissuey Bible pages. Once she set her palm just above his kidney as she leaned around to rinse the cookie sheet from dinner. Beating the meringue to the required "stiff white peaks of virginity" required fifteen minutes (one must suffer for one's faith, the recipe insisted—no electric mixers). They took turns stirring, rotating in a circle that shrank as their comfort increased. By the end, it was as if they were one set of hands. The bowl and spoon were warm from their mutual touches, and Vada could feel her breast pressing his shoulder, her breath down his jawline.

They folded in the broken nuts, pressed each teaspoonful of batter onto two drops of chocolate they'd set on a wax-lined cookie sheet. Finally they turned the oven off, and Vada asked Darla to place the boulder before the tomb. She looked at him blankly.

"The beanbag chair," he said.

"Are you sure that's safe?"

"Just don't put it too close to the vent. We don't want the miracle of a melted boulder."

It wasn't a tight seal, but it would do. They stood back. "You may feel sad to leave the cookies now," Vada read.

"What do you mean, leave the cookies?"

"We have to leave the cookies overnight. If it's any consolation, it says here that the disciples were crestfallen when they closed the tomb."

"Crestfallen?"

"That's what it says."

"What kind of recipe has the word 'crestfallen' in it?"

"This kind. Are you finished? In the morning you can get up and bite into the cookies, and they'll be hollow . . ."

"Except for the chips."

"They'll be hollow *except for the chips*, and we can alleluia."

"Alleluia!" Darla plopped down into the beanbag.

"In due time."

"But I want them *now*," she said.

"See," replied Vada. "Everybody's in a hurry. That's exactly the kind of thinking that spawns Apocalypse Nights."

"Help me up, then," said Darla, and she was beaming, and she held out both her hands. When Vada lifted her, she went straight through arm's-length and into a hug, and she kissed the side of his neck and said, "Good night, you sweet man. Thanks for everything."

*   *   *   *   *

This is the problem with artifacts. What Vada wants is to preserve that moment, that tone. But what's up in the barn isn't a tone, isn't the feel of her nose brushing his ear or the dizzy swaying-in-wind feeling he was left with a moment later when she headed down the hall to—he insisted—his room. What's up in the barn are the recipe (#5), Bible (#6), beanbag chair (#7) . . . and then the breakfast tray (#8) on which he brought up a plate (#9) of eggs and sausage, a glass (#10) filled with his special gross-looking-but-delicious mix of cranberry and orange juices, and a porcelain egg cup (#11) and hand-knitted cozy (#12—thanks and farewell, Celeste). Inside the cozy he nestled an Easter drop. He piled half a dozen more around the base of the egg cup, and as she savored her breakfast, he sat on the edge of the queen-sized bed, fully four feet away (morning having restored things to their proper distances, alas), watching.

And then she went home.

104

Subtract One

But Vada was wrong, just a second ago—a half-second ago, a hundredth. The retreating Wyatt footsteps he thought to hear must have been his own heart, one last tattoo, because now his friend—nearby, almost directly above him—shouts toward the open exterior door, "Help, Darla! It's Vada!" The tone is panicked, and Vada can't help feeling a surge of elation—*This was all it took to set Wyatt to quaking like the rest of us? I should have died years ago.* He knows that even through her wrath, Darla cannot fail to hear that fearful, plaintive, unprecedented note, and the combination of *that* tone, *this* name invoked, will stop her, spin her, send her hurtling back to the house.

Very soon Wyatt, with the superhuman strength people are said to possess in such moments, will wrench the grizzly free, and he and Darla will kneel alongside, and there will be pleading whispers and then Wyatt, putting his hunting skills to use one last time, will lay two fingers to Vada's neck and turn to Darla and instead of shaking his head with the usual Wyatt sureness will let his eyes drop and his chin sag. And then, still on their knees, they'll hurl themselves into each other's arms so fervently that it might tip them over and drop them onto . . . but why dwell on that? Vada won't be here.

Fare well, Darla and Wyatt. Does he mean that, one word and two? He tries to. Does he wish them every happiness? Come on. But he wishes them no ill. He hopes his death won't ruin the wedding, or hopes it'll ruin it only around the edges . . . ecstasies need a *little* ruining, to show them in relief. He wishes them little ruinings they can handle. He's probably helping out by haunting the trophy room, which they'll have to get rid of. He's done Darla at least that favor.

Then again, maybe Wyatt will have *him* stuffed and mounted, and he'll stay here forever, adornment in the house, trophy of trophies, nodding across the aisle every morning to his old nemesis the grizzly. He'll be dusted weekly by Señora Estorino, spoken of in the intimate cant of marriage. "Lumpykins, Vada's coverall is getting mothy. Should we change his clothes?"

Vada imagines himself on a pedestal—yes, Wyatt, he remembers, he was half-paying attention despite himself while you babbled all these months—he imagines himself on a *plinth*, skin lovingly stretched over a frame of plastic. From time to time Darla will open the hinged rear door of his display case, lean in to clear his hair of cobwebs or polish the brass fitting of the hose he grips. Wyatt will have paid extra to have the taxidermist crook Vada's thumb at the knuckle to concentrate the imaginary spray. Every Easter Darla will make forgotten cookies, and she'll set one on a plate inside Vada's case for three days, just in case. And every year Wyatt—knowing now the whole story of Apocalypse Night, theirs being that kind of marriage, and doing his part because that's what you do if you're lucky enough to find yourself in such a marriage—will eat the cookie and replace the plate, the same way Vic and Celeste used to fool Vada into believing in Santa Claus. Darla, like Vada back then, will consent to be fooled.

One Saturday a year, in the dreary stretch between Thanksgiving and Christmas, season of the winter pig-picking, Wyatt will brush Vada's teeth. He may, as he rubs the dentifrice in with a rag, get a dust mote in his eye now and again, motes being all that will remain of Vada.

Vada imagines himself under glass, rampant, gleaming teeth bared, hose confidently trained. Still shedding motes, just like anyone else in the land of the living. Yes, he'll be at home here.

He holds still. And then still isn't something he has to hold.

Acknowledgments

I am grateful to more people than I could possibly name on this page—but that won't stop me from trying. Special thanks go to the National Endowment for the Arts and the Charles Phelps Taft Center at the University of Cincinnati, both of which granted generous fellowships that made this book possible. I cannot overstate my debt to the friends who agreed to read the mess-in-progress and pretend it was better than it was: Chris Bachelder, Brock Clarke, Trent Stewart, and Jillian Weise. Heartfelt thanks, too, to my colleagues and students at the University of Cincinnati; to the wonderful people at Northwestern University Press (among them my delightful editor Mike Levine, the terrific copy editor Xenia Lisanevich, and Rudy Faust, Anne Gendler, and Marianne Jankowski); and to the many friends who helped and encouraged me during the seven years this novel was in progress, regress, ingress, aggress, and especially digress—and now, at last, egress. I'd also like to thank the editors who published (often in different form) excerpts from the novel: Charles McGrath and David McCormick at *Golf World*, Mary Flinn at *Blackbird*, Dinty W. Moore at *Nightsun*, and Kirk Curnutt at *Ocho*. A shout-out across the unbridgeable divide to the late, great Richard Seaver, my former publisher, a brilliant and kind person without whom this book would never and could never have been undertaken. Most of all, my love and gratitude to Nicola Mason, without whom I could undertake *nothing* without soon getting undertaken myself. I rely on her for everything, both literary and personal, and have been doing so for twenty years. Here's to several more decades of grateful dependency in all things.

About the Author

Michael Griffith is an associate professor of English and comparative literature at the University of Cincinnati. He is the author of *Spikes: A Novel* and *Bibliophilia: A Novella and Stories*.